THE VALLEY

the valley

GAYLE FRIESEN

KEY PORTER BOOKS

Library and Archives Canada Cataloguing in Publication

Friesen, Gayle
    The valley : a novel / Gayle Friesen.

ISBN 978-1-55470-001-1 (bound)—ISBN 978-1-55470-223-7 (pbk.)

    I. Title.

PS8561.R4956V36 2009   C813'.54   C2009-902117-X

ONTARIO ARTS COUNCIL
CONSEIL DES ARTS DE L'ONTARIO

The publisher gratefully acknowledges the support of the Canada Council for the Arts and the Ontario Arts Council for its publishing program. We acknowledge the support of the Government of Ontario through the Ontario Media Development Corporation's Ontario Book Initiative.

We acknowledge the financial support of the Government of Canada through the Book Publishing Industry Development Program (BPIDP) for our publishing activities.

Key Porter Books Limited
Six Adelaide Street East, Tenth Floor
Toronto, Ontario
Canada M5C 1H6

www.keyporter.com

Text design: Marijke Friesen
Electronic formatting: Alison Carr

Printed and bound in Canada

09 10 11 12 13 5 4 3 2 1

For my friends: silver and gold.

one

In God's green pastures feeding, by the cool waters lie. Soft in the evening . . . then something I don't remember.

Waters cool, that was the girls' part, *in the Valley* was the boys' part. *Pastures green* (girls), *on the mountain* (boys) . . . then something else.

I shake my head like it might loosen the lyric that's been dogging me since Salmon Arm. My daughter, Julia, glances sideways, earphones lodged firmly into her ears, and gives me a quizzical look. "What's your problem?" she says.

I consider offering her my theory about how we all have neural pathways in our brains, etched by time and biology, and that these pathways connect our nervous system together with neurons called white matter and that this white matter is meant to communicate with the distant areas of the brain. Local communication in the brain, however, is handled by grey matter. This is not a theory, of course, this is fact. My own personal theory is that my white matter has lost its ability to travel to distant places. And that it's all turning grey.

Marci, my therapist, would shake her head at my unscientific interpretation. But Marci isn't here. I am. Heading home for the first time in twenty years. With homework: *what do you want and what makes you happy.* (Galling, being thirty-eight years old and still doing homework. One of the many indignities endured in regaining full mental health.) "Two things?" I asked. "You can do this," she answered, brimming with encouragement. "You're up to this." Easy for her to say at a hundred and fifty bucks an hour. Either way—whether I'm up to it or not—she wins.

I started therapy a few years ago. I was organizing my library one day and couldn't help but notice the disproportionate number of shelves allotted to self-help books. I looked at the rows of titles and had the brilliant notion to pile them up and calculate the cost. When the dollar sign approached a down payment on a cute little cottage up at the lake, I turned to Mark, who was grading papers in the living room. "I think I may need therapy," I said. He smiled, a little tired. "You think?"

Marci is a big fan of happy. She believes in it the way other people believe in family or country or war. She is committed to happy. I believe she would die for happy. I love this about her even when I hate this about her. It sounds easy— it's not. The list of what makes me happy, thus far, reads: my bed. (It's a great bed, to be fair. King-sized, posturepedic. You can jump on it without spilling a glass of wine, though we never do. Quilt with a thread count of a thousand, fluffy feather tick, more pillows than we ever use.)

Before I left our session, I tried to explain to Marci that the Mennonite tradition from which I spring tends to distrust happy. Glad is fine but fun is suspect. Giddy, silly, whimsical?

Unnecessary. Euphoric, ecstatic, blissful? Bordering on blasphemy. Joy? Oh, joy counts, but there's a cost. *The joy of the Lord is my strength*. That's a song. It goes like this: *The joy of the Lord is my strength, the joy of the Lord is my strength, the joy of the Lord is my strength* and . . . finally . . . wait for it: *The joy of the Lord is my strength*. It's not such a bad song when you hear it sung by a congregation, each strand finding a harmony that could make you weep with its beauty. But the lyric itself? What does it mean? I'm happy if *You're* happy. That's what it means. Capital Y, capital You. Me doesn't matter so much.

"I don't have a problem," is what I say to Julia.

"Whatever," she says.

As I drive, *God's green pastures* slinks back into my loopy brain. Some songs never leave, no matter how hard you try to rid yourself of them. I have a theory about this as well. Music is like water: it seeps into places—crevices, corners, caverns—where even a neural pathway can't follow. But words are solid. I often get the words wrong, as Julia so often tells me with a look of pain. But they feel like the right ones, I tell her. She says it's not the same. (For instance, a KT Tunstall song: "Well, my heart knows me better than I know myself" is not "My heart knows my sweater when it's on my shelf.") It can drive you crazy trying to remember the right words, that's all I'm saying.

Something, something and then: *All the sheep of his pastures fare so wonderfully fine. His sheep am I.* His sheep am I? No wonder I forgot.

"What are you singing?" Julia dislodges one earphone.

"I wasn't singing."

"Yeah, you were," she mutters.

"I was humming."

"Because that's so different from singing."

"How could you tell I was humming?"

"Your face goes funny."

"Thanks."

"You're welcome." She replugs herself.

"What are you listening to?"

She points to her ears, shakes her head, and mouths, *I can't hear you.*

"Touché," I say.

She smirks. I wonder what she's thinking. Sometimes, when I'm feeling brave, I ask. I tell her it's a game, like being home free when you're playing tag; like being the confessor and I'll be the priest. Once she said that she sometimes pretended I wasn't her mother—Kate was. That ended that game. It's only fun until somebody loses an eye. (Or a tooth.)

Did I ask Kate to pick up the mail while we were gone and Mark was at his conference? It was on my list. Yes: after she expressed shock that I was actually making this trek, I asked her to pick up the mail and feed the cat until Mark returned. She said, "Of course, aren't I always there for you?" She was.

It was because of Kate that I'd had the courage to leave the Fraser Valley—which she referred to as the Valley of the Shadow of Death—and move to Winnipeg. We both had reasons to leave our homes and families, but Kate had the car. She also had impressive powers of persuasion. She convinced my parents that I needed to get away after my brother, Jake's, death and that she would take care of me. Years later, after she became a principal, she found a job for me as school secretary. She was also godmother to Julia and, when the occasion warranted it (me, in my king-sized bed, unable to rise), surrogate housekeeper and chef. Kate had kept her word. (What Kate hadn't mentioned to my parents was that she was leaving her mother, whom she detested. Just as well. In our community, hatred went over as well as happy.)

My foot eases up on the gas until even semi-trucks and RVs hauling ski boats are passing us. A kid in the back seat smiles; I smile back. He sticks out his tongue. I pull over to the side of the road at a viewpoint.

"What now?" Julia sighs dramatically.

"I have a cramp."

"Don't get out. I want to get there."

"We are there, if here is there, which it was ten minutes ago."

"Thank you, Deepak Chopra. Can we get moving?"

"Do you want to massage my foot?"

"Yeah, I want to massage your foot."

She's so sarcastic, but I don't mind—not really. If it weren't for sarcasm we'd have no way of communicating at all.

I get out of the car and walk over to the guardrail overlooking the lazy Fraser River. At least, this time of year it's lazy. I'd forgotten how shamelessly lush the valley is: bright emerald, overripe, fed by rain that falls continuously throughout the year, though not today. Today is a postcard day, a decoy.

"Can you see the farm?" Julia asks, coming up behind me.

I shake my head. "Are you excited to see it?"

She doesn't hesitate even though, these days, excitement is reserved for half-price sales and emails from tall, truculent, tattooed boys. "I am." She puts her arms around me—arms that are pudgy in her opinion but remind me of the child she still is. "Are you?" There is hope in her voice.

"Of course I am," I lie.

"What are you looking forward to the most? Seeing Gramps and Gran or the farm?"

"Well, it's kind of a draw," I hedge.

"And after so much time . . . I bet it's changed a lot."

I resist saying that time and change both have a way of standing still in the Valley. "Your grandparents were just out last Thanksgiving."

"I know, but we've never been here. Never. That's weird, Mom," she says, drawing her arms away from me and leaning out over the guardrail. It's a flimsy bar and I hate edges.

Automatically I put my arm out to pull her back. She laughs at me and leans even further. "Julia," I say. "Don't fool around."

She rolls her eyes and steps back. "It's so beautiful," she says. "The mountains are awesome, aren't they? How could you leave this place?"

I look beyond the green to the mountains, and one in particular. Jake's mountain. A shudder passes through me like a Winnipeg wind. Julia doesn't notice; she's too busy taking it all in.

"Just roughly . . . where is it?"

"What?"

She groans. "The farm."

I point to a bend in the highway.

"I can't believe we're almost there," she says. "*Finally*," she adds, with a meaningful glance at me. She's begged for this moment since she was ten years old and developed a crush on cows. She couldn't believe her very own grandparents owned cows and that she'd never seen them.

"Believe it," I say, realizing that there is no turning back now. At almost every exit throughout Saskatchewan and Alberta I had considered it. At the BC border I even considered offering Julia a quick dip south, where I would distract her with the promise of Disneyland.

But my mother had been insistent on the phone. Both she and my father had been asking us to come for a visit for years, but this time my mother was firm. "We're not getting any younger, Gloria," she said. "It's time."

"Are you all right?" Guilt emerged like a dandelion—impossible to kill. Guilt: a crop as cultivated as raspberries and corn in this place.

"Oh, phht, don't be dramatic. We're fine."

Phht was my mother's favourite response. I once asked her if my father had carried her over the threshold to the farm and she answered, "Phht." It was her answer to almost every question. She is a very certain woman. There is her work on the farm—from dawn to dusk—there is her family, and there is her Lord. It is, in particular, her Lord who is responsible for this. Everything falls beneath his jurisdiction (The Lord's Will), thus rendering questions moot and answers: phht.

The night my mother called I had a dream, which is unusual. Or, at least, it is unusual for me to remember my dreams. Marci says that everyone dreams. If the woman has had a doubt or a wondering moment in her life I would drop dead on the spot. Don't get me wrong, I like her. She means well and that's something. And I think she has probably saved my life on half a dozen occasions. I mean this metaphorically, or maybe hyperbolically, because I have no suicidal tendencies. None. We established this early on. "It's never the answer," she said, matter-of-factly. "No kidding," I said. We were on the same page. I am in no rush to get to the great beyond, meet my maker. We have issues, he and I.

The dream was a two-parter. In the first part, a woman showed up at my door. She didn't look like anything or anyone, a typical dream character. Except for her creamy white throat. I remember her throat because, when she walked into the house, I could feel the pulse of her heart in my thumbs as I attempted, unsuccessfully, to push her away. I ran around the house then, screaming, "There's an intruder in the house." I yelled for my mother and father, Julia and Mark and Jake, to come inside. I was pretty directive, now that I think about it. Not typical. Until I realized that neither Jake nor Julia had made it. I panicked, felt the slippery sheen of sweat on my chest. I called 911 but got an answering machine. *Odd*, I thought. Even in a dream I knew that a person should answer, a real, live person. But what could I do? I left a message: Help. When I turned around, I saw a policeman in my house. He had long hair and he wore sandals and a gentle expression on his face. Whew, I was saved. I called out to him. "Officer? Officer?" Finally, he looked at me and I repeated, "Officer . . ." I expected him to give his name but he looked amused and said, "Cool."

"Officer Cool?" I repeated.

"No," he smiled. "It's cool you think I'm an officer."

The intruder stood there the entire time, saying nothing, touching her creamy white throat, which surprised me since I thought I'd given it a pretty good twist.

Part Two was more of a painting. The backdrop was inky black and I knew it was supposed to be the sky, even though there were no stars and there should have been stars. It was midnight and the sky was slit open like the belly of a fish.

Inside, a golden light shone but it didn't stream and I knew this was wrong because light should stream. It was beautiful, the most beautiful thing I'd ever seen. But I woke in terror, my heart fluttering like a trapped hummingbird, and I couldn't breathe.

I shook Mark awake. "I have to go home," I said.

"You are home," he said, reaching for me. "Go back to sleep."

"Not this home," I explained. "And I don't want to go back to sleep."

He raised himself up onto his elbow and stroked my hair. "Ah," he said.

I tried to explain my dream and he did his best to listen, but really, there's only so much listening one human being can be expected to do, and he wasn't, unlike Marci, being paid a handsome fee. If anything, quite the opposite. He was a good man and deserved better.

When I finished he leaned close and kissed me in the crook of my neck. Sometimes this worked, though not lately. I pushed him away, hating myself for it. "I need a glass of milk." I reached for my robe and wrapped myself in it. "Do you want anything?"

He shook his head. He was hurt.

"I have to go," I said. "It's time."

"Go home," he said, pulling the covers up around him. "Then come back."

two

I feel Julia's warm hand on my shoulder. "Mom? Where'd you go?"

I force a smile. "Right here."

"Phht," she says, reminding me so much of my mother. She shakes her head and runs back to the car, yelling, "Let's go, let's go, let's go!"

I take a swig of Revelstoke water, picked up at our last gas stop, and follow her to the car. I enter the stream of traffic and begin the descent.

The countryside passes in a blur: a waterslide that wasn't here before; an amusement park that used to be Flintstone's and is now a generic dinosaur park; Bridal Veil Falls; cow-dotted pastures; verdant fields. Marci's question—what makes you happy?—chugs along with each landmark.

I realize that Julia is talking. I adjust my posture to appear as if I've heard everything she's said, hoping to catch up. She's furious when I don't hear every word.

"So then Amber says, 'I had to let him go. He was depleting me.' Can you believe it?"

"Kind of a reverse Jerry McGuire?" I say, hopefully.

"Yes! Exactly. That's what I said—sort of. Then she says she doesn't know what I'm talking about, and I say, 'Remember when we watched it, like, eight times in a row because we thought the guy was so cute . . .'"

"Tom Cruise?"

"Yeah, Mom. I'm into geezers now."

Tom Cruise, a geezer? "Who then?"

"The little boy, the little cutie pie. The do-you-know-how-much-a-human-head-weighs kid."

"Right."

"Anyway, now she's not talking to me because it's like the worst thing in the world if I don't believe her, but it's a total joke if I pretend she made it up because she didn't."

"Maybe she thought who said what wasn't the point."

Julia swivels her entire body, and I prepare myself for a roll of the eyes. She doesn't disappoint. "But that's not the point. The point is . . . what's the truth? Who said what."

My daughter's grim determination to pursue truth unnerves me at times. It's going to bring her pain.

"Mom? Are you listening?"

"Of course I am." I manage to look insulted.

"It's just that I totally kick ass when it comes to remembering who said what. I'm just never wrong. I can't help it," she adds, almost to herself.

"Yeah, about that," I say, remembering a semi-prepared speech on my list of things to do. "You might want to lay low on the whole kicking ass, kissing ass, big ass—anything with ass in it, really—way of expressing yourself while we're at Grandma and Grandpa's."

"Why? They're cool."

"No, Sweetie, they're not. You're wrong. You're great

with movie lines, but really wrong about Grandma and Grandpa being cool." I say this a little louder, a little faster than I intended.

She cocks her head sideways, as though receiving body language tips over a secret headset from Marci.

I take a breath and begin again. "I'm just saying that it's different here—they're different here. Narrower. You've only seen them at our house." Julia doesn't know about the whispered side conversations in the pantry about why we don't do something about the clothes strewn all over the carpet in her room, why she isn't at youth group on a Friday night, or the more pointed glances at our admittedly well-stocked liquor cabinet.

"Narrower? What does that even mean?"

"They're more . . . well, less, actually." I rely on a cookbook that was the second-most important book in our house: *More with Less*. It was a guide more than a cookbook. How to eke the most from the least, use everything, the first shall be last, etc. It's an avalanche of tumbled instruction.

"While I'm young, Mom, while I'm young."

"Well, for starters, there's no MSN here, no DVDs, no CDs. Nothing requiring abbreviation."

"TV?" she smirks.

"Black and white—maybe."

She starts like a filly in a thunderstorm. "Okay, now you're scaring me."

"Be afraid."

"Oh my God, you're serious?"

"That's another one. No saying the Lord's name in vain. Did you know that, when I was a kid, this place was in the Guinness World Records for most churches per capita in the world?"

"Thus the reason for calling it a world record. What's your point?"

"They're just very religious here about . . . being religious."

"Okay, Mom, okay," she says in her faux soothing voice. "No ass talk." She puts her hand absently on mine.

I look at the land around us, at how encircled we've become by the tall, imposing mountains. "Nineveh," I say, as the edge of mountain flattens to valley floor.

"Nineveh?" Julia repeats. I can feel her probing eyes.

"Vineyards. They tried growing kiwis out here a while back, but I don't think they did very well. Maybe they knew they didn't belong. Anyway, you probably don't say kiwi vineyard. It's probably orchard."

"You said Nineveh."

I want to ask her if she believes in time travel. I want to warn her that's where we're headed. Instead, I offer a sheepish smile. "Whatever."

She has the grace to smile as she plugs herself back into her IPod. "Whatever," she says, but she says it differently: weary calm and a little sarcasm. Zen with an attitude.

As I drive along the narrow road fringed by familiar mountains, the words trickle in.

In God's green pastures feeding—

The sun dips behind the mountain and the sky turns mauve.

By the cool waters lie.

The pungent odour of manure and rain-soaked earth seeps into the car.

Soft in the evening—

I wonder if my mother will have made soup for dinner.

three

I must have read the Jonah story a hundred times when I was a kid. We had this tattered yellow book of Bible stories; it was a bedtime staple, along with night lunch. The stories bored my brother, Jake, so there was no need to take turns; it stayed in my room even after my parents gave up reading bedtime stories to us. They said I was old enough to read for myself, but I think they were just tired of all the questions. My mother used to say that I would give God a headache with my questions. She meant this as a joke, but it made me nervous. Did God get sick? Who took care of him when he was sick? Did he have a mother who took care of him? Was Mary his mother? No, that was Jesus's mom. But if Jesus was also the Father and the Holy Ghost, did that make Mary his mother, his wife, or his dead sister?

The stories came with vivid illustrations in case you weren't getting the picture: slain giants, murdered babies, a prince who dangled from a tree branch by his hair; an entire world covered by water except for one, lone, floating ark, which didn't seem big enough for all those animals and birds, let alone Noah's family. For years I dreamed about the drowning townsfolk who watched Noah sail away. Sometimes he waved, sometimes he didn't.

As I grew, I kept reading about this God, this Jehovah, who moved in fire and cloud and spoke through flaming shrubs and sent ten terrible plagues when one might have done the trick. I read the stories over and over and always hoped things would turn out differently, that Pharaoh would take a look at the river of blood and say to Moses, "You know what? Changed my mind. Go ahead." But it seemed like everyone in the Old Testament had to learn the hard way: Jehovah did not like to lose.

When I needed a break from the gore I read the New Testament, which had pictures of lambs and loaves and fishes and gentle Jesus. These stories, at least, had banquets and picnics and people springing back to life with gusto: Lazarus, a sick little nameless girl, and finally, Jesus himself. It hardly seemed to me that the Jehovah of the Old Testament and the Jesus of the New Testament could be related, let alone be father and son.

But the Jonah story really mesmerized me. I liked the name, Nineveh, for one thing. It was one of those words you could say over and over again without tripping once: Nineveh, Nineveh, Nineveh, Nineveh. Like car tires over a bumpy road. And Jonah impressed me. He was so disobedient. Jehovah told him to go one way, so Jonah went the other. Who would ever be that brave? Who would dare to defy Jehovah? Of course, it didn't last long. Three days inside the smelly belly of a fish would curb anyone's resolve, but still, Jonah tried—you had to give him that. Even so, I figured that God must have things under control. What was the point, otherwise, of being Jehovah?

I see the turnoff to my parents' farm and ease up on the

gas. Slowly, we make our way through the tall, golden fields of corn, past the ditches filled with fireweed, buttercups, and red clover. And then I see the farmhouse. As expected, nothing has changed.

My parents are as much a part of the farm as the old apple tree out front, the raspberry fields, the faded red barn, and the prolific garden. Every Thanksgiving they drive to Winnipeg with their car packed full of coolers stuffed with frozen vegetables and boxes of canned fruit. Their own suitcases require a minimum of space.

Julia sits up straight, then slumps back against the seat, woozy from her music-doze. She tugs at her hair, pushing back stray strands. "We're here?"

"Yep."

She wriggles in her seat and reaches for the handle as soon as we turn into the long driveway. The car creeps toward the farmhouse, tires crunching on the gravel like the last bits of popcorn. Two figures wait in the twilight.

"There they are," she says, pulling the door open before the car has stopped. She runs to them.

My mother's arms open wide for her granddaughter, and then the parable of the Prodigal Son slips into my head, except it's wrong because a son isn't returning. I close the passenger door and make my way to the porch, where my parents are clucking at how Julia has grown. She's eating it up. She's excited to see the big BC mountains and the small BC mosquitoes that, for the most part, mind their own business. She's outgrown her love for cows, perhaps, but she's thrilled to be here. She throws herself into my father's arms. "Gramps!"

"Well, there, Susie-Q," he says, as always.

"It's Julia," she says.

"Well, well." He thumps her back and, despite dusk, I see his smile.

"Well, well yourself," she says, completing the routine.

The car keys dig into my hand.

"Gloria." My mother embraces me. "So. You're here."

"Mom. The place looks great." I say this quickly, giving only a cursory glance at the house I used to return to a thousand days and nights. It's just a house, I tell myself, feeling an unwanted prickle of tears. I take in the simple white stucco, two storeys, painted every two years by my father, and the wraparound porch—slightly sagging now—flanked by hydrangea bushes. The old apple tree is taller. The trellis under Jake's window is still there. Mine was taken down after I snuck out once too often. The house had a lopsided, winking appearance after that, as if it knew things I didn't.

I give my father a brisk hug. He doesn't thump my back. "How was your trip?" he asks.

"Good."

"How'd you come?"

"The, uh, Number One."

"So, you paid the ten dollars," he says. His steel grey hair bobs stiffly up and down. He and my mother always take the longer, cheaper Number Three. It's prettier, they say, and ten bucks is ten bucks.

"Yep."

"Hmm."

I steal another look at the house. I know every inch of it, every settlement bump, every crack in the pavement (I avoided the one in the garage every day so that I wouldn't break my mother's back), the count of every staircase (twelve up to the back door, thirteen to the basement; this never made sense to me), the best hiding places (the crawl space or the wide basement window wells; it was a draw). I know this place and it knows me.

My mother steps forward briskly. "Let's get your bags inside and have some supper. You must be starving!" Her voice is all business now: feed a cold, feed a fever, feed everything.

Inside, I leave Julia sniffing joyfully at a pot of borscht and freshly baked buns and follow my father up the stairs to my old room. He places the suitcase on the floor and painstakingly explains how to open the window as though I hadn't lived here (and snuck out the same window) for eighteen years.

"Thanks, Dad."

"Mmm hmm." He hesitates at the door, looking like he wants to say something. "So, you're here."

Please don't, I think, *say more. Let's pretend this is an overdue visit.*

"The shower nozzle sticks a little," he continues as I expel a breath I didn't know I was holding. "You still like to take long showers?"

"I'm afraid so."

He nods. "We have a new water heater."

"That's good." I smile at him. "I promise I'll turn off all the lights when I come downstairs."

As he smiles I get a sudden, vivid glimpse of what used to make me happy. Take that, Marci. Not so hard after all. I now have two things on my list. This might not be so bad. Maybe I have moved on. Or maybe I'm experiencing a spontaneous remission of my unresolved past. The unresolved past is Marci's belief (she doesn't have theories). She calls it my unattended sorrow. She's sure I should be over Jake's death by now—it's been twenty years. Or, if not over it, then farther down the road. She likes to say, *When travelling through hell, it's best to keep moving.*

"You don't get through hell," I'd responded. "That's kind of the point of hell."

She just crinkled. Crinkled and furrowed over hell and said it was simply a metaphor for resistance. After that, she couldn't get enough of religious imagery. It was as though she'd discovered some new form of aversion therapy. She talked about the crown of thorns surrounding my sacred heart and the boulder of sorrow that needed to be rolled away from the cave of my, I don't quite remember, suffering? Or was it the tomb of my tight belly? At one point she told me that I needed to deny my pain three times before dawn. I told her I needed a break from the metaphors. Actually, I told her to give me a fucking break. She didn't miss a beat, launched immediately into my anger, which was like a tiny ball that, when swallowed, grew barbs so that you had trouble hacking it up. And the longer it sat, the sharper and longer the barbs became. We argued for most of the hour about why anyone would swallow a ball, or more to the point, try to hack up a ball covered with spiky barbs. She repeated that I needn't be so literal. (She would never say "shouldn't." This is how I know she's not religious.)

As I look out the window at the fenced pasture lined by poplar trees and the red barn just beyond, I remember how often I climbed out this window to meet up with Des and Kate, my two best friends, even after my father removed the trellis. Des would lean a ladder against the house, giggling while Kate shushed her, worried that someone would hear us.

Des, Kate, and I became friends in the fifth grade. Kate—Katharine Doerksen—walked into our Sunday school classroom—fresh from Vancouver, which was as exotic to us as if she'd flown in from Paris, France—with the same poise she would carry with her into every room she would ever enter. Her clothes were different: flared pants and wedged shoes. She wore her hair in a neat bob that made it obvious that her mother didn't cut her hair as ours—judging from the severe bangs—did. Our fathers were farmers, while Kate's dad was a doctor. This occupation caused a stir, initially. Honest, hard work was the cornerstone of the community—the more backbreaking the better—and while being a doctor wasn't dishonest, it was presumptuous and this was sometimes the same thing. The most telling difference of all was in the way Kate scanned the room as our Sunday school teacher introduced her. She had such an air of worldliness about her that it was impossible not to stare. Everyone wanted to be her friend. I was honoured, and baffled, when she decided to sit next to me. She smiled prettily and complimented both my plain white sneakers and my straight brown hair. By the time Des arrived, late as usual, flying into the room with her golden curls poking out in every direction—dirt on her knees from climbing one last tree before her mother found her—Kate was ensconced. Des said, "Who are you?" Kate told her with a slight lift of her chin. Des shrugged. It was that easy to become Des's friend.

Apart from inappropriate giggling in church, Des and I had been a fairly tame duo. But when we strode up to the double digits, and gained Kate as a friend to boot, we became

a force. We immediately created a secret language that baffled the boys and tormented the adults. In our elementary
years alone, we went through three Sunday school teachers,
breaking Des's brothers' measly record of two. It wasn't that
hard. Incessant giggling drove them to the edge—a touch of
blasphemy tipped them over.

For instance, Mrs. Peters always started her lesson with a
reading from Scripture. "Yea verily," she would read. Well,
this could be set to music so easily: *Yea verily we roll along,
roll along, roll along. Yea verily we roll along, along the
deep blue sea.*

Then there was the time that Des forgot to memorize her
weekly verse and thought it might be a good idea to distract
the teacher. She pointed to a puffball cloud outside the window and shouted, "Look, it's Jesus. He's back." She was
sent to the Sunday school superintendent over that one.

Our parents spoke sternly with us, but it made no difference. We were fearless when we were ten.

I look again at the barn, with a piece now missing from
the roof. I do a double take. I immediately recognize the
onset of a migraine but, still, I always do a double take, no
matter how often it happens. My mind refuses to accept that
my brain is saying *something is missing.* I look again, con-
centrating on what should be there, but a chunk of the barn
is most definitely gone.

Julia flits through the door and part of her face is missing.
I shift my head so that I can see all of her, but I can't.

"This is like a movie set," she says, throwing her arms
around me for the second time in one day. I hug her, grateful
that she feels real, but she disentangles herself quickly and
darts around the room like a butterfly, lighting first on the bed,

then a chair, and then on the steamer trunk at the foot of the bed. "It's just so—*Little House on the Prairie*, isn't it? I love it. I have an afghan on my bed. Gran's grandmother made it. That's, like, my great-great-grandmother, right? Or my great-grandmother? Anyway." She stops talking and hugs herself.

"Great-grand, I think." Julia is one of those people who loves family—the bigger and louder the better. Being an only child is the reason, I guess, though she has dozens of cousins on Mark's side. (His relatives populate southern Manitoba like gophers.) Even so, Julia's always felt cheated on the sibling side of things.

"Gran says dinner's ready. Can you smell it? Let's go, let's go, let's go!" She reaches for my hand and pulls me to the door.

I hold it for a second before releasing her. "You go down. I'm not that hungry. Tell them to start without me, okay?"

Her face shifts. "You're okay, right? You're probably just tired from the trip, right? It was a long drive."

I stroke her head, feeling the warmth of her skull, the bumpy texture of her curls, and smell the scent of wildberry shampoo from this morning's shower at the motel. "I'm fine, Sweetie, just a little tired." Her eyes remain locked onto mine. "I'll be down in a few minutes."

She hesitates for only a second, long enough for me to see the exuberance leaking out of her. "Whatever," she says as she leaves the room.

The first sign is a subtle one. If I'm driving, I find myself studying the licence plate on the car in front of me, trying to figure out why there is nothing between the first and last letter. Then I look around, thinking that things are still normal. But every other licence plate is the same: two letters flanking nothing where something used to be. For a second I think this makes sense: life is written in code, a mysterious code that is profoundly true and impossible to crack—a mean practical joke. That's when the alligator brain kicks in and says, *You idiot, something is missing.* That's when I start to panic.

You find yourself slowing down because part of the landscape has fallen away and you don't know where to stand or where to look, what you can trust. You are in the centre of the jigsaw puzzle, and it's as though the pieces are being removed one by one. Continuity is shot, edges blur, and you need to find footing on the fragmented remains. You close your eyes, find your way to a darkened room, and wait for the pain. The pain always comes. My doctor reassured me that this is good. "That's how we know it's a migraine. Otherwise there's trouble." That's the bitch about migraines—the pain is the good news.

I close the curtains and lie down on the twin bed, which doesn't fit the way it used to. With my eyes shut, I feel the room move in ever-shrinking circles until it slows and the vice tightens. Now there's only the waiting.

Marci thinks my headaches are due to stress and that I'm suffering a "mild" depression. She smiles when she writes a prescription. "It's like making our way through a tunnel," she explains, as though she was planning to accompany me. "We know there's a light at the end, but sometimes we need help to get there. We all need a little help from time to time, surely."

I pull the blanket up around me, and another old song plays over and over in my head.

Surely goodness and mercy shall follow me
All the days, all the days of my life.
And I shall dwell in the house of the Lord forever,
And I shall feast at a table set for me.

I should have told Marci that it's not that I can't make it to the light. There is no light—that's the thing. Just a really long tunnel.

I wait a little longer and there it is, smack between my eyes: the pain.

four

Julia doesn't look my way when I enter the kitchen the next morning. It's hard to say how long the cold shoulder will last, usually a day. But there are distractions here: grandparents to charm, a barn to explore, kittens to discover, boys too, hopefully. She'll get over it; she always does.

The kitchen is exactly as it was twenty years ago: blue and white ruffled curtains, avocado-coloured appliances, flowered wallpaper faded but still intact. The room is spotless. Plaques hang on the walls: *God is Love* and John 3:16 in its entirety. Even the macaroni art that I made in Pioneer Girls is here, although the "f" has dropped away, so instead it reads: *I come to give abundant li e.* Finally, the biggest plaque of all is reserved for Menno Simons, father of the very best faith of all: *True evangelical faith cannot lie dormant. It clothes the naked, it feeds the hungry, it comforts the sorrowful, it shelters the destitute, it serves those that harm it, it binds up that which is wounded, it has become all things to all people.* It is a lengthy motto, almost poster-size.

I look around for the coffee pot, but it's nowhere in sight. I had prepared myself that there wouldn't be any alcohol on the premises, but I was counting heavily on caffeine.

"You look well rested." My mother approaches, teapot in hand.

"Good. Is there coffee? Somewhere?"

"It's bad for your father's nerves."

My father, who is reading the paper, shakes his head almost indiscernibly. "Blood pressure. Your mother calls it nerves."

My mother dismisses the comment with a *phht* and hands me a cup of tea. "Have something to eat."

The table is groaning with platters of food: pancakes, scrambled eggs, bacon, and biscuits—plump, warm, and brown—and jam, three different kinds: raspberry, apricot, and plum. I take a pancake and some eggs. "Wow, Mom."

"Well, how often do my daughter and granddaughter drop by for breakfast?" She says this with only a pinch of re-proach—chastisement light. She can't help herself, not being one for direct criticism. But she has a point, so I eat my break-fast in silence.

There was always an abundance of food at our house—Jake had an enormous appetite—but it was gluttony to eat too much. Our bodies were temples of the Lord and so, even in the presence of plenty, we were expected to show restraint. *Moderation in all things.* There's probably a plaque on the wall to this effect.

Julia hasn't heard about restraint. "Isn't this great?" she says, with her mouth full, bits of biscuit flying. Her cold shoulder is warming.

"It is." I finish my breakfast and pour another cup of

tea. Three more and maybe I'll have enough caffeine to fuel the day.

My mother reaches for my plate. "That's all you're eating? You're so thin," she says, glancing disapprovingly at the scraps of leftover egg and half-eaten pancake. I wait to see if she'll bring up the starving children of Bangladesh, but she doesn't.

"I'll clear up."

"No, you relax."

My father is still hunched over his newspaper, and I wonder how to begin a conversation with him. We could talk about the sticky shower nozzle, I suppose. Mark and he usually talk about golf and local politics for hours, taking the pressure off of me. "So, Dad," I begin.

He looks up with an expression that's not unfriendly.

"How's your golf game?"

He folds the paper neatly, careful to place each section back in its original spot so that it would appear to have not been read. "Pretty good."

"Great."

We look at each other and smile.

Julia considers us curiously as she swallows a large mouthful of food. "You know what you need around here, Gramps?"

He flashes a quick smile. "What? What do I need, little one?"

"Well, first of all, I'm practically five-five." She straightens in her chair. "And second of all . . . what's with that puny black-and-white TV? Hello? It's the new mill."

"Mill?"

"Millennium. Has been for a while now. You are in serious

need of a large-screen TV and DVD player. How do you watch movies around here?"

Silence. I grab a biscuit and take a sizeable bite. I chew and smile apologetically. To my knowledge, the sum total of my parents' movie-going experience has been to watch *The Sound of Music*, and they weren't impressed. War is a serious business, with no musical numbers.

"I should get out to the barn," he says, rising from the table. He rubs my daughter's hair as he leaves.

"Catch ya later," she yells after him.

"Don't forget that I want to go see Agnes later on," my mom calls out.

He lifts a hand to show that he's heard, and the screen door clatters shut.

"Mr. Nickel had a stroke a few days ago. He's still in the hospital. I want to bring some bread by."

I scan my brain. "Jarnelle's dad? He had a stroke?"

"Two days ago. Just an episode, really."

"How bad was it?"

"It affected his speech." She wipes down the clean counter-tops. "But, you know, he wasn't much of a talker anyway."

My mother has a real knack for finding the bright side of things. That's not quite it. It's an obligation, a cove-nant, because it's unchristian to complain. It might not be on the same plane as pride or jealousy or sloth, but it's on the list.

"Really, it could be a bit of a blessing," she says. If any-thing, she's getting speedier at locating the silver lining.

"Why's that, Mom?"

"Well, Agnes has been after him to retire, and maybe this will give him a little shove. The Lord has mysterious ways."

I might have known the Lord would be behind this. Des, Kate, and I used to make a game of it. We called it: Now That's a Blessing! We'd go up to the hayloft with something from our mothers' kitchens and mull over the possible spiritual upside of every likely predicament while eating something— I have to say now, not being a baker of things—amazingly scrumptious. Their bakeoffs were legendary, and all the more so because the competition was never acknowledged, competition ranking up there with complaint. My mother would praise Mrs. Doerksen's cinnamon buns and then march home with the intent to improve on them. Conversely, Mrs. D would claim that my mother made the best pies in the valley and then produce a crust so flaky that my mother would have a tough time keeping the smile on her face. "Mmm," she'd say, leaving a telltale bit of crust on her plate. "You use lard?" The ever-so-subtle inference being that any-one might make a flaky crust with animal fat as opposed to the healthier option of Crisco, a vegetable fat: a dilemma as old as the feud between Cain and Abel. We learned the art of passive-aggressive baking from our mothers. But mostly we devoured the results and played the game.

"Our cow died," Des might say.

"But not the herd," Kate would add.

"Now that's a blessing!" we'd shout.

"Looks like the valley might flood this winter."

"But we could swim to church—"

"Now that's a blessing!"

"Helmut Wiebe took his shirt off on the church workday."

"But not his pants."

"Now that's a blessing!"

We lasted as long as the baking did and laughed until our

sides ached. I don't know how we could laugh so long and so hard at so little, but we did.

"What are you smiling at?" Julia asks, reaching for another biscuit. Is that three now? She'll be grumbling about how fat she is later in the day. It takes every ounce of willpower I have not to say anything. But I've read the books. I don't want to be the one she points to, years from now, about an eating disorder. There's going to be enough legitimate blame without that.

"Nothing," I answer. "How about we drive into town this morning? I could show you my old haunts."

"Okay," she shrugs, piling jam on her biscuit.

"Mom, do you want to come with us? We could pick up some groceries for supper."

"I need to keep an eye on the bread. You two run along."

The big yellow ceramic bowl on the counter is filled with rising dough. It's cracked slightly on the side but not enough to be discarded. "Is that the same bowl?"

"Why wouldn't it be?"

The dough is covered with a crisply ironed, but faded, red and white tea towel. The same tea towel from twenty years ago? I look closer. It is. "And the same tea towels?"

She shrugs.

"Quit harassing Gran," Julia orders.

I bring my cup over to the sink. "You always made the best bread, Mom," I say. "Far superior to Mrs. Doerksen's."

"Who's Mrs. Doerksen?" asks Julia.

"Kate's mom."

"That's not true," my mother says, but she's smiling at the thought of it.

On an impulse, I give her a hug around her shoulder.

There's less of her to hug now. "It's good to be home," I say. And it only feels like a partial lie. "Are you sure you don't want to come?"

She shakes her head. "There's too much to be done."

Grocery list in hand, Julia and I drive off. My mother gave me directions before we left; I guess she thought I might have forgotten the way. But the funny thing is, the directions are wrong. She always did get north and south mixed up. It doesn't matter. This road is seared into my brain as permanently as the brand the cows wear on their rumps.

"Why do they call you Gloria?" Julia asks.

"Apart from it being my name?"

"Yeah, apart from that." She scrunches up her nose and scowls. "Everyone else calls you El back home."

"Well, Dorothy." I turn my head to watch for traffic. "We're not in Kansas anymore."

"Fine." She folds her arm across her chest and stares out the window—the classic disgruntled teen pose. She's sure she's invented this.

"I'm sorry," I say. As soon as the words are out of my mouth it strikes me how often I say them. *I'm sorry* I didn't make your lunch today. *I'm sorry* I didn't fill out that field trip form. *I'm sorry* I didn't wash those pants. *I'm sorry* I spend so much time sleeping. Honestly, when said too many times, sorry becomes grotesque. "I never really liked the name Gloria, so when I moved to Winnipeg I just abbreviated it to El. Grandma and Grandpa never got used to the idea."

"You always make jokes when you don't want to talk about what's really going on, did you know that?"

"Thank you, Dr. Phil."

"You're doing it again! You know, one day I'm going to stop asking. One day I'm just going to not care."

We drive in silence until we reach the older part of town, the part that cradles the memories. "Okay, there," I say, pointing to a restaurant on our left. It has probably changed ownership a dozen times since I lived here, but it looks the same. "That used to be Smitty's. We used to go there—my friends and me—and eat bran muffins. We were completely addicted."

"See, that's the kind of thing I want to know: where you got your fibre. Was that so hard?"

I reach over to swat her, but she's too quick and leans out of the way. At least she's smiling again.

"Seriously fascinating, Mom. Sometimes, when you were feeling wild, would you order a blueberry muffin? Or maybe, God forbid, chocolate chip? And I thought you didn't know how to have fun."

"Oh, we had fun, my sarcastic girl. We made sure we got the booth closest to the cutest boys and flirted like crazy. We never let them know that was what we were doing, mind you. Overt flirting was outlawed in this town, but we'd raise our voices a little, flip our hair, you know. Let them know we were there." I smile at the memory and then at how subtle I thought we were being until this very moment as I hear myself explaining it to my daughter. We would have been as subtle as Julia and her friends.

Julia's face is a perfect hybrid of disgust and morbid fascination. "*You* flirted? For real?" There isn't even a trace of caustic in her voice now.

"Don't sound so shocked."

"I totally can't help it. I can't even imagine it."

We're well past the restaurant formerly known as Smitty's, but my mind drifts back and I feel the pulse of the forgotten.

"Which friends?" Julia asks, apparently having digested the news that her mother, at one time, flirted.

"A girl—woman now, of course—Desiree Penner. Des. You've never met her. And Kate. You know, Aunt Kate?"

"You and Aunt Kate were friends when you were kids?"

"You knew that."

"Yeah, Mom. Your life's an open book. What about this Des person?"

"Oh, just a childhood friend. She was—fun."

She sighs and waits.

"*Very* fun."

"Stop," she says, holding out a hand. "Too much information. My brain is overloaded."

I leave the comment alone and Julia turns on the radio. I'm relieved. The farther we travel, the more landmarks we pass, the closer the past feels.

~

Des lived on the neighbouring farm with her parents and three older brothers, but it wasn't until we were old enough to cross the creek bordering our land that our friendship really began. I would have been five or six years old when I ran into her—on my own—at the creek. Jake wasn't trailing behind, which was unusual. I remember that first feeling of exhilaration that only guilty freedom can bring—being somewhere on my own. It seemed like such a brave thing.

Des was standing beside a spot in the creek, her wild blond curls dancing in the small square of sunshine. I knew her from church, but she was a tomboy—all those boisterous older brothers, I guess—so we'd never played together. She had a tendency to climb trees, and this particular activity never made sense to me. But on this day she ran up to me and said, "I know where there's a dead bird."

My knees went weak with jealousy. "Where?"

"That's for me to know and you to find out," she said, smugly, but then she started giggling. "Want me to tell you?" She never got any better at keeping secrets.

As she led me to the location of the deceased bird, she added that she also thought the bird might be a fairy. This stopped me dead in my tracks.

"There's no such thing," I said, sternly.

"Oh yeah? What about Tinkerbell?"

"That's just a story."

"Yeah, I know." She stuck her chin out, and our fledgling friendship nearly ended before it began.

"It's not real," I explained patiently. My mother had read *Peter Pan* to me only the year before and was quite clear about this. There were Bible stories—all true—and then there were made-up stories.

But Des refused to budge, and I saw my chance at seeing the dead bird slip away.

"If it's a fairy then it will wake up if you laugh," I said.

"You're right!" She raced off, and I did my best to keep up, but she got there first. By the time I arrived there were tears glistening in her eyes. She looked at me beseechingly, "You try."

I looked down at the prone robin and then back at Des. I didn't want to be right but I knew I was. I mustered up a laugh even though I had absolutely no faith in the exercise and despite the fact that it felt wrong to even try. As expected, the bird remained dead. I tried to comfort Des by suggesting that we give it a proper burial. I'd been to my grandfather's funeral only months before, so I knew what to do.

We scooped up the bird, quickly named Bert Bergen, and carried him over to the willow tree that brushed the stream we shared. I delivered a moving eulogy about his brief but carefree life and finished with: "Here lies poor dead Bert Bergen. We didn't know him but we loved him so. Now our Bert is flying in heaven with the angels. Amen." We threw dirt on the feathery corpse, fashioned a cross from twigs and string, and our friendship was forged.

On the way back to the farm, Des asked, "So angels are real but fairies aren't?"

I could see in her blue eyes that she trusted me completely. "Oh, yes," I said, emphatically.

Des nodded sadly, but I could tell she believed me. I felt bad about her sadness, but it was better that she knew the truth.

"So what happened to her?" Julia asks, startling me to the extent that I wonder if I've spoken my thoughts aloud. "This Desiree person. Cool name."

"Oh," I say, turning into the grocery store parking lot. "We just lost touch." Julia looks disappointed but I shrug my shoulders. "It happens."

This is true, I tell myself as we make our way to the front door. People lose touch with childhood friends all the time. You aren't even officially out of childhood until you forget someone you thought you would play with forever. It happens all the time. Twenty years of unread, unanswered letters. Then, a few years ago, a Christmas card to which I responded in kind. It was what I could manage: a civil, acceptable facsimile for what was once the truest friendship in my life.

five

When we arrive home, I go directly to my bedroom and lie down before dinner. A poster of David Cassidy hangs on the wall. I put it opposite my bed so that his would be the last face I would see before sleep. There's a smudge under David's nose where Jake drew a Hitler moustache and I made him erase it. Actually, he refused. I had to erase it myself.

I loved that poster the way Julia loves her punk-band spiky-blue-haired rock stars. The difference is that Julia can see herself inside that world, at least in her imagination. Not me. David lived in a world I couldn't even imagine being a part of. He was of the world. I was instructed to be in, but never of, the world. I was meant to skirt the periphery like a satellite, keeping a constant vigil for needy, lost souls. I was never sure if this was a Mennonite thing and so expected because of who we were, or if it was a Jesus thing, and so expected because of who we were meant to become. Maybe not so much to become—that would be prideful—rather, to compare ourselves against and be forever found wanting.

Unlike the who-is-God question, my parents enjoyed the who-are-the-Mennonites question. Especially my mother. She could talk about the subject for hours, and a kind of glow came over her when she did. Who they were: non-fighters, non-drinkers, non-spenders, non-dancers, non-card players, non-graven-image-havers, non-child-baptizers, non-doubters. This, above all, was what we were: non-doubters. There was no need to even think about it—the thinking had already been done. Menno Simons had figured it out in 1500.

It was very important to my mother that Jake and I know this was who we were. We weren't just part of a community; the community was who we were, knit into the fabric of our being.

It made no sense to me. I couldn't understand that being born into something made it who you were. Or that God would create a whole entire world and then say we couldn't be a part of it. I remember spending hours poring over the Bible, trying to find evidence of the Mennonites. We weren't listed in any of the twelve tribes of Israel, nor was there a prophet or disciple named Menno. When I brought this to the attention of my mother, she asked me why it was so important to me. I confessed that there was a dance at school that I wanted to attend. She nodded her head in such a way that the disappointment in the room was palpable and said that I should follow the Spirit's leading. I was ready for this, quickly pointing out several Old Testament scriptures that clearly indicated that dancing was not only allowed, it was a common practice of worship. She reminded me that this was the Old Testament. Emphasis on old. We, on the other hand, had been washed in the blood of Jesus from the New Testament, thus breaking the old covenant. Then she brought out the *Martyr's Mirror,* which was chock full of our ancestors who had given their lives for their faith, taken a stand. One story, in particular, stood out: Dirk Willems.

Back in the day, Dirk was tried and convicted for his religious leanings. Cleverly, he escaped from his prison window with a rope made of knotted rags that dropped him onto the ice that covered the surrounding moat. Luckily, due to prison rations, he was as light as a sprite and was on his way to safety when the prison guard broke through the ice in his pursuit. Dirk, compassionate to the end, turned back and rescued him. Not so luckily, the guard turned out to be a rule-following fellow unmoved by pity and Dirk was subsequently burned—due to shifting winds—to an excruciating crisp. In conclusion, my mother said that I could dance or I could take a stand. But by this time she had the Holy Spirit and Jesus and Dirk Willems on her side and, though this was one of the few times I felt Jehovah was on my side, we'd been outnumbered.

Jake, on the other hand, said he'd prayed about it and felt that Jesus would really want him to go to the dance. I didn't speak to him for a week.

I hated that who I was had already been decided, but, more than that, I hated being defined by what I wasn't. But it didn't matter. We knew the way. It was the right way and the only way. Everyone else was wrong. Everyone.

I roll off the bed gingerly because of a swelling wave of pain and dig through my purse for my prescription. I pop one of Marci's most recent cures into my mouth and wait for the jagged peaks to flatten, for holes to fill. I wait until I feel nothing except the rocking back and forth and a faint buzzing in my ear that continues regardless.

A knock comes at the door and a groggy glance at the clock tells me I've slept. It's five o'clock. Julia should be home from school. I need to wake up.

"Gloria?" I hear my mother's voice. What's she doing in Winnipeg? Where is Mark? Is he still at work? I have to tell him that my mother has come for a visit. She should have called first; normally, she calls first. The house is probably a mess and I haven't done any baking, not that I bake. I should, though, I should bake. I would be a better person if I baked. I try to get up but my head—a bowling ball—falls back against the pillows.

It's when she enters the room that I remember where I am.

"Dear?" She's worried. She only calls me "dear" when she's worried.

I wonder if Des called. Did she tell my mother about how she tried to explain and that I wouldn't listen? That she paused beside me that day in church and I wouldn't follow her? That I just sat there and wouldn't take a stand? What kind of Mennonite was I, anyway?

"Are you all right?" she asks. She sits beside the bed and hands me a cup of tea.

I prop myself up on my pillows and take the steaming cup from her. Through the thinning fog, I see my reflection in the mirror and remember that I'm not eighteen years old. I wonder if I ever was.

After I take a shower to clear the sticky medication cobwebs from my head, I help my mother set the table for dinner. "Use the china," she says.

"On a weekday?" I tease, but she's busy stirring the gravy. "The roast smells delicious."

She grunts a response. Her jaw is set the way it always is when she has a hundred things to do at once. But it doesn't matter what she does—stop to tie a shoelace, settle a fight, stir a white sauce—her dinners are always perfect. You'd think I'd understand it now, but I don't because Mark always helps with the dinners. I handle pasta with bagged sauces. It was something we started doing when we first married because I'd never paid attention to my mother's domestic lessons, and Mark enjoyed eating. But now, twenty years later, I find myself envying my mother's competence in the kitchen. In the last couple of years I've even wished that I'd paid more attention to her insistence that I learn how to make a pie. What an odd little rebellion that was: refusing to make pastry.

"Mom, can you come in here?" Julia calls me to the living room.

It's a small room, shut off from the rest of the house by sliding doors on one side and an entrance to the front door of the house on the other. We never used that entrance except after Jake's funeral. It doesn't seem possible, but it's what I remember.

This was also the music room and, although it is fifty years old, the upright Heintzman is as shiny as the day my parents brought it home. They were so excited to show it to us; it was a huge purchase. Jake and I were optimistic. Mrs. Lepp was going to teach us how to play and we figured that within weeks, or maybe even days, we'd be playing duets

46

every bit as well as the Bensler children—probably better. Jake ended up being the musician. Technically, I could play every bit as well and I often had the pieces memorized before he did. The way Mrs. Lepp put it was that I played with my head; Jake played with his heart and everything else. I don't think she meant it as a compliment to either of us.

"Mom, who's this?" Julia points to my brother's graduation photo. "Is this my uncle?"

I nod, thinking how much he would have loved the sound of that. Uncle Jake.

"Were you guys, like, close?"

"Sure." My hand reaches out and strikes a note on the piano. It sounds harsh, tinny—ghostly. Had I never told her he was my twin? It doesn't seem likely, yet even now the words stick in my throat. I always wince when people— usually Mark's relatives—introduce me as Mark's better half, because I know better. "We were twins, Sweetie."

In the second it takes for her to react to this news, I wonder if she'll be angry that I haven't told her this sooner. But she slides next to me on the piano bench and pushes herself against my arm. "Oh, Mom," she says. "How do you lose a twin?"

I squeeze her hand, unable to speak. She doesn't push, and so I don't tell her that when you come as a pair you make certain assumptions. If we arrived together we would likely leave together and, in the meantime, we would take care of each other. I was twenty minutes older than Jake. I lorded it over him occasionally, but mostly I thought of him as my kid brother. Jake was far too trusting. He never understood what a wicked world it was.

On the day of his funeral, Mrs. Braun approached my

mother and me at the cemetery. She clutched my mother's hand in her two plump ones and said that Glory was having a good day with the arrival of Jake and that he'd been taken home. She said it like she was discussing the weather.

I was horrified that Glory would be happy on this day. All I knew was that Jake had left home, not gone home. And that someone should have been paying closer attention.

I stopped believing in angels the day he died, but not in Jehovah. He was there when Jake died and had done nothing. He was supposed to be our Heavenly Father, but even an earthly father would have known better, held on tighter. Done something. But to think that he was happy about it was a cruelty I hadn't expected.

I waited for my mother to set Mrs. Braun straight. She, of all people, would find the right verse to send her packing and to restore sense, at least. But my mother only nodded, her head bowed. And it was official: Jehovah really did not care.

"Did he play the piano?" Julia swivels on the piano bench and plays "Heart and Soul" with two fingers.

"He played well."

She continues to plunk out the song and each note brings a memory: Jake spying on Des and me; Jake begging me to go hiking with him; Jake making me laugh so hard I thought I'd pee my pants.

"How did he die?" she asks, looking at the keyboard.

"He fell off a mountain."

My mother enters the room, wiping her hands on her apron. She watches Julia on the piano. For a brief moment our eyes meet and I wonder, again, how she could have just stood there and said nothing. Her boy had not gone home.

"Dinner's ready," she says, returning to the kitchen.

Julia stops playing and looks at me, her eyes full of questions.

"It smells great, doesn't it?" I get up and follow my mother.

sit

The next morning skids in drenched and sopping. According to the weatherman, we're experiencing a low-pressure system. It sounds appealing. No pressure, no big deal—low pressure. Truth is, it is tough to get out of bed on a day like this. The damp burrows into you and settles in the bones. *Healthy food for the body; healthy thoughts for the mind.* Marci strides across my foggy brain to deliver this earth-shattering advice. I pull myself out of bed to avoid her absentee cheerleading. *Whatever is true, whatever is noble, whatever is right, whatever is pure, whatever is lovely, whatever is admirable—if anything is excellent or praiseworthy—think about these things.* This old memory verse that I haven't thought of in years suddenly surfaces. It's clear that my mother has joined Marci and is now stitching plaques inside my head.

I dress in sweatpants and a T-shirt and make my way downstairs where I sit at the breakfast table. My father enters the room shortly after. The bemused expression across his face—teacup suspended in mid-air—informs my alligator brain that I'm sitting in his chair. I move without a word and he seems relieved.

"When did you give up coffee?" I ask him.

"Few years back. Your mother read something," he says, with a miniscule rise of his bushy eyebrows. He takes a sip of the tea and looks like he's still getting used to the taste.

"Tea is better for you anyway, Gramps. It's an antioxidant. Excellent decision." Julia munches on a thick wedge of toast.

"Well, if you say so, Doctor Susie-Q." His smile is really one of the all-time great ones. I've missed this smile.

My father is a man who moves slowly, considers his words carefully. He left the decision-making up to our mother—although, officially, he held onto the head of the household title due to Scriptural imperatives—but Jake and I knew where the real power lay. If you could get Mom onside, Dad offered no resistance. He never yelled unless we came too close to farm machinery, and then his voice was sure. You never questioned how much you mattered when he shouted for you to get away from the teeth of the combine or the whirring blade of the lawn mower.

His smiles, however, were easy. Our mother was always busy doing something: canning, freezing, baking, cooking, or cleaning, but our father would stop anything to pick you up in his strong arms and kiss a scraped knee. Now, watching him joke with Julia, I remember the gentle man, the one I would ride with on the tractor for hours or follow to the barn, where I would perch on a bale of hay and pepper him with questions. His answer was almost always the same, some version of "Trust and Obey." And even when I didn't think it was enough, it was reassuring that he believed it.

At Jake's funeral he stood beside my mother and held onto her arm. It was she who held him up, his strength undermined by a force he had no will to resist. I saw who he was that day: a kind and gentle man but powerless and broken.

It's only when my mother enters the kitchen dressed in a grey suit with a crisp, white blouse and pantyhose and sensible black pumps that I realize it's Sunday.

"Church starts in a half-hour," she says, pointedly glancing at my sweatpants. "You're coming, aren't you?"

She has the grace to frame this as a question, but it's a mere formality. I consider asking her if I have a choice and, for a second, we share the equivalent of the squinty-eyed showdown.

"I thought that maybe afterwards we'd go down to Sears and pick out a TV and one of those DVD thingamajigs," my dad says to Julia.

"What? Gramps, really? You are so totally and completely the best, I can't believe it. You don't have to, you know," she adds. "But you can, if you want. You too, Gran, also the best."

My mother smiles uncertainly. "Well, but not on a Sunday, Abe."

"Oh," Julia exclaims loudly. "You guys are so much like Marilla and Matthew Cuthbert, except, obviously, not brother and sister."

"Who?" my father asks.

Julia's eyes grow wide. "Oh my God! I mean, gosh. Oh my gosh. This is great, isn't this great, Mom? We can rent *Anne of Green Gables*."

I take a sip of my tea and look at my mother, who is glancing at her watch. Julia's assessment is bang on.

"I'll go get dressed," I say.

I take my tea upstairs and go straight to the closet. I sip slowly as I examine what I've brought along. I finally choose a simple navy suit because it's not too fancy and that's good. Fancy would indicate that I think too highly of myself. On the other hand, you can't dress too casually, because everybody knows the Lord is prone to having hurt feelings when people don't dress for his day.

Long ago, I tried wearing denim overalls and a bandana to church. My mother went purple in the face. "Don't you have any respect?" she asked.

"Didn't Jesus wear sandals to church?" I responded.

There was another squinty-eyed showdown and I changed my clothes, but it was after Labour Day, so I wore white shoes. My mother's Jehovah has definite opinions about Sunday morning attire.

The subject of church has been a sore one. My mother's letters always ask where we're attending. In the early years, I told her that Mark and I were shopping around. But when Julia was born she grew increasingly concerned. Julia needed guidance, values, and the good clean social environment of a youth group; each letter bulkier than the last with Scripture she included that was underlined in felt pen. My father's postscripts were always short. We needed to be part of something—the body of Christ. He thought we needed to find our home.

When I told my mother that we had settled on a United Church (Christmas and Easter, but I didn't mention this) she was horrified.

"They're barely Christians," she said.

But at least we were going to church and we were still saved—if barely.

~

My dad gets us to church exactly fifteen minutes before the service. The building is unchanged except for a wheelchair ramp out front and the trees, which have grown taller. The A-frame structure is modest, resolute, and plain, a perfect dwelling for a God who demands humility, steadfastness, and simplicity. Julia strides into the building; she knows from experience that any gathering includes the potential for cute boys.

I'm glad I've chosen a shirt with a high neck because, as we climb the front steps, I feel myself grow red and my heartbeat accelerating with adrenaline. There really is no upside to anxiety except that you can't argue with it; it wins every time. And you can't tell yourself to settle down and buck up. You would, obviously, buck up if you could. All you have, during the interminable moments of anxiety, are the moments themselves, and what you are feeling—dammit—is what you are truly feeling. If anxiety tried to play hide and seek, you would find it first every time.

Now, standing at the edge of my old church sanctuary, a feeling of being smothered comes over me and I need to escape. I tell my mother I'm going to the bathroom, and she looks as suspicious as she used to when I would develop a persistent thirst just before the sermon. Now, as then, she nods grimly.

In the cubicle, I lean my flushed face against the cool metal door and breathe in the industrial-strength disinfectant cake that's as much a part of this room as the peeling beige wallpaper and cracked linoleum floor. Two or three people enter the room, talking, laughing, but the conversation is indistinct, as though through water. When they leave, I take a sip from the fountain and think that a stiffer drink would be better.

As I wash my hands, I avoid the reflection in the mirror. I don't like to see myself when I get like this. I don't look like the person I think I am. But I can't resist; I've been in this bathroom too many times. I take a peek and the first thing I see is fear. But there's another reflection as well: younger and unafraid.

I grew up here. There should be a spot on the doorjamb that records the growth. We attended services twice on Sunday and midweek for Pioneer Girls—who *crossed the Prairie in the days of wagon trains; pressing on to new horizons, in our hands God's precious word*. I remember prayer meetings, choir practice, youth group, and committee meetings where we did nothing but nominate future committees. Then there were banquets and potlucks and socials where we honoured the committees, whose number rivalled the length of any of the beget lists in the Bible.

This was something else that Kate, Des, and I found endlessly amusing: the beget lists. We would scan the congregation and whisper about who had beget whom (and how) until Mrs. Peters found it necessary—through thin, disappointed lips—to remind us that Jesus himself was the only *begotten* son of God and so it wouldn't do to laugh about such things.

But there was something about church that did beget laughter. All those rituals: prayer, baptism, communion. Hope. Faith. Love. It was all so big and important and serious that there were times we couldn't take, or hold, it all in. It began as a chirp and a sputter—usually Des—and then a giggle would break out. Soon we'd be shaking helplessly with laughter that could be contained by a pressed hand as effectively as rising floodwater by mesh.

Our parents said our behaviour was disrespectful and they would separate us until we earned back the right to sit together again. We'd be good, for a while, but eventually the whole cycle started again. What we could never explain to our parents, because we hadn't the words, was that the laughter was never about disrespect. It was about joy. We didn't need to be taught how to worship; we already knew. And I always imagined that the Holy Ghost was laughing with us. Of the three of them, the Holy Ghost seemed like the fun one, the relaxed one, the easygoing one. Like he could take a joke and maybe even laugh at himself. Of course, I never passed this theory on, not even to Des. Both she and Kate already thought I took the whole thing more seriously than I needed to. I realized this one day when I said "Isn't it fun when you're in the bathtub, making waves, and then you hold out your hands and say, like Jesus did when he he walked on water, *Peace, be still*. Isn't that fun?" I asked again. They stared at me. Des giggled. Kate just said, "You're a strange kid, you know that?"

I return to the church foyer and find my family at the entrance to the sanctuary. My mother enters the room first, and I can tell by the forward thrust of her head that she's excited to introduce her only grandchild to her friends. Someone with silver hair calls her over to one of the pews. "Is this Julia?"

My mother nods proudly, or happily, I guess. It's hard to know what happiness looks like on my mother. Glad is better; grateful is best. Julia shakes the hand of first one grey-haired person and then another. She's wearing a denim skirt and a sweater that she borrowed from me. Her hair is tied back in a loose knot and her makeup is discreet. She didn't need to be told how to dress. I can see from the smiles and the nods that she's making a good impression, and I'm about to join them when someone touches my hand. I turn to see Des smiling at me.

My throat constricts, and I feel the heaviness press down on my chest. How can she be here? After everything that happened, how can she be here in this place?

She says it first. "You. You came."

seven

"Des?" I say, as if there's room for doubt. But of course there isn't. Instant, liquid recognition travels from the tip of my head to the soles of my feet, where it tingles. *Sole mates forever,* we used to say, holding our feet together, laughing hysterically.

She shakes her head. "I can't believe you're here. Your mom said you might be coming."

"You've talked to her?"

Des laughs, the same tinkling sound that could revive a fairy. "It's a small town, an even smaller church. You remember."

I shake my head. "Yeah, of course. You're here, though."

"We're both here. I think that's official."

"Okay," I finally smile. "I didn't know you were living in the valley again," I say. "I thought you were still in Israel."

"We go back and forth, but these days we're mostly forth. Maxi, that's my daughter, has this thing about graduating with her friends. We've pulled her around too much."

"I knew you had a daughter," I say, quickly. It's not as

if I haven't kept up with Des news. My mother has kept me informed, although, clearly, not up to date. "How old is she?"

"Sixteen," she says, just as Julia arrives.

"Hey, Mom, Gran's wondering where you are."

"Of course," I say, pulling her next to me.

"This must be Julia," Des says.

"Oh, I'm sorry . . . yes, this is Julia," I say. "This is Des."

Julia takes Des's outstretched hand and shakes it. "Desiree?"

"Not very often. Mostly it's Des. You're gorgeous. You must have a beautiful father."

"Nice," I say, smiling.

Des smiles back and suddenly she's sixteen, eighteen, and ten years old all at once.

"Sweetie, can you tell Gran I'll be there in a minute?"

"Tell her we won't miss the sermon," Des says, twinkling.

"Sure, sweep the offspring away. No prob. I live to serve," she says. "Nice to meet you," she adds as she walks away.

Des watches her leave. "She's fun."

"She is," I say. "How are your parents?"

"My mom's fine. She moved back east when my dad died."

"I'm sorry. I liked your dad."

"He was sick for a long time."

"Your daughter, she's sixteen?"

"Driving now. It's terrifying. She's parking the car."

I smile, desperately groping in my mind for something more to say. I try to arrange my body in a way that looks like it's natural to be chatting here in the foyer of the church after twenty years without even one conversation.

"There she is," Des exclaims and I'm relieved. I think we

both are. She waves to a girl coming through the door, and I finally take a good look at the woman in front of me. Her hair is the same frizzy tangle of golden curls, although now streaked softly with grey, and she's a good twenty pounds heavier. She looks so womanly, so grown and womanly. Actually, she looks like every single Sunday school teacher we used to send shrieking from the room.

Des drags her daughter across the room. Julia returns with a five-minute warning from my mother.

"Okay, okay, you don't have to yank," the jet-haired girl grumbles.

"Maxi, this is Glo and her daughter, Julia. Julia's fifteen?" She looks to me for confirmation. I nod. "I've told you about Glo."

"Yeah, a million times." She smiles briefly, nods to Julia. "Hey."

"Hey," Julia responds.

As much as I'm able, I try not to stare. It's not the nose ring or the barbell in her eyebrow or the thin strand of electric blue among the inky black. It's the eyes. Her father's eyes.

"It's nice to meet you," I say. I wonder, for a bizarre moment, how she would respond if I added: You might have been my daughter, you know, if I'd slept with your father when I wanted to.

Des wraps her arms around her daughter's shoulders and hugs her tightly. Maxi just stands there, not looking in the least discomfited. It's as though they're one person—the old and new. The past and present.

"Is Gabe here with you?" I ask, casually.

She shakes her head. "Oh no, he'll be in the barn. That's his church."

"Maxi has his eyes," I say.

Des nods. "Julia has Jake's mouth."

For a moment we just look at each other, and I wonder how we can move past this. It doesn't seem possible.

"My mom said you guys did some crazy shit together," Maxi says from within the stranglehold.

Ah, that's how. "Oh, not so crazy."

"What kinds of things?" Julia asks, stepping forward.

I can't meet Des's eyes, so I concentrate instead on her nose, but even this brings a wave of memories. She used to ask: What about God's nose? Everybody talks about his eyes, his hands, his feet. What about the nose of God?

"Did she ever tell you about the time she decked Harvey Bruchner? Grade seven, I think it was." Des's eyes glint.

"You didn't," Julia says.

"I did not," I say, at the same time.

"Oh, yes you did. Laid him out flat. Mind you, he wasn't expecting it, but still."

"Cool," Maxi says, warming up now.

"Why did you hit him? You hit him?" Julia asks, still shocked.

"I didn't hit—" I begin, but Des's smirk stops me. She never did lie. Then it comes back to me. "I did," I say, incredulously.

"Yep. He told your mother that he thanked God he was not born a woman."

"I think that was the only verse he ever learned. I might have slapped him."

"Oh no," Des laughs. "You always wanted to slap someone and say, 'How dare you'; you also wanted to throw a martini in someone's face." She turns to Julia. "Your mother had quite the list of things she wanted to accomplish. But you decked Harvey. He had it coming."

"Huh," Julia says, still digesting the news.

"Listen, you two have to come over for a proper visit. We have so much to catch up on." I let this monumental understatement catch up to me as she continues. "We're living up at Ryder Mountain now. It's beautiful there. You have to come." She looks at me and I see the dare in her eyes. It's the same look she had when she climbed a tree and called me to join her. The same look she had that day in church—the last time I saw her.

"That sounds like a good idea," I say slowly.

"I'll show you my horse," Maxi says to Julia.

"You have a horse?" Julia squeals and then looks embarrassed.

"Your mother used to love horses."

I had loved horses? Really? "We should be getting in now."

"Of course. But you'll come." She states this as fact as Maxi takes her mother by the shoulder and steers her toward the balcony. "I'll call . . ." She catches my eye and I nod imperceptibly.

"They're nice," Julia decides, as we move to the entrance of the sanctuary. "Isn't it cool that she has a horse? Did you see her tongue piercing?"

I allow her to push me along. "I didn't notice her tongue."

Julia catches my mother's eye and steers me over to the pew where my mom and dad are sitting. My mother scowls briefly because the pastor is already welcoming the congregation, but once we're seated, she looks ahead, smiling as broadly as I've ever seen. My father reaches his hand across her lap and touches mine briefly, also staring forward, also smiling. *God*, I think, *this makes them happy*.

The heat in my face is, thankfully, subsiding, but I still feel like I could use a stiff drink. I look around at the room: the vaulted ceiling with its broad supporting beams; the narrow windows along the panelled sides; the one stained glass window at the back that ushers in a brighter light; the hard pews filled with people. Some of the faces are the same, though older, but many are new, and they are tan and taupe and black. This surprises me; it used to be a sea of white. And the pastor has a goatee. This surprises me as well. He's not wearing a tie or a suit. I lean over to my mother and point this out because I'm not a very mature person. She only shrugs as though I've made a valid point.

And then the congregation stands in one smooth movement and a thrum of conversation fills the room. I am startled at first until I remember the ritual: passing the peace. I shake the offered hands as my mother introduces Julia and me. Then I feel an urgent pull on my shoulder. I turn with its insistence. Evangeline Doerksen, Kate's mom, is staring up at me with soulful eyes.

The Doerksens were our church's royal family, but we were torn between being honoured that such beauty had made its way into our humble congregation (they often wore coordinating outfits) and being concerned over their materialism. My mother refused to gossip about them (which could not be said for some of the other ladies who visited our house; those kitchen walls were thin), but when Evangeline stood in front of the church and wept for the state of the unsaved world—her *great sorrow*—I saw my mother roll her eyes at my father, who smiled and patted her hand.

Kate was the middle child. Lester, her older brother, was omnipotent in school and Lydia, the youngest, was omni-adorable everywhere else. It didn't matter how perfect Kate was, her siblings managed to out-omni her. If I left my family's sadness for the frozen tundra of Manitoba, Kate fled the constant reminder that she had to fight for a place in her mother's perfect sun.

"Gloria, dear." She reaches over and embraces me weakly with her frail, spidery arms. She probably weighs a hundred pounds soaking wet. "How wonderful to see you." Her eyes shine with unshed tears. (Man, that lady knows how to cry, Des used to say.) "This must be Julia." She turns to Julia and embraces her as well. "Kate has told me so much about you."

"Oh, you're Aunt Kate's mom? I love her," Julia says. I smile.

The tears now threaten to fall. "Yes, it's such a tragedy that she couldn't have children. She would have been a great mother."

"Oh," says Julia. "For sure."

"But the Lord knows best. His ways are not our ways."

"Uh, okay."

"How long are you here?" she says to me, her tears magically gone.

"A week or so," I say.

"Oh, so short? After all this time." She shakes her head.

"Well, Julia has to get ready for school."

"Of course. You look well," she says, pinching my upper arm with her hand. "Very healthy."

My mind is whirling with Kate stories, the last of which was her theory that her mother had been receiving secret beauty treatments. (*There's Botox in them there hills,* were her exact words.) When Kate got divorced, her mother's idea of support was to send literature from bald evangelists to her doorstep along with the admonition that God had told her that Kate needed to work on her marriage. God spoke regularly to Evangeline Doerksen. I was Bible-versed by my mother; Kate had been Bible-thumped.

"I try to eat well," I say.

"I can see that," she smiles.

The congregation, I see with relief, is returning to their seats. Before she leaves, Evangeline grasps my mother's arm as well. "Such a blessing," she whispers. I think my mother stiffens, but I'm not sure.

After the singing, accompanied with loud drums and electric guitars, the announcements begin. A young man in shorts (bare legs in church!) regales us with upcoming events: a potluck dinner, a budget meeting, and the baptism classes that will be starting in the next week. When someone tries to sneak in late, he booms out, "Thank you for joining us," and, when he catches someone taking a catnap, he says, "Hope we're not keeping you up, Brother Pete." Humour. I have to admit that, perhaps, change is catching on here.

But when the pastor takes the pulpit—he practically bounces with vigour—his first words are. "We are sinners. Oh yes, we are. Could we *be* more sinful? I don't think so." And I think, *Ah. Here we go.*

As he proceeds to describe the narrow path of salvation, I let myself drift back to a similar, if less sitcom-inspired, sermon.

When we were twelve years old, Kate and Des and I began baptism classes along with the other girls in our class. It was time to be officially saved. (I had been saved at five years old and roughly every year after that—just to be safe—but this was official.) In our little town that had the most churches per capita in the world, there were only two types of people: washed or unwashed in the blood of the Lamb.

One sunny afternoon after we'd completed our third session with Pastor Reimer—a lesson on salvation—we waited outside in the parking lot for our parents to pick us up. Jarnelle Nickel was standing beside me, wearing a moss green Fortrel pantsuit that picked up the green in her eyes, which would have been noticeable even if she hadn't pointed it out as often as she did. Leaning against the white stucco wall of our church, she looked like the fig tree in my mother's living room.

I was mulling over the last conversation I'd had with Pastor Reimer. He had read the story of Nicodemus to us and patiently explained the need for every sinner to be born again. I raised my hand and asked if everyone was a sinner. He said yes. Right off the bat? I asked. He smiled and said yes again, adding that this was called original sin. So, what happens if you sin again and again, I persisted. Do you have to be born again and again?

He said that wasn't necessary, but his smile wasn't quite so cheery. (He was probably recalling all those weeping Sunday school teachers.) He explained, again, about Jesus and the whole cross business, as if this should settle the matter, but I really just wanted to get the rules straight. There was a lot riding on this. He repeated that everyone sinned and came short of the glory of God; it was the human condition.

It perplexed me that we needed to be saved from what was, essentially, ourselves—especially since God Himself put us together—but first things first. So I said, "After you're born again, is the fresh sin new or original?"

He tabled the conversation for the next week, saying we would pick it up again (we never did), and I was still stewing about this when Jarnelle said, pulling a sausage curl straight with her hand and watching it bounce back, that there were going to be a lot of people in hell. A lot.

"What do you mean?" I asked. It hadn't even occurred to me that everyone wouldn't be going to heaven. I mean, as far as things went, it was a fairly simple procedure: *Dear Lord Jesus, come into my heart.* It was the logistics that had me baffled, not the act of repentance itself. I never minded saying sorry if I really was.

"Well, the Japanese aren't going," she said. "No way."

"Why not?"

"They have idols."

"What about the Arabs?" I asked, concern mounting. I'd always been uneasy with the way things had gone with Ishmael. He was a son of Abraham, after all. It seemed like he and his mom had gotten the short end of the stick.

"Wrong mother," she said, another curl bouncing back.

I was prepared to go through the story with Jarnelle, verse by verse, and show her that it wasn't really Ishmael's fault that he had to start a whole new tribe since it was Abraham's wife, Sarah's, idea that her husband and his mom got together in the first place. But she was already on to the Hindus with their too many gods and the Mormons with their suspect prophets and the Seventh Day Adventists with their, I don't remember, something to do with seven days. She might as well have listed most of the churches on the billboard at City Hall. But my head was spinning and, while

I had to admit that her comparative religion knowledge was vastly superior to mine, my heart was settling deeper and deeper into the pit of my stomach as each fate was so neatly decided. Finally, barely able to speak above a whisper, I asked, "What about the Catholics?"

She appeared to waver here and I held my breath. Victory was in my grasp, the truth at stake, lives hanging in the balance. But in the end she shook her head and said, "Nope."

"Why not?"

Her curls bounced sideways like a Slinky. "They care too much about Mary. It's not normal. And, also, they think you can get out of hell." Her friends giggled at the absurdity. "Purgatory? As if. No way."

"The Pope, you think? For real? The Pope is going to hell?"

But Jarnelle remained unmoved. She was sorry, she said, but this was the way things were. She didn't make up the rules, did she? And then her parents arrived to pick her up.

As she climbed into the car, I called after her. "But they believe in Jesus, too." She had no response to this.

I remember the conversation for several reasons. For one, it started a series of nightmares about the tens of hundreds of thousands of millions of eternally burning souls. But, at the same time, I felt a small sense of accomplishment because, although I had lost the Buddhists, the Muslims, and the Hindus—and admittedly, this was huge—I may have saved the Catholics.

eight

I follow my father to the car—thankfully he's never been one for loitering in the foyer—while my mother remains behind to introduce Julia to every single member of the church. He hums a few bars of the Benediction and we wait in companionable silence.

He starts the car when they get in and we drive off toward home, where a chicken dinner is waiting.

"I can't wait for lunch," Julia says, stretching her arms happily. "That was a nice show," she says.

"Service," I correct, before my mother can, almost adding that Julia's word might be more apt. I press my lips together, remembering Julia's continual admonition to be nice.

"Well, the drums are always too loud," my mother says. "And I don't know why we need electric guitars. Did you see how many people had to adjust their hearing aids? But the sermon was fine."

"I liked the band," says Julia. "They were rockin' out."

My father laughs out loud and even my mother smiles at this. I just look at Julia and shake my head. At times like this

she reminds me so much of Jake. He could always wrest a
smile while I . . . *Never mind*, I think, before Marci can complete her sage advice to let it go. *Let go and Let God,* she
said once. And only once.

"When do you think we'll go to Maxi's place?" Julia asks.

My mother turns at this. "You met Maxi?"

"Yeah, and her mom. She's nice."

My mother faces forward again. "So then you saw Des?"

"Yes," I say, thinly. "That was a nice surprise. I didn't
know they were back in town."

Julia scowls at the tone.

"Didn't I mention that?" my mother says.

I think I see a faint blush creep up her neck. My mother
is a terrible liar and only a moderately good prevaricator.
This statement wobbles between both. "Why, no, you didn't.
I think I would have remembered."

"I've invited them for dinner next week."

As these words settle into me, I feel my blood rise. "So
then you did know that I saw her today. She must have
mentioned it."

"Oh, Gloria," she sighs.

"Now, you two," my dad says. "This is like old times."

"What's the big deal, Mom? She was your friend, right?"

"Yes," I say. "I just didn't want this visit to be a big
event."

Julia reaches forward and taps my mother on her shoulder and says, sotto voce, "We better cancel the parade."

My parents laugh. I stare out the window and mutter
inwardly, like a chant: *Let it go, Let it go, Let it go.*

Julia doesn't come down for breakfast the next morning. It's a meal she often skips at home, but not here. Yesterday's lunch had been strained, and we'd spent the day playing an intense game of Scrabble, with Julia doing more than her share of the talking. I wonder if she's taking a well-deserved break from her duties as intermediary and comic relief.

My parents and I eat waffles and sausage as if nothing has happened. We're good at this, practised at avoiding head-on collisions. After I slip the final plate into the cupboard, the telephone rings. My mother answers it, then hands it to me without a word.

As I take it, she whispers, "It's Des."

Wow, I think. *Mom: 2, me: 0.* Too late to pretend that I'm not here. I take the receiver from her with a scowl.

"Glo?"

"Hey, Des," I say, casually. False, but convincing, I think.

"Hey, um, hey." She's nervous.

I take the phone and enter the next room, stretching the cord as far as it will allow. "How's it going?" I say.

"Good. Great. Listen, Maxi's dying to have Julia come over and see her horse. And I thought maybe you could stay for lunch, if that's okay? I mean, I know you're here to visit your parents and all, but it's a gorgeous day for a ride. And I thought, maybe . . . but if you're busy, it's . . ."

"Sounds great," I say, wanting desperately to save her from herself and the way she always talked too much when she was nervous. It's the least I can do. "Julia will love that."

"So, see you then? Your dad can give you instructions, okay?"

"Yep."

I hang up the phone and leave the kitchen without a glance at my mother.

"Des called. Maxi wants to show you her horse," I say to Julia.

"Okay," she says, making no move to get out of bed, her face toward the wall.

"I thought we'd leave in an hour or so."

"Okay."

I climb in bed with her the way I used to. She's still turned away from me but I can feel the warmth of her body through the cotton sheet. It's a muggy day. I expect to be rebuffed but it doesn't come. "You all right?"

"It's just—nothing . . ."

"Just what?"

"Just really weird here sometimes. Like . . . quiet."

"Yes." I want to tell her how it's sadness she's feeling and that we don't talk about that. We don't have sad here; we have faith. "Yes, it is, quiet." It's not enough; I know this.

She sits up in bed, suddenly, cross-legged. The bed bounces. "More importantly . . . what should I wear?"

"I can't believe you think I'm going to fall for that. Do I look like I was born yesterday?"

She eyes me up and down before leaping off the bed. "Not hardly." She throws open her closet and begins riffling through her clothes. I watch her, knowing that I've disappeared now as she decides on the perfect outfit. Her ability to bounce out of weird is well honed. Sometimes I think she's gotten scarily good at it.

A half-hour later, Julia emerges in a pair of tight jeans, darker than usual eyeliner, and a sequin-encrusted T-shirt that says BOY CRAZY. I'm glad my mother is in the barn. I recently read a parenting book by a woman who'd clearly read a lot of Shakespeare. The final chapter was entitled "To Be or Not to Let Them Be." I decide now to keep my mouth shut, even though it is painfully obvious that she is being herself in the image of Maxi.

"I wish I had a tattoo," she mumbles as she checks her reflection in the hallway mirror.

"We could see if your grandfather could warm up the branding iron."

Her lip curls.

"Just a joke," I add.

"Technically there should be humour involved," she says, distracted by her reflection in the hall mirror and the way her hair is flipping on one side. I let her fuss and tell myself again that it's good she doesn't need my approval—healthy, even. But I hate it. I see the little girl in her eyes, the still-round arms, the shine of her hair, the bulge of a tummy she tries to disguise with folded arms. I still want to protect her and I wonder if this ever goes away.

"Earth to Mom," she says, catching my eyes in the mirror.

"I'm here."

"No, you're not," she says, matter-of-factly.

~

On the drive to Des's place, I try to make up for last night's dinner of weirdness. As we make our way along back roads threaded through cow-dotted fields, I tell Julia about some of the things Des, Kate, and I used to do: roller skating, hay rides, choir practice, youth group, Missions Fest.

"Missions Fest?"

"It's hard to explain."

"Try."

"It was a . . . festival of missions."

"Nice effort."

"Seriously, Jewel, it's . . . this place is hard to explain. It doesn't always seem real to me."

"Didn't you grow up in the seventies? The Beatles, drugs, free love? What happened then?"

I reach the road that leads to Des's house on the hill. "We didn't have the sixties or the seventies here," I say. "The town voted against it."

Julia looks mildly put out at this, but busies herself with reading my father's instructions, directing me as we climb higher and higher, until she shouts, "Hey, that's it!" She points to the address on a mailbox. "Wow. What a gorgeous house."

The house is magnificent, with gables and dormers and wooden shutters, wide picture windows. A porch wraps itself around the house; creeping wisteria and flowering clematis wind their way through trellises. Elk Mountain and a forest of ancient cedars frame the valley below. Fog clings to the lowlands; it gives me vertigo to look at the shifting carpet of mist beneath. It's something from a fairy tale. Des is written all over it, but so is Gabe. For the first time, I allow myself the possibility that he might be here. For not the first time, I wonder at my ability to skirt the obvious.

Des waits for us, alone, on the porch, sitting in a chair fashioned from willow branches. She puts down her teacup and waves as we approach.

"The lady of the manor, I presume?" I say.

Des grins, sending a battalion of lines to flank her eyes. "I know. Isn't it a hoot?" Her voice is the same one I've known since we were five years old. "I'm so glad you're here. Maxi is in the barn, Julia." She points to a lavender-lined path and the weathered grey building beyond. "Roy will show you." She taps the Border collie at her side; he leaps forward with a yip. "Barn, Roy."

Julia squeals her own yip, off-setting the stern effect of her makeup. "Cool," she amends quickly. "Come, boy." Her authority dissolves as the dog licks her face and she giggles.

"Do you want me to come with you?"

"I'll be fine, Mother." She tosses a sharp glare in my direction, then runs up the path with Roy leading the way.

I mime an imaginary gun to my head. "When will I learn?"

Des laughs. "They're here to drive us insane the same way we did with our mothers. Mother karma, I guess."

"I guess."

I climb the steps. Neither of us says anything. This is different from running into her at church. This is intentional, and it accentuates the years of silence that have separated us. At the same time, the wide berth of time disappears altogether, leaving me with an entirely different type of vertigo.

She breaks the growing silence. "Do you want some ginger tea?" Now she sounds every bit the grown-up.

I take a cup and sit in the tall chair beside hers that remind me of thrones—the king and queen surveying the wooded kingdom beyond. "It's just gorgeous here, Des. How perfect for you." I sip the warm tea.

"We lucked out. Bought some land at a good time, sold at a better time, and then we found this place. Dumb luck. But we're here now, and it would take a stick of dynamite to get us out."

We. Us. The tiny words jump out at me. I leap over them. "I never thought I'd hear you say that. You with the wanderlust."

"I did my share of wandering, I guess." Her voice is thoughtful. "What about you?" She passes a plate of biscuits. The pottery is heavy and rough; a design of olives, blue and cream.

"Not so much. But you've actually lived away. What was that like?" I ask, determined to steer the conversation toward the bland, impersonal, safe. I hear how forced and heavy my words sound. I tell myself to stay afloat, tread for an hour or so. I rub my knees to keep the blood moving.

"It's so good to see you," she says, instead of answering my question.

I take a sip of tea. "It's good to see you."

The screen door opens with a creak and closes with a crash as a man steps out onto the porch. Not just a man, of course. It's Gabe—but he's a man now. I, on the other hand, have just tripped over a crack in the universe and am sixteen again. But he is most definitely a man—tall, lean, handsome, with the same ridiculous pool-blue eyes. Des's man. And I need to grow up now. "Glo," he says. In the fraction of time that is mine to respond, I remind myself that he is Des's man. "You look great," Gabe says, moving forward. "Doesn't she look great, Des?" Gabe squeezes her shoulder before reaching me. I rise uncertainly. Handshake or air kiss? I don't know the appropriate greeting for the boy I thought I'd love forever. Before I can decide he gives me a hug.

All I think is, *How is it possible he smells the same?* Soap, clean sweat, horsehide. It picks me up like a rock and tosses me into the field. I murmur something about how he looks great as well, just great, and then I force myself to pay attention to the words coming out of his mouth. I try to catch hold of them the way I used to grab at the bars of a merry-go-round: carefully, watching each one go by until I made the huge leap.

"—long in town?" he is saying. There is a pause and a gap. I leap.

"How long are we in town?" I guess. He nods and relief fills me. I'm on the merry-go-round. All I have to do now is hold on tight. "A few more days."

"Your parents are well?"

"Older but pretty much the same."

As we carry on a stilted non-conversation about aging parents and real estate, Des watches us, leaning back in her chair.

"How does it feel? Being back," Des asks, suddenly. Gabe shoots a look across the table. The question catches me off guard, but the intimacy of the look is even more disconcerting. I ask myself if I still expected Gabe to be standing next to the porch in the rain where I left him twenty years ago.

"It's completely the same," I say. "They haven't changed a thing."

"That's not exactly what I asked," she says.

"Slow down there, girl." Gabe's voice is faintly patronizing. I remember this.

"Okay, if you could remember that I'm not one of your horses."

"I think I can do that," he laughs and immediately the tension dissolves. He was always good at that.

"Sorry," she says. "Gabe says I'm a little intense sometimes. A little impatient."

"You never were." I recall the trusting eyes when I told her that fairies weren't real. Trusting but disappointed. The trust is gone now, though. Of course it is.

nine

Des tells Gabe to show me around the property while she makes lunch. I say that I'll stay and help. "Go," she instructs. "You guys should . . . go."

Gabe gives her a light kiss on the side of her face. If she registers it, it doesn't show.

As I try to keep up with his long-legged stride, I search for things to talk about. Something other than how great he still looks in Levi's bootcut jeans, how he still has the greatest ass. It seems absurd to talk about anything other than the fact that we haven't seen each other for twenty years and that the last time we spoke I told him I didn't love him anymore. "It's gorgeous here, Gabe."

"We like it." Again with the *we*. He pushes a gate open and waits for me to pass through. As I do, I smell him again and it reminds me that we used to belong to each other. I move ahead quickly.

"Glo?"

"Yes?" I say, far too eagerly.

"I asked how Mark was doing. Is he going to join you?"

It's strange to hear Gabe say Mark's name—the past talking about the present. And the present is that Mark and I are together; Gabe belongs to Des. "Uh, no," I answer. I pluck a buttercup from the ground and sniff it, remembering—too late—that buttercups have no scent, only the mystical ability to predict whether or not you like butter. *Keep up*, I warn myself. *Hang on.* "He's at a conference now, and then he needs to prepare for the summer session. He's up for tenure this fall."

Gabe nods. He has such a strong profile. I used to call him my Marlboro man. His hair is greying at the temples but, other than that, twenty years sits lightly.

"University?" His mouth is moving.

"Pardon?" I feign a hearing impairment as an alternative to crazy.

"He's still at the University of Manitoba, I said, but it was a dumb question because I knew the answer. It's weird to see you, Glo, I have to say."

"I know."

As we walk, Gabe shifts the conversation smoothly to the local vegetation. "Pearly Everlasting," he says, pointing to a white weed. "Night-Flowering Catchfly," he says, pointing out another.

I smile, remembering his impromptu botany lessons.

When we reach a grove of alder trees between the house and the barn, Gabe points to a gash in the side of one of the trees. "Black bear. Comes around every spring to let us know he's still around. See here—" He touches a succession of marks, each one higher than the last. "Like a kid showing us how he's grown," he says. "You can change the land all you want, but he doesn't see that. It's still his territory. His wild memory."

I look beyond the grove to the farmland below. You could almost see my parents' land. "I know how he feels."

Gabe smiles his slow smile. It brings me back to another mountainside. "So, you found your big wide world in Winnipeg?" he asks.

This was the reason I'd come up with for not loving him anymore. That big wide world out there. Not my finest, or most original, moment. "Well, it's wide, anyway," I say. "Let's go find the girls."

"Good idea."

The barn smells like every other: the sweetness of hay mingles with the heavy sweat of the animals and the unyielding sour of manure. The stalls have bridles hanging beside them. At a glance I count eight stalls. "You breed horses?" I ask, reaching over a door to rub a beautiful chestnut muzzle. The pungent aroma of horse sweat fills my nostrils and brings me back to all the trail rides with Gabe. "You lucky duck."

"Lucky duck," Gabe grins. "Haven't heard that for a while. Do you still ride?"

"Oh no, not for years. Not since I lived here. Well, apart from a couple of dude ranch horses that Julia insisted on riding while we were camping. But those poor creatures hardly count." Creatures? Did I really just say creatures? I shake my head, caught. Gabe smirks and I have this irresistible urge to touch his face, just one stroke on the side of his stubbled cheek.

"Pops." A voice trickles down from the hayloft. I look up. A face appears, upside down, with black and sapphire hair splayed about like petals of a flower. Then Julia's blond mane is alongside. Inverted, they both look much younger.

"It's so cool up here," Julia says. "Come see."

"Not right now."

"Hey, hi there." Gabe waves. "I'm Gabe. You must be Julia. You're as pretty as your mother."

Julia smiles, colours slightly, and pulls herself quickly out of view. Maxi makes a face at her father. "Gross, Father." Then she disappears as well.

Gabe shrugs. "I go from Pops to Gross Father in seconds these days."

"Tell me about it." We laugh. *Stay here*, I think. Marci would deeply approve. *Be in the moment*, she would say, beaming with her borrowed wisdom.

Lunch is an eclectic Mediterranean feast of hummus and tzatziki, tapenade and pita bread. Des lived on the stuff, she says, while she was in Israel. There is also tabbouleh and stuffed eggplant—a reminder of Gabe's time in Lebanon, when he and Des were only a border away from each other. The wine is from Italy, the only place they hadn't been and I had.

"Mark had a conference in Rome, so I tagged along."

"Did you love it?" Des asks.

I nod half-heartedly, finishing my wine too soon. Gabe pours more into my glass. "I'm not much of a traveller, as it turns out. It was all too disorienting for me. I thought I would love it, but I didn't. I felt like an outsider."

The wine has loosened my tongue; my words sound tired and defeated. They don't describe how I felt when I wandered the streets of Rome while Mark was busy in sessions. Every day I would get myself a cappuccino and walk through the monuments and ruins, arches and aqueducts, bridges and roads that had seen the passage of slaves, martyrs, apostles, merchants, tourists, and travellers for thousands of years— through a civilization that had the world talking still. On a tour of the Coliseum, the guide spoke gushingly, waving his umbrella around his head to make the point that the Romans were the first to use cement in construction and the knowledge was then lost for hundreds of years. But they were the first: he was emphatic, practically giddy, about this. It became the refrain I was to hear over and over again: the mighty Romans. All very impressive, but I was disappointed. The very name, Roma, woke up old, romantic notions. I thought I would find answers waiting, buried in the rubble, but instead I found names engraved on monuments: names of ancient men who lived hundreds of years before and left only a monument to themselves. Jesus never went to Rome, of course, but the Roman world had shaped his destiny. Yet I saw nothing of him there, and that was what I had hoped to find.

"The food was great, though," I add.

The girls flit out onto the porch now. They ate leftover pizza earlier, unable to wait one more minute for food.

"So," says Maxi, sitting on her father's lap and taking an olive from her mother's plate, chewing it like gum, then spitting the pit into her hand. "How's memory lane?"

"We haven't gone very far down that road," says Des, sipping her wine.

"Julia, what do you think about the valley?" asks Gabe, smoothly.

"It's beautiful. It's so . . . green."

"It is that. Do you like it?"

"It's weird that we haven't been here before," she says, almost urgently.

This startles me. Julia is a good conciliator but not much of a blurter. She is careful. Or so I thought. I give her a warning glance, but she evades it and looks, instead, to the mountains beyond. "This place is kind of a mystery."

"That's funny," says Des.

I have to agree, thinking there is no more sure place in the world, and so I smile. Des smiles back.

Gabe watches us. "Did your mother ever tell you she defended my honour?"

"What?" Julia asks, her eyes trained on Gabe's.

"I'd only been here a couple of weeks when I was outed for being a Jew."

Julia looks at me.

Gabe's mother was Jewish; she moved them here after his dad died. Between being Jewish, cute, and almost an orphan, he was irresistible to me. I decide not to say any of this.

"It's kind of ethnocentric here. Not a lot of diversity," says Des.

"That's one way of putting it," I smile. "There was only one way, Sweetie. Everything else was suspect."

"English," Maxi says, spitting another pit onto her mother's plate, "would be helpful." She looks to her father.

"Some loudmouth was on the playground—"

"Harvey Bruchner?" Julia says, like she's figured out a *Jeopardy!* question.

"No," I say. "I don't think it was Harvey."

"Just some loudmouth," Gabe continues, "who thinks it's his job to inform the town that a Christ-killer is in the house."

"And my mom?" Julia sounds like she's eight years old, wondering how this story could possibly turn out.

"Your mother decides that it's her job to enlighten our villain . . ."

"Paul," Des says, suddenly. "Paul Braun."

"That's right," Gabe and I say, almost simultaneously.

"Your mother says—shouts, actually—that, for his information, the Jews were the chosen people and Jesus was a Jew and that he, Paul Braun, was a stupid-head."

"Ignorant stupid-head, I believe," Des says.

"Yes, I did," I admit, "say that."

"I can't tell you how helpful that was," concludes Gabe. "Being the new boy *and* chosen by God."

"Always glad to help," I say.

Gabe smiles. "Your mother was fierce."

Maxi winces. "Dad, we've talked about this, remember? No trying to be hip?"

"Now that's ironic, *hip* being a word from my generation."

"He means it, though," Des says, patting Julia on the hand. "Literally, your mother was fierce."

"Well," I say, "literal, anyway."

"Punching out Harvey Bruchner and now this," Julia shakes her head.

"When parents get nostalgic, it's time to vamoose," Maxi says, hopping over the railing and landing neatly on her feet.

"No kidding," Julia agrees, jumping up as well.

I watch them walk up the hill, laughing like they've known each other forever. Gabe gets up from the table after receiving a not-too-subtle eyebrow arch from Des. He disappears with an armful of dishes.

"What a great place for kids," I say, going for the soccer-mom voice instead of the nervous, guilty ex-friend option.

"Maxi pretends that she's all grown up, you know, with the eyebrow and the tongue, but she's still a kid, really."

"Julia, too."

"Our daughters," Des shakes her head. "We have daughters!" She says this as though it's breaking news. "Us!"

"I know. It wasn't exactly our dream, was it?"

"No, it was Kate's. How is she?" she asks, a slight edge to her voice.

"She's a principal now," I say.

"That makes total sense."

"She's good at it. Really good. You heard about her divorce?" This is a mere formality. There's no way that this wasn't front-page news, if not literally in the town paper, then at least on the church prayer chain, which was the more efficient method of communication.

"I was sorry to hear about it. And shocked. Kate was always so careful about love. I mean, she had a list."

"I know."

"An actual, physical list."

I smile at this. "Athletic, handsome, tall . . ."

"Good head of hair."

"Of course. Rich, funny . . ."

"No," Des shakes her head. "I don't think so. Not funny."

"Really? Because Preston was funny."

"Well, there you have it. Nothing funny about perfection." Des smiles over the lapis blue wineglass that matches her eyes. "Remember skinny-dipping in McGann's pond? That was fun. You always had the best ideas."

"My idea? That was your idea."

Des shakes her head. "Oh, no. Don't you remember? You were reading *Anne of Green Gables* back then, and you couldn't stop talking about the scene where she floats down the canal, pretending to be . . . whoever. You were in deep, that's all I know. I'm not sure where the skinny-dipping fit in—maybe that was my idea, that sounds like me—but you started it. You had to talk Kate and me into it."

"Really? I thought it was your idea and Kate agreed."

She finishes her wine and places the glass on the table. "Oh, yes. Kate had to agree. That was the requirement. She was afraid that someone would see us. What would people think?" She raises her brows. "I'll get some coffee for us."

Skinny-dipping in McGann's pond was my idea—Des is right. I suggested it to Des, who giggled, and then we looked to Kate, who hesitated. During the fearless years, Kate and Des and I imagined we were a version of the Trinity. In our own created cosmos, Kate was probably God, Des was Jesus, and I was the Holy Ghost. We thought it was funny but true at the same time. Kate was bossy, organized, and, in lots of ways, perfect; Des was accommodating and trusting; I floated somewhere between the two.

Finally Kate bestowed her benevolent half-smile and we knew she was in. We tiptoed across the field, even though it was midnight and no one was around. A new family had moved onto the property only weeks before, but the house was far from the pond. By the time we reached the edge of the water—after passing the familiar creek that seemed haunted in the deep night, and the weeping willow branches that clutched after us—we could barely breathe.

Kate hesitated at the edge of the pond, her hands at her collar. "What if somebody sees us?"

Des glanced down at her chest. "There's nothing to see . . ."

"Now that's a blessing," I finished, and we shattered the spell with giggles.

We proceeded without any further thought for slumbering monsters, man or beast. The moon was full and it unleashed something in us. Des grew braver in the moment: diving and doing cannonball jumps off the dock in only her pale pink underwear. Kate, never one to be outdone, joined her. I entered the water slowly, letting my temperature catch up to the cool. I floated a distance away, buoyed by the sound of their bubbling voices. The pond surrounded me and, with my ears submerged, became a muffled fusion of music with crickets and owls and frogs thrumming the rhythm; Kate's and Des's squeals provided the melody. As I bobbed in and out, I wondered if this was what the womb felt like, that before-world, where everything was safe and warm and easy.

When I heard a sound in the woods, the crack of a twig, my first thought was of some lonely, hungry bear. But before I could warn Des and Kate, I saw the shaky beam of a flashlight on the path, and then it was gone. The moonlight took over and I saw the scrawny boy. I ducked immediately beneath the water and began to swim to Des and Kate to warn them that we were being spied on. In the next few seconds I thought about our lost moment and I became indignant. When I resurfaced for air I was fully prepared to yell at the intruder. But the boy was already backing up the path—I could see the toothy grin in his shadowed face—and he waved before turning. My indignance melted away, replaced by something new and undiscovered.

At school the following Monday, I discovered that his name was Gabe and that he was our age and in our class. I braced myself. It would have been a perfect opportunity for him, the new boy. But he didn't say a word to me and, as the days passed, neither did anyone else. I hadn't told Des and Kate that he'd been there, because I didn't want to spoil their fun and also because I knew Kate would find a way to blame Des, even though it was my idea. Kate's reputation was already very important to her, and Des had a tendency to get into trouble. But there was another reason I stayed silent. I didn't want to share that sliver of moonlit mystery.

Years later, I asked Gabe if he remembered that night.

"I'll never forget it."

"Why didn't you tell anyone?"

He looked awkward at first, and then he grinned. "You were mermaids. I didn't know if you were real." It was the same toothy grin as that night, and I fell in love with him on the spot.

ten

Des returns to the porch with a tray of coffee and biscuits. Gabe is wearing a cowboy hat and boots. This makes me laugh.

"Are you laughing at me? You laughing at me?" he asks, doing a bad version of Robert De Niro.

Des groans as I laugh. "Oh, not the impressions. Please don't laugh or it will be Sean Connery next and Maxi and I will have to ban him from the house."

"It's just, well, you always wanted to grow up to be a cowboy. It's so rare that people actually stick to their original plans. It's nice," I amend. "Not funny at all."

Gabe clumps down the stairs. At the bottom, he leans against the railing, his eyes squinting up at us, thus cementing the image in place. "Has Des told you about the day Maxi was born?"

I shake my head as Des groans.

"I had to go home for her special scarf and some goofy whale music. When I came back they'd moved her into the labour room. I didn't have to ask for directions. You could hear her in the parking lot."

"I was doing fine until Pastor Reimer showed up."

"Oh, no. If this was a movie, this is where the music would change."

"Exactly," Des smiles. "He was visiting someone and heard I was there, so he decided to pop by to see how I was doing."

"A move I'm sure he's regretted since," Gabe adds.

"What happened?" I say.

"He comes in and decides to remind me that pain in childbirth was ordained by God. He even quoted the verse, 'You will suffer greatly when you give birth.'"

"He didn't."

"He did."

"So," Gabe continues. "I'm walking down the hall and I see an old man leaving the room, covering his ears and knocking nurses out of the way in a desperate bid for freedom."

"Not quite," Des sighs.

"And in the background, I hear Des yelling, 'She took an apple. She didn't cut down the fucking tree.'"

"I was in transition," Des explains.

I laugh but I'm also a little thrilled. The man had handed out his own share of curses over the years.

Gabe chuckles and says he's off to the Co-op to buy feed. He leaves us with a wave.

"I was in transition," she explains again, taking a sip from her coffee cup. "Now, tell me about Mark. We have so much to catch up on."

I leave this monumental understatement alone, deciding in an instant that the present, no matter how uncomfortable, is better than the past. I rifle through my brain to compose the facts that I'll release. Anything other than my suspicion that Mark and I were through. "We met in university. He's a history professor now, but then he was just, well, a goof-ball."

"I like him already," she says. "Say more."

"I was working in the cafeteria and he just sort of wandered in and asked me out."

"How bold."

"Yeah," I say. "So I went and we hit it off and that was that."

"Ah, how romantic," she smirks. "Just like the movies."

I smile. "Life isn't so much like that, as it turns out."

"Well, not when you leave out the good parts," she smiles like she knows. "I'll go get dessert. You work on your story. You were always good with stories."

～

She's right, of course, and I've been busted. My courses weren't going well and my parents' cheques were beginning to reflect how much higher education they thought I required. I missed Jake and I missed Des and I missed Gabe. I missed my life. But I can't say this to Des. That's when Mark wandered in with his infectious, goofy smile. He started flirting with me, but all I really wanted was to give him his hamburger and fries and keep the line moving. He asked me if I wanted to go out for a drink sometime. I said I wasn't thirsty. He said "Never?" I said, "That's right, I'm never thirsty." "So, you're like a camel," he said. I said that was ridiculous, of course camels got thirsty. He managed to take that as a yes, because later that day he was waiting for me outside the cafeteria.

I was not looking to fall in love; I was certain about this.

I hadn't fallen out of the old love. I can't say this to Des either. When Mark ordered his third beer and flirted with the waitress, I tried to find an excuse to leave.

"So, Mark," I asked, even though his head was twisted around, watching the waitress leave. "What do you believe in?" I thought this line of questioning had a good chance of cutting the evening short.

Mark didn't blink. "Besides lust?"

"Besides that," I said. (Although I thought it was a good answer.)

"Nothing."

"Nothing?" I was a little intrigued by this.

He leaned forward so that I could smell the beer on his breath. "With all my heart. Everything comes from nothing, right? I mean, we're all pretty much agreed on that, if nothing else." Then he grinned stupidly. "No pun intended. But religious or not, we're all agreed. There was nothing—the abyss—and then there was something." Then he leered, "And you're something," which made me groan and smile.

"Go on," I said.

"That's it. It's what I believe. I'm here, you're here." He lifted his glass. "So here's to the nothing that brought us here."

I laughed, said he was drunk and, despite myself, almost fell in love—or as close as I wanted to come again. I really liked that Mark believed in nothing. Later, when Julia was born, he changed his mind. He believed in us. And that's when I knew we were in trouble.

My parents accepted him even though his educational aspirations were a little "grand." (Somewhere in Proverbs.) But he had a plan and a future and was from good stock, if not Mennonite. His parents were farmers though, and this almost made up for it.

Mark wanted me to continue studying after we got married, but it made more sense if I worked, I thought. I was big on letting sense rule and, the fact was, I didn't have a plan except to forget. And, for a time, it worked. Jake became the brother who died in a tragic accident. Simple. Gabe, a first boyfriend; Des, a high school buddy. Mark knew none of them, and so I could reconfigure my history to match his impression. It wasn't that hard. I became adept at sitting still when a bad memory came along, so still that it didn't notice me and I couldn't feel it. Eventually, it would pass. Marci believes my numbness has wrapped itself around my unattended sorrow. I tell her that numb is not the worst thing in the world.

And then I got pregnant. Mark listened to me rant about how completely clear I had been on the subject of me not wanting to have a baby. When I stopped to breathe, he nodded and sensibly pointed out that I was on the pill and we had used condoms. Then he hugged me and said this baby was determined to be.

I kept my panic and fear to myself, although there were days when I had to lock myself in the bathroom until the shaking subsided and my breathing returned to normal. Kate tried to understand, but it was hard for her since she and Preston had been trying to conceive for two years.

I was the most disagreeable pregnant woman ever. I drank, took up smoking and ran down stairs. In the seventh month I realized that this was really going to happen, this being was inevitable, but nothing could make me love it. I would take care of it for eighteen years and then I would let it go. *Eighteen years*, I thought, *I'll give you that.*

And then she was born. Too small, lungs not quite formed. They had to revive her twice and worried about liver function. After a week, the doctors said that I could go home but Julia needed to remain. With a voice I didn't recognize as my own, I told them I wasn't leaving her.

It wasn't her tiny toes and fingers that did me in. Or her rosebud mouth and the froth of black hair that stood straight up. Or her bleating little cry. It wasn't even her, exactly—I didn't know who she was yet. It was her life that undid me. How alive she was; how she simply was, in spite of my ill attention.

I devoted the next fifteen years to protecting her. I checked her while she slept in her crib, once every ten minutes. I didn't turn my back while she was on the change table; I chopped her food so fine a worm could have ingested it without choking. I don't think she knew that wieners didn't come in little pieces until she was eight years old. When she was enrolled in kindergarten, I took the job at her school as secretary. Mark wanted another child, but I couldn't see how I could be in two places at once. By then he had already figured out that I was damaged and didn't insist.

I tried to protect Julia from all the things I feared as a child. When, for instance, she walked into the kitchen and didn't find me there, she didn't think: Oh, must be the Rapture. *Man and wife asleep in bed. She hears a noise and turns her head, he's gone. I wish we'd all been ready*. That's what I wanted—to raise her in a world where these fears didn't exist. To keep her safe.

⌣

Des returns to the porch with more coffee and chocolate, which she dips into immediately. "An obvious weakness," she says.

The rain starts pouring in earnest. "Let's go find the girls," I say. "It's really coming down."

As we walk up the lavender path to the barn, the wind pushes against us, carrying with it the scent of rain-soaked earth. I pull my sweater close around me and remember how slippery the earth could be—how easy to fall.

"Gabe is right. I am intense and impatient. And blunt— that's the other thing."

"I remember you being completely fluid."

She laughs. "What does that mean?"

"Free, I guess. Brave, for sure. You'd do anything on a dare."

"Do you remember Truth or Dare? You always chose truth."

"And you always chose dare."

"Kate wanted to play Secretary."

I laugh. "No, Kate wanted to play Boss. We were always the secretaries, remember?"

"And now you're the school secretary. That's a little funny."

I don't quite know what to say to this. Probably because it's the first time I've put these two pieces together. I needed to keep an eye on Julia; Kate was Julia's principal. It just made sense. "It is," I allow. "A little."

"You know," she says, suddenly, facing me. Her hair is even curlier in the rain. "Listen, I knew you couldn't come with me—that day."

The abruptness of her words hits me like I've walked

headlong into a glass wall. Should have seen it coming but, well, it's a glass wall.

"Sorry," she says. "That's the blunt thing I was talking about."

"I should have," I say, slowly.

"Maybe. Maybe not. That's not the point. The point is that, deep down, I knew you couldn't follow me. It was somewhere I had to go alone."

"I'm so sorry." I struggle for something better. "Des, really . . ."

She shakes her head. "No, you're not. But you want to be."

We continue walking in silence until we've reached the corral. Two horses stand tied to the fence, and Maxi is saddling up the chestnut mare I saw earlier.

I try to arrange my face into something that resembles normal. "What's going on?"

"We're just going for a quick ride down to the stream," Maxi says.

"She's never been on anything other than a dude-ranch horse. She's pretty inexperienced."

"Hello," Julia waves a hand. "She's standing right here."

I offer a grimace as an apology. "Shouldn't they be wearing helmets?" I ask Des. Julia rolls her eyes at Maxi, who just smiles.

"You're just going to walk the horses, right, Maxi?" Des asks.

"Sure." She pulls on the horn and hoists herself up onto the saddle.

I look above the mountain to the gathering clouds. The rain isn't going to let up. If anything, it's going to rain harder.

"We should really get home before it pours, Julia. You're not dressed for this and, besides, your grandparents like to eat early."

"Are you serious?"

"Maybe another time."

Julia's neck hyperextends; disbelief paralyzes her for a moment and then, with one quick motion, she throws the reins at Maxi. She storms off to the car without a word.

"I'm sorry," I say.

"Don't worry about it. Maxi gets pissed off at me every couple of hours."

"Mother."

"Gabe could go with them." She puts her hand on my shoulder and I feel its warmth through my jacket.

"I'm just . . . Julia says I'm overprotective. That's what she says."

~

As we make our way down the winding road, rain falls in diagonal sheets, pressed by the wind. The vehicle strains against it and my knuckles grow white on the wheel.

There's really no way to explain rain. Over the years, I've tried to describe it, but rain bores the people of Manitoba. They prefer the direct, no-nonsense approach of snow. Snow makes you hardy and tough; it tests you. Rain endears itself to no one. Rain is an uninvited guest. It sits too close, asks nosy questions, gets under your skin. Rain creates its own set of commandments, carves its way through stone. Eighteen years of rain is the reason I love the Manitoba cold. You can protect yourself against cold; all you need are layers.

I glance over at Julia, wondering if I should say something, but she's stony quiet, wrapped in her own layers.

"Did you have to embarrass me like that?" she says, once we're off the mountain.

"Let's talk about this later."

"Why can't we ever talk about something when I want to?" Her voice shifts, and it jars me. She ages twenty years when she uses this tone.

"Right now I'm just trying to get us back in one piece, okay?"

"Fine."

"Fine."

We continue the drive with the pelting sound of the rain on the car roof. When we arrive at the farm, I tell Julia that I'm going to pick up a few groceries and to let her grandmother know I won't be long. I don't mention that if I see a pub along the way I won't be disappointed.

"Are you mad at me?" she says, once she's standing outside.

"No, you're mad at me," I explain.

"I'm not mad, I'm frustrated. Why do you have to be like that? It's raining, for God's sake. It's rain . . . it's water. I'm not made of sugar."

Dust, I think. *Same difference.* "Yes, you are."

She groans loudly.

"Go inside, you're getting soaked."

"Well, would you look at that?" She spreads her arms wide, catching the rain. "And I'm still here."

eleven

Locating a pub isn't as difficult as I thought. The church/drinking establishment ratio has apparently evened out in the last twenty years. Pulling up at the Jolly Fellow, I look around for familiar faces, hoping to see none. It's an instinctive reaction. Des's dad used to buy beer at a liquor store thirty miles away and back his car into the driveway so that the neighbours wouldn't see. Sometimes a sin is only a sin when it's seen.

I find a seat at the end of the bar, the most dimly lit section, and tuck myself in. I've just received my drink—cranberry and vodka—when Gabe walks in. I watch him greet two men in matching trucker hats. I quickly bow my head and try to think invisible thoughts.

It doesn't work. He's looking straight at me when I glance up. He grins and shakes his head when I pretend I've just noticed him. I smile back—busted. When he slips onto the stool beside me—beer fumes and fried foods aside—I can still smell the earth on him.

"Of all the gin joints in all the towns . . ." he says, flashing his smile at me.

"Except you walked in, so that's my line."

"But it's my joint. My town."

"Fair enough. How's the Co-op?" I ask as he orders a beer, settling in.

"Pretty exciting. Prices look good for corn this year." We take sizeable gulps of our respective drinks. "Mr. Loewen said to say hello to you."

"Oh." His stool is a little too close to mine, and our legs are almost touching. When I try to shift, the leg wobbles, and Gabe holds out a hand to steady me, which was not the purpose of moving farther away. "He still runs the place?"

"Yep. He was very excited to hear you were back. The whole town is buzzing with the news."

Dismay has obviously travelled across my face, because Gabe laughs. "Just kidding." He shakes his head. "You look guilty. You always look guilty over the strangest things."

I don't comment on his use of the present tense. "I just don't want this visit to be a big deal."

"Sounds like somebody thinks she's a big shot."

"No, I didn't mean that. I just . . ."

"There you go again. Being guilty. Relax."

I take a slow sip. "Telling someone to relax is the most counter productive thing you can say in a moment of tension. It actually produces a state of anxiety because the person thinks, oh great, now I've failed at being relaxed on top of everything else."

"I am deeply sorry if I've created a state of anxiety for you," he says contritely, bending his head too close to mine. "But it is a big deal." He takes my drink and smells the contents. "Cranberry juice and vodka? All the better to be undetected."

"Stop thinking you know me," I say, regretting it immediately.

He leaves this alone and asks me about life in Winnipeg. *Small talk*, I think, drawing my first easy breath since he sat down. I launch into a travelogue of the city that the chamber of commerce would be happy to endorse: its tough, pioneer people, thriving arts community—cultural mecca of Canada, according to its citizens—the climate that makes a man out of everyone. I've just started on Louis Riel and the Red River Rebellion when Gabe holds his hands up in surrender.

"I get it. You're a convert."

"Well, you wouldn't know anything about that." Damn vodka. Odourless but not without influence.

"Not for your lack of trying. How many times did you recite the Three Spiritual Laws to me?"

"Four, actually. Obviously not often enough."

"Four then. What were they again?"

"I don't remember."

"Yeah, you do. C'mon, for old time's sake."

Of course I did. "I'm going to pass."

"Remember that crusade you tried to drag me to? What was his name?"

I laugh. "Why, why are we wandering down this particular path? What about that barn of yours? Now there's a beautiful building."

"What was his name? He had black hair, like a crow was sitting on his head? Larry, Randy . . ."

"Barry Moore, okay? The Barry Moore Crusade. I was a very earnest person, is that what you're getting at? An earnest, guilt-ridden, Bible-thumping teenager who wanted to save your lost soul. But you know what? That was a long time ago, and I think your soul is probably just fine—likely always was. And probably none of my business." I finish my drink. "Likely never was."

"You and your speeches," he says, giving me a look that almost makes me dizzy. "Anyway, I don't want to tell you to *relax* because I know how *tense* that makes you, but I was going to say that I went. That night."

I swivel to face him. "You did not. You said you'd rather be trampled by wild horses, buck naked, dragged through the street by your curly hair before you'd—"

"I said *by my curly hair*?"

"I might have added that. But you swore—"

"I swore a lot of things back then."

"You swore you'd never buy into organized religion. Wild horses were definitely mentioned."

"It was important to you, so I went."

Doubt is obviously the predominant expression on my face, because Gabe sighs. "You were wearing a red top with little sleeves and a jean skirt . . ."

"Des must have told you."

"Your hair was in a ponytail, and you were wearing cowboy boots, I think, and no, Des didn't tell me. We don't . . . she didn't tell me." His jaw tightens when he says this but, just as quickly, he laughs. "You still don't believe me? You need more proof."

"No," I say slowly. "It's just you were so stubborn about it."

"Me? Stubborn? I have a mule who's less stubborn than you are."

"You have a mule?"

"Okay, I made that part up," he smiles. "More proof:

They started singing a song about the dark blot of sin in your soul. You went to the front and some little old lady creaked over and sat down beside you . . ."

"What was she wearing?"

He smiles slowly. "I have no idea. But you looked really happy afterwards and I just didn't get it."

"Well, you see, my sins had all been forgiven. Again. You were paying attention. *Just as I am, without one plea, but that thy blood was shed for me.*" The words trip off my tongue as though they'd never left.

"Yeah, at sixteen years old. Then they sang 'Amazing Grace.' *Poor, wretched and blind.* I remember thinking: but she's perfect."

There's nothing clever to say to this. He's looking at me the same way he looked the last time I saw him, when I told him that I didn't think I loved him anymore. Disbelief and honest confusion. *You don't think?* he asked. Buying time, or ever literal, I said of course I thought. He persisted. *You* think *or you* know *that you don't love me anymore?* I told him that we didn't want the same things and that I needed to go out into the big, wide world. He said he'd come with me. I said that what we had wasn't true love and that did it. I broke his heart with a lie. Except it wasn't really a lie. What I couldn't tell him was that the moment I saw Jake's body, lifeless on the side of that mountain, I stopped believing.

The pub is filling up now with the after-work crowd and growing louder. Gabe finishes his drink. "You want another?"

"No, I need to get back. I should get back." I grope for my purse but Gabe touches my hand.

"Let me."

I let his hand rest on mine and remember how good he

was at touching. One of Marci's hopes for this "journey" (she uses the word more often than all the people on reality television combined) is that I will be able to recover some of my early memories and polish them like a rare stone. It has something to do with grieving. But this memory, I think even Marci would agree, is just a bad idea. So I make an inelegant dive for my purse, almost falling off the stool, and fumble for my wallet. "No, let me. Lunch was so lovely." I pull a couple of bills out and place them on the bar. "It's the least I can do."

He nods at this ridiculous comment. "Well, thank you very much," he says politely, mocking me.

"It was great seeing Des again, both of you, again. Really, great." It's as if I'm having an out-of-body experience from the ceiling, screaming at myself to shut up and ignoring myself completely. "I wondered, of course. But it was just . . ."

"Great?" He leans back on the stool. "I just remembered who you remind me of."

"Who?"

"Your mother."

I finally meet his eyes and stay there.

"Ah," he laughs. "There you are."

I leave the building with the sound of his low, rippling laughter. Outside, I let the rain cool my face.

"Gloria?" A large woman moves purposefully toward me.

"Mrs. G," I say, receiving her warm hug. Maggie Goodwind is my parents' neighbour and my mother's closest friend.

"I heard you were coming."

It's official, then, the second coming of me, the prodigal daughter. Fleetingly, I think how proud Marci would be of my mixed metaphor. We chat briefly about the weather and my trip across the Rockies. I edge closer to my car and say that I should be getting back.

Mrs. G glances over at the pub. "Don't forget your groceries."

I must look confused, because she adds, with a grin, "I was just chatting with your mother."

CNN *has nothing on the quick reporting of news, I think, compared to this town.* I smile sheepishly, busted yet again, and she hugs me goodbye.

A pound of coffee later, I pull up in my parents' driveway. I look in the rear-view mirror to see if I look normal, whatever that might be. And I wonder if I'll ever stop being guilty here.

twelve

I strip off my sodden coat and shoes and leave them in the mudroom. Inside the kitchen, I try to identify dinner.

"Chicken noodle soup?" I ask. The smell reminds me of coming home from school.

My parents and Julia are playing Scrabble at the kitchen table. Julia's face is glum and I wonder if she's still upset with me. "How's it going?" I stand behind her and stroke her hair. She doesn't push me away.

"Grandma and Grandpa are so good at this. They're totally kicking my . . ." I press a little more firmly on her head. "Bum." She looks up and rolls her eyes at me.

"You just haven't gotten the good letters," my father comforts her. "Do you want to play?" he says to me.

I take a seat beside Julia. "I'll just watch."

Julia shows her letters to me. She has the q and the z. "They're totally playing down to me and it's still not helping. I suck."

I notice my mother frown at this and my stomach clenches involuntarily. Julia just smiles. "Sorry, Gran. What I meant was that I am not very gifted at this game." She manages to get a grin—an actual grin—out of my mother. *Just like Jake*, I think. *You take her too seriously*, he used to say to me. *How do you not*, I would counter.

The phone rings. "Mark," she says. My mother's tone is friendly and warm. She likes Mark. He could elicit the same reactions that Jake could. I used to think it was a male thing but now, adding Julia to the list, it's apparent that it's an anything-but-me thing. I hear Marci chastise my victim stance as my mother hands the phone over to Julia.

"Hello? Oh, Daddy." Her face lifts. If she could patent that look she'd give Botox a run for its money.

I look down at Julia's letters as she chirps happily about the day. Her end of the conversation is dominated heavily with Maxi news: Maxi's dog, Maxi's horse, Maxi's barn, Maxi's hayloft, and, finally, Maxi's tongue. "Yes, Daddy, a tongue ring. No, she doesn't lisp. She's very nice." There's a slight twang of indignation here. "Mom? She's fine. Really good." Her voice is false as she spins a better version of me. She does it without thinking. I block out an unsolicited flash of Marci wagging her stout finger at me as she tells me that Julia and I overprotect each other. I place *qat* down on a triple letter and my father smiles approvingly.

Julia puts her hand over the phone. "That's not a word," she mouths.

"Yes, it is." Satan plays cards; we play Scrabble.

"Gotta go, Dad. Mom wants to talk to you. She misses you. We both do. Love you."

She hands the receiver to me and meets my eyes. There's that warning in hers—be nice. Worrying about Mark and me is second nature.

"Hello, Mark?" I'm suddenly aware that my mother and daughter are both watching me like I'm a segment on the evening news. "I'm going to take this upstairs." I hand the phone to Julia. "Hang up for me, okay?"

Upstairs, I settle into a chair beside the phone in the hallway. I've spent hours, days probably, on this phone. It's one of those solid black rotary telephones you find in museums now. The curved receiver feels warm and comfortable in my hand. I take a deep, cleansing belly breath and pick up the phone.

"Okay, Julia. You can hang up now."

"Bye, Daddy. I love you."

"Love you too, Bug."

With a click, Julia is off the line and the air across the miles is stilted. It's been this way for the last year as the fighting has stopped, replaced by an uneasy détente. In the past, we mostly fought over how to raise Julia. Mark wanted to sign her up for soccer (head injuries), swimming (drowning), and dance (eating disorders). He said he wanted her to live; I said I wanted to keep her alive. Once, Mark suggested we sign her up for knitting except, oh wait, those damn needles. So easy to puncture a lung. Julia's done her best to provide sound to our muted home, but she's only one person. This is probably why people have more than one child.

I feel pain nudge the bones of my eyebrows. I hear: "El, are you there?"

El-are-you-there? The words hang like laundry on my mother's wash line. How many names is it possible for one person to have? With my parents I am Gloria. Old friends call me Glo. My daughter calls me Mom and my husband has chosen El. Eventually, I suppose, I'll simply be G. Then nothing.

I've read that people with brain tumours sometimes experience moments of such clarity and lucidity that the rest of the world fades into white noise. Is this sudden clarity the work of a tumour? El-are-you-there. Is it a new name? It seems quite likely that my husband has no idea who I really am.

"El?" he says again. His tone is clear and sure, and it reels me back.

"Oh, Mark. I'm sorry. I'm here."

"Right. How are you? How was the trip? I tried calling you on your cellphone, but it rang in our bedroom. And your parents don't seem to believe in answering machines."

"I forgot my phone. And my parents don't believe in the twenty-first century, although Julia is trying to change that."

"Don't worry about it," he says.

"What?"

"The phone."

"Oh. Right. Sorry about that."

"No," he sighs. "I am. It's just I was worried about you guys and I couldn't seem to get hold of you. Christ, it seems like we're always apologizing to each other."

"I meant to call."

"Doesn't matter. Tell me, how are things going out there? What have you been up to?"

I wonder where to start: lunch with a friend I've only mentioned in passing or drinks with an old boyfriend. Hmm, tough call. "Lots of farm stuff. Catching up with my parents. Scrabble. Food, oh God, the food. Julia's having a great time, though. She can't get over how my parents compost everything. She says they're completely green."

Mark laughs at this.

"How was the conference?" I say, moving right along. "Did they like your paper?"

"I think so. It's hard to tell. Nobody likes to seem too impressed at those things."

"I'm sure it was great." I struggle to remember the title of his paper, the one he hopes will staunch the ever-increasing pressure to publish or perish. "Has Kate been by?"

"Of course. The mail is collated and placed conveniently beside the telephone."

"Alphabetical?"

"And by order of importance."

I smile into the phone. "That's our Kate." Not for the first time I think that Mark should have found a Kate. Someone whose bark matches her bite. Kate, like Mark, is completely consistent; she knows what she wants and who she is.

"So, how are you?" he asks, the teasing gone, replaced by the more familiar concern. The kind of tone often used to inquire after an ailing relative or pet.

"I am terrific, actually." I hear the cheerful note in my voice, and I'm almost convinced. "It's not as bad as I thought it would be. Maybe Marci's right . . . you just have to keep moving." I cast about in my mind for a suitable aphorism. Failing, I try to remember a book title: *Wake Up to Your Life*; *7-Day Detox Miracle*; *Book of Secrets*; *The Road Less Traveled*. Ah. "You know, further along the road less travelled." Technically, this is also the title of the sequel, but I don't think Mark will notice.

"Really? That's great," Mark says, sounding relieved. "So, Julia is having a good time?"

I smile, also relieved, and we have an authentic conversation, as we always do, about our daughter.

"Love you," he says, after a brief pause when we've run out of Julia stories.

"Love you, too," I say. As I hang up the phone I hear the missing *I*. It wasn't always this way.

When I stood at the altar with Mark, I didn't have cold feet, not even a baby toe. I had picked out my white dress in an hour, chosen the flowers via the eeny, meeny, miny mo method, and settled on the menu in less time than that—chicken was fine. Who cared, really? Were there people who cared deeply whether the entree was chicken or salmon and, if there were, did I care about them? I didn't understand the fuss and I had no second thoughts about marrying Mark. Gabe was part of my past. Mark was my future. When I said *I do*, I did.

And then it was time for the candle ceremony. We moved over to the table where two vanilla-scented candles burned, and still no second thoughts. A third candle, unlit, stood between them. We were to pick up the slender, individual candles and, in unison, ignite the stout centre one as a symbol of our newly created oneness. I wasn't nervous about this. I wanted to light that single candle; it was what I had longed for my entire life. I wanted to be united. I wanted to be whole.

But, as we tipped our two candles toward the new wick and newer oneness, I had thoughts: second, third, and fourth. We were supposed to blow out our candles afterwards. I lit the middle candle as Mark did, but when I raised my own candle to my lips, I couldn't bring myself to blow out the flame.

My parents were there, aunts and uncles, cousins and crying babies. Kate was there, beside me, and I knew this was wrong, and suddenly everything was wrong. Des should be beside me, holding my bouquet along with her own. And then I went dizzy with all the others who should have been there.

Mark noticed my paralysis, and his eyes searched mine for an explanation, a clue on how to proceed. I could tell he wanted to help me. He was so young, as young as me. I remember standing there until he smiled a sweet, worried, and very naked smile. And so I thought we would be okay.

We blew out our own candles and our old selves. Mark kissed me before the minister said he could. People applauded and I pushed my doubt aside. I sat at the table to sign the marriage certificate and, as I wrote my new name, I gave the last of myself away. The smell from the candles was strong and for years, when I used vanilla extract, I remembered that moment and how I had wanted to keep that flame alive for just a little longer.

I'm considering a little nap when Julia comes up the stairs to tell me that dinner is ready. I look at my watch. It's almost six thirty, which means I've detained dinner a good hour. I reconsider the nap.

"Fresh buns and homemade soup," she announces like a waiter reciting the specials. "Homemade. All of it. Even the noodles."

"Surely this can't continue to surprise you," I sigh. "Just say it, I'm a bad cooking mother."

"You're a bad cooking mother."

"You know, that hurts."

She grins and pushes me toward the stairs. On the way down she says, softly, "How's Dad?"

"Fine."

During dinner, which is predictably delicious and fresh and homemade, Julia keeps up a running monologue about her life in Winnipeg and her friends, keeping it all impressively G-rated. After dessert—a delicate fruit crumble and ice cream—my father brings out a puzzle. As my parents set it up on the coffee table, I say that I'm going to my room to read. Julia beckons me to the corner of the room, a sombre look on her face.

"What is it?" I say.

"You leave, you die."

I burst out laughing. My parents look our way and I smile back. "Getting a little gamed-out, Sweetie?"

"Seriously. Leave and die." Her eyes are a little wild. "What's with all the family time? I just want to watch a video. Not that I can. And why are there no computers here? I thought . . . why didn't you tell me to bring my laptop?"

"You are a good person," I say, holding her shoulders. "Remember that. You've just hit a wall. You need to breathe." I kiss her forehead and walk over to the coffee table. "You know what? I'm suddenly in the mood for a puzzle."

Julia gives me a grateful look and takes the seat beside me. I may not be a good cooking mom but I have my moments.

We're somewhere between the sky and the earth—lots of blue and brown pieces; my parents love a challenge—when Julia says, "What's this about Maxi's mom and Uncle Jake?"

The three of us look at her and then at each other. The freeze-frame in the room is almost comical. Almost. Julia, searching for a piece of sky in sky, doesn't appear to notice. She looks up eventually. "Maxi said they used to date. That's kind of cool, isn't it?"

Wow, I think, *from the mouths of babes*. I search for something to say, but my father gets there first.

"They were sweethearts."

"Oh, Gramps. I love that." She's content with this answer and more intent on finding an elusive piece of the sky.

My parents and I hold the gaze only a moment longer before we, also, return to the puzzle.

~

Des and Jake didn't start going out until high school, but he fell for Des long before, during the Christmas pageant. The moment shines in my mind more brightly than the star of Bethlehem, which, in our church, was a piece of cardboard covered with gold foil and glitter—hauled out of storage year after year until it was ratty with use.

Mrs. Wiebe was the Sunday school superintendent that year—actually, every year that I can remember. In July she would tell my mother (who was on the Nominations Committee) that she might not be back in the fall, yet every September she emerged from the summer break capable and hopeful and ready to serve again. She wore ruffled polyester blouses and pantyhose so thick that we were mesmerized by their density. Her hair, which looked like the helmet of a Roman guard, remained unaltered in all the years I knew her, and I think it would have been disturbing if she had changed it. For all that, she was a woman who gave the impression of having been pretty once. We all wondered why she had married Helmut, a stern, humourless man with the jawbone of an ox, who could silence us with nothing but a glance over his shoulder. Only great tragedy could make a woman settle for a Helmut, I thought.

By the end of November a worried expression crept over Mrs. Wiebe's face, replacing the softer, yearning one we all preferred. As the first Advent candle was lit, the lines were already growing deeper in the middle of her brow, and we remembered that celebrating the birth of the Christ child was dire business indeed.

Jarnelle insisted on being Mary, Mother of God, because everyone said she looked just like her and also because she owned her own costume. (I didn't point out—kindly, I thought—that Mary would turn out to be a doomed Catholic.) In any case, neither Kate, Des, nor I would have wanted the role. Sitting still and saintly would have been an uncomfortable stretch.

There was a shortage of boys in our class, and so Jake was conscripted to be Joseph. He was reluctant, but Jarnelle insisted he would be the handsomest Joseph ever. Vanity won and he agreed. Kate was to be the Angel of the Lord; Des and I were shepherds. All in all, not bad casting.

On the afternoon of the dress rehearsal, the usual chaos ensued: forgotten or inappropriate costumes (silk bathrobes); rambunctious sheep (the primary division); microphones knocked down with ear-splitting reverberation or, worse, used for impromptu performances. As the day wore on, Mrs. Wiebe's face assumed a hunted look. She was keenly aware of the parents who drummed their fingers on the pews behind her, many with presents to be wrapped and stuffing to be prepared.

Des and I behaved ourselves. There had been a snowfall the night before, and we were dying to go sledding as soon as possible. Valley snow had the lifespan of manna and so the better we behaved, the sooner we'd be sliding down the hill at the nearby cemetery. We shuffled about the stage with our robes and discreetly used our staffs to keep the sheep under control.

And then the Angel of the Lord was upon us, and light

shone all around (Marvin Peters on the spotlight). This was Kate's cue, her big moment. But instead of saying, "Fear not, I bring you tidings of great joy," in a normal voice, Kate thundered the words in a guttural, threatening tone. We all jumped, terrified.

This was too much for Mrs. Wiebe, who was expecting a more circumspect, less demon-possessed, angel. She clapped her hands to her face and said, "Good God in heaven," and immediately turned bright fuchsia, a shade we hadn't yet seen that day. Concerned parents rushed to her side while we shepherds muttered. Des was surprised that Mrs. Wiebe would take the Lord's name in vain, but I said she was probably literally calling upon God for protection from Kate's angel. We did start giggling then.

Kate tried to repeat the performance in a softer, gentler manner, but she just couldn't manage it. Finally, Jake whispered to her, "You're not supposed to scare the crap out of them," but it didn't help. It was decided that Kate's interpretation was too intense and she was replaced by Des, who everyone agreed couldn't terrify a lamb let alone a crew of mangy shepherds.

Kate's mom was upset. Her face lost its beatific expression as she drew Kate over to the side of the stage, where she told Kate that she was sure the Angel of the Lord would be more ladylike. Kate rolled her eyes. Her mother then pinched her daughter on the tender underbelly of her arm, keeping a thin smile on her face the entire time. Kate didn't cry out, which made me think it wasn't the first time it had happened. Kate's mom then reminded her that a Doerksen was a light, a shining example for others.

On the night of the pageant, there was the regular noise and confusion as halos were attached, burlap arranged, and makeup applied. Props were organized and the SSSST (Secret Service Sunday School Teachers) were dispatched throughout the balcony to keep order among the prospective troublemakers (Des's brothers).

Outside the church walls a more remarkable backdrop was taking form. The snow had not melted and was, instead, clinging heavily to the fir boughs and streetlights. As we prepared ourselves for the celestial birth, fat flakes wafted from the sky to join the white quilt that had spread itself across our unaccustomed town. If we hadn't been at church, I would have sworn magic was afoot.

We couldn't wait to stand beneath the lamppost and watch the falling snow, but Mrs. Wiebe looked so discouraged that our pity defeated our excitement. Newly demoted Kate (relieved, she said, because the other costume didn't show off her boobs) and I repeatedly told the younger ones to be quiet. Mrs. Wiebe seemed grateful.

The church was filled to capacity that night. Christmas carols reached every part of the sanctuary and the lights of the Christmas tree blazed in the corner. All was set for the story to be retold in the glorious tradition of its inception.

Things went smoothly, for the most part. One of the wise men forgot his myrrh at home and decided to improvise with a stuffed animal from the nursery, which leaked little foam pellets down the aisle, making him appear less like a King of the Orient and more like Hansel. Babies cried and had to be spirited to the soundproofed nursery in the back of the church. Finally, it was time for the shepherds. Kate and I herded our flock of sheep to the middle of the stage as the choir sang, "Hark, the Herald Angels Sing," the end of which was Des's cue.

With the last lingering note of the song, Des's garland-encircled curls popped through the curtain and she smiled her huge, dimple-creased smile. There was never such a sweet-faced angel, I was sure. Her eyes sparkled as she announced: "Fear not! I bring you tidings of great—"

But then, before she could complete the line, the star above plummeted and landed squarely on her haloed head. (Later, people would see this as foreboding: the fallen angel.) There wasn't a sound in the room, corner to corner. Des looked stunned but not hurt—it was only cardboard—and I knew what was coming next. She managed to utter, "Joy," before she collapsed into a fit of giggles.

Kate and I joined in almost immediately, as Des drifted to the floor in a whoosh of white chiffon. Little kids snickered and the older ones in the balcony joined in. Wave upon wave of laughter crashed over the sanctuary as man, woman, and child merged until it was one sound, one sole resonance. My parents laughed, Mrs. Wiebe's drawn face loosened as she surrendered to the laughter, and even Helmut was smiling. In that moment I was sure that this was what the Christ child was meant to do, and it *was* magical.

I glanced over at Jake to share the wonder with him, but he couldn't stop looking at Des. He couldn't take his eyes off her.

thirteen

Julia shakes me awake the next morning. My eyes are still blurry from sleep as I glance beside me: nine o'clock. I've woken to the sight of this alarm clock, this room, for how many days now? Forever.

"Maxi called. She wants us to go riding." Julia yanks the curtain open. Sunlight pours in. "It's a beautiful day. The weather channel says there's very little chance of a hurricane. Can we?"

I pull the covers back up to my chin. "I'll think about it. But no death threats, okay?"

She grabs my hands and pulls, doesn't let go until I'm sitting up. "I need this."

"I can see that."

"So?"

"So, we'll see."

"Gran's making coffee; Gramps bought a DVD player," she announces. "Woo hoo, what a day of grace."

"I beg your pardon?"

"It's what they say around these parts," she says, dryly.

"Wear this." She tosses a shirt and jeans onto the bed.

I rise from the bed grudgingly, but heartened by the promise of coffee. "You'll have to wear a helmet, you know."

The sudden shift on her face is immediate. "Mother, I'll look like a geek."

"A geek with brain cells intact, Daughter."

"You aren't serious. You can't be serious. You can not," she states, as if a contraction is what stands between her and mercy.

"Take it or leave it. I'm not bending on this one."

"Like you ever do." She leaves the room in a huff.

I fall back against the pillows, tempted to remain, wondering at how quickly I turned from her saviour into her Jehovah.

⌣

With three cups of coffee percolating through my bloodstream, much to the dismay of my mother who frowned after two, we climb the winding road. It isn't just the caffeine that's making my pulse race, it's the prospect of seeing Des and Gabe again. It doesn't seem likely that we can keep things casual for much longer.

What happened between Gabe and me was an adolescent romance, but it was never casual. And what happened between Jake and Des was more than sweethearts. Love was uncomplicated in these parts; sex was not.

Miss Blanchard, another Sunday school teacher, a single woman who had a "heart for the youth," did her best to lead the girls through the murky tributary between these two rivers. (The boys were sequestered in another room with Mr. Kroeker to discuss the spilling of seed. Jake filled me in until I begged him to stop.) At our end of the church basement there was talk of being virtuous women, which involved spinning wool and making belted linen garments to sell to the merchants. The closest Miss Blanchard came to actual advice was when she told us to gird ourselves in the armour of the Lord. It was, I suppose, the theological version of the chastity belt and, all in all, a lot less practical than the instruction the boys received.

Des balked at the armour of the Lord advice and, even though Kate was a rule follower, she balked as well. She was the most beautiful of us. I was baffled, as usual. From what I could see, sex was fairly unromantic and bore little resemblance to the growing sense that there was something in the world we weren't being told about.

And then I discovered the Song of Solomon. Instantly, that book became the most read book in my tattered Bible. Admittedly, King Solomon was overtaxed in the romance department. With seven hundred wives and three hundred concubines, not to mention a kingdom to tend to, I couldn't imagine that his would be an easy house to come home to. But the language he used for love. Oh my. Now here was a guy who understood.

> *Your lips, my bride, drip honey;*
> *Honey and milk are under your tongue,*
> *And the fragrance of your garments*
> *Is like the fragrance of Lebanon.*
> *A garden locked is my sister, my bride.*

Your breasts are like two fawns,
Twins of a gazelle.
How beautiful and how delightful you are
. . . your mouth like the best wine.
Your lips are like a scarlet thread,
And your mouth is lovely.

I couldn't believe this stuff was in the Bible, and I couldn't imagine that Jehovah was okay with it. Jesus wouldn't be any help here, because he'd never even been married, let alone had a girlfriend, although we did wonder about Mary Magdalene. I read the slim book over and over again, turning the onion-skin pages with a trembling hand.

Somewhere along the way, between that world and mine, passion had become of the world.

As we pull into the driveway, Maxi tears around the corner, Roy barking at her heels. With the jet black hair and multiple piercings, she should look tough; her flushed face and her mother's dimples make this impossible. She waves to Julia, who opens her door before the engine is off. Julia greets Roy, buries her face in his silky fur, and then flies off with Maxi to the barn. Maxi shouts over her shoulder that Des and Gabe are waiting there.

When I turn the corner in the path, I see Gabe saddling up the horses. Des waves to me, a cup of coffee in her hand. As I walk over to join them, I overhear Maxi tell Julia that she's borrowed a friend's jacket, boots, and helmet for her to wear. She adds that Julia will look awesomely equestrian. Julia gives me a sour look. She didn't appreciate the call I made earlier, voicing my safety concerns.

"We'll be twins," Maxi adds.

Julia scans Maxi, who is at least a head taller and considerably thinner. "Hardly," she says. When she sees the jacket she shakes her head. "I'll just wear my own stuff."

"Give it a try. She's the same size as you, I'm sure."

"Poor girl." Julia reluctantly sheds her own coat.

Maxi scowls. "Oh, pul-ease. I'm way too bony and flat as a board."

"And frankly, we're a little concerned," Gabe says from behind a grey, dappled horse.

"We've begged her to get implants," adds Des.

"Or sign up for one of those makeover shows."

Maxi turns to her parents. "Okay, you both need to stop talking now." She faces Julia again. "Seriously, I'd kill for your boobs. I'm not joking. Try this on."

Julia takes the jacket; it fits perfectly.

"You look great," I say, venturing an opinion. Julia seems pleased. And relieved.

"Now try the boots," Maxi orders. She hauls Julia over to a bale of hay, where they sit. Julia rips off her sneakers, and their tittering becomes confidential and indiscernible.

"You have an amazing daughter," I say to Des.

"She is," Des agrees. "So is Julia. Maxi's been raving about her all week, how funny she is, how smart—"

"She's a lot like Jake," I say, without thinking. Des doesn't respond, and I wonder if I should apologize for bringing up his name so casually.

"I wondered about that," she finally says. "She has his laugh, isn't that something? I wouldn't have thought you could inherit a laugh."

"The things we inherit, hmm?"

"My mother was kind enough to pass her saddlebags on

to me," she says, with a grimace.

"Speaking of saddlebags," Gabe interrupts, "we're almost ready here."

"He hears everything," Des says.

"Knows everything too," he smiles, cinching the saddle tight.

As he leads the horses outside the corral and ties their reins to the fence, I realize he's saddled only four horses. I look quizzically at Des.

"It's not really my thing," she says. "I'll get lunch ready."

"Oh, that's too much. Let me take you guys somewhere. It's my turn."

"Even Steven?" she says. She used to tease me about how I needed to make everything fair. I told her it came from being a twin, everything split, down to the womb. "You can take me out to dinner sometime if it will make you feel better."

"Okay," I agree. I look at the horses, the next hurdle at hand. "I'm not sure about this, Gabe. It's been years."

"It's like riding a bike, except it hurts a helluva lot more when you fall off."

"That's comforting." I walk over to the grey mare and stroke her soft muzzle. She snorts and snuffles into my open palm. Her familiar scent reassures me. I breathe the smell in as though it's perfume and pull my fingers through the rough, tangled mane.

"Should I leave you two alone?" Gabe asks.

"That'd be nice."

Des watches us and gives me an uneasy smile. I wonder if Gabe has told her about running into me at the Jolly Fellow.

The girls tromp across the field in their tall black boots and English riding helmets. There isn't a scowl or a complaint from Julia.

"How brilliant are you?" I whisper to Des.

"It was Maxi's idea," she says, but I know she had a hand in it.

Julia does a quick pirouette in front of me. "Do I pass inspection? Did you bring the bubble wrap in case I fall?"

"It's in the car."

"Was my mother always this nervous?" Julia asks Des.

"Kind of. Very nervous about falling out of trees and coming across bears. But she was brave, too."

I can't believe Des has said this. Of all the things I wasn't, brave would top the list. Julia, rightfully, looks skeptical. I imagine she has an image of me—huddled in bed, curtains drawn—in her head.

"About what?" Julia persists.

"Truth," Des answers, quietly.

This, too, stuns me. Thank God for Maxi, who pushes her way into the conversation. "What about my mom? What was she like? Pushy and overbearing?"

"Your mother was the best person to be in Sunday school with."

Maxi smirks. "Did she ever stop laughing?"

"No."

"That's not true," Des says. "Oh, do you remember Bob?"

I shake my head. "Sounds like a bad movie."

"One of our Sunday school teachers."

"We had a male Sunday school teacher? No, I don't remember."

"Well, we had him for a week and then he mysteriously disappeared."

Julia looks surprised at this comment.

Maxi shakes her head. "That's my mother's idea of humour."

"What happened?" Julia asks.

"He was the best teacher ever, that's what," Des says. "He wore shorts in the middle of winter and big Hawaiian shirts. He taught us the Golden Rule and I actually listened to him. He said, and I think this is a direct quote: 'If you give shit you're gonna get shit back.'"

"Oh," I laugh. "I do remember him now. Whatever happened to him?"

"Banished," Des says. "Kate's mom found out."

"Ah, corrupting the morals of the youth," I say.

"Plato? Or Socrates?" Des says. She could never keep them straight.

"Aristotle," I say.

"SPA." Gabe comes up behind me. "Socrates. Plato. Aristotle. Isn't that the lame way you remembered?"

"Just lame enough to get me an A in Philosophy," I say.

"I'm going to hate myself for asking, but why SPA?" says Julia.

"Roman baths."

"But the philosophers were Greek," Gabe says, as exasperated now as he was when I came up with the acronym.

"But I remembered," I say, maybe a little smugly.

"Your mother and your father were excellent students," Des says to Julia and Maxi. There is a slight pull to her smile, a frozen quality. "Not me, so much."

"Are we ready to shove off?" Gabe asks quickly.

"Wait!" Des runs to the side of the barn and rifles through a bag. She returns with a camera and hands it to Gabe.

Maxi and Julia stand taller, bite their lips, pinch their cheeks and stick their chests out. "Lip gloss!" they cry. Des throws a tube of something from her purse. Gabe leans his head on the fence and groans.

"Daddy, be quiet," Maxi orders as she dabs.

Gabe lowers the camera. "Did you just say 'Daddy'?"

"No," she scowls. "I said, 'Loathsome Father.'" Then she smiles brilliantly, her arm around an equally smiling Julia, and Gabe snaps the picture.

"The four of you now," he says.

I stand behind Julia; Des stands in front of Maxi and the shutter clicks, cementing the surreal moment forever in place. Des and I never dreamed of having children.

"Life's funny, huh?" says Des, as though she's read my thoughts.

Maxi mounts her horse with intimate ease. Julia is less eager. She stands back and eyes the horse up and down as though she's noticed for the first time how big it is.

"She's as gentle as a lamb," Gabe promises. He helps Julia up and gives advice in a slow, constant stream, taking time for her questions.

What would it have been like if Gabe was her father. It's a thought that's disloyal on so many levels—to Julia, Des, and Mark—but there it is.

⌣

Sunshine ripples through the trees, causing the path below to appear textured and uneven, but the horses move with confidence. It doesn't take long to adjust my body to the feel of the saddle and the motion of the horse, although I'm pretty sure the muscles in my butt and thighs will say something different in the morning. Gabe takes the lead, followed by Julia and then me. Maxi pulls up the rear.

The towering trees are ancient and magnificent, loamy air spiced with pine and fungus, dirt and rainfall. I feel my lungs swell as I take the air in greedily. It gives me a sensation of being bigger than I am; I have more space inside me than I know. Foreign yet familiar. I breathe again and again, unable to get enough of it.

"Do you mind if we trot?" Gabe asks Julia.

"Uh, okay."

We trot for a bit and then the horses break into a canter. Gabe continues to give instructions in his low, teen-whispering voice. I can see Julia's body relax in the saddle.

"Let's go faster," she says.

Gabe laughs. "All in good time."

When we reach a clearing, with a stream that trickles through, we dismount and let the horses drink their fill. The girls stand beside them.

"She's a natural," Gabe says.

"I love it, Mom," Julia shouts over to me. Her voice is shaking with emotion. Her cheeks are ruby red. "I love it, I love it, I love it!"

She's not trying to hold herself back, to be cool. She's spilling over. It's been too long since I've seen this. The tension between Mark and me has crept up on her. But here she's back to being only Julia.

The girls stay with the horses, cooing and whispering secrets into their velvety ears like young lovers; they stroke their necks and tell them what lovely beasts they are. Gabe and I sit on a log and watch.

"A little scary, isn't it?" he says. "Girls and horses."

"I've never seen Julia this way."

"But you remember."

"I guess I do."

"Maxi doesn't try to disguise it, not even in front of the old man." He places his hand over his heart. "I'm being replaced."

"It's the nature of things, isn't it? We raise them to let them go."

"Crazy system."

"Yeah."

He smiles at this and the twenty years dissipate like morning dew. I wonder if he remembers how much time we used to spend in the woods. The forest was where we kissed for the first time; I wonder if he's thinking about that now. It was almost brusque, as if he thought it was about time. Our teeth had bumped and that made me laugh, which relaxed him considerably. His lips were so much softer than they looked. *A scarlet thread*, I wanted to say, but was far too timid. This is not good to be thinking about now. It would help if he looked different. Old boyfriends are supposed to be pot-bellied, bald, and worn. You are supposed to look at them and wonder what you were thinking.

His profile is the same, except for the grey at the temples, and he's filled out some. His limbs are under control now. He used to have a vein on the side of his head that protruded and pulsed when he was upset.

He turns to me, aware of the scrutiny. I feel my chest grow hot. "I was just wondering if that vein still goes crazy when you get angry," I say.

"Nobody gets me that angry anymore."

"I'll take that as a compliment."

He laughs, but I'm not really joking. It's been a long time since I've had the energy to even annoy anyone, let alone provoke rage. The most I seem to get out of Mark these days is exasperation, a lesser emotion by anyone's standards.

Besides kissing, the forest was where Gabe and I would argue. and our most passionate arguments were about religion. After one particularly gruelling debate over whether or not Jesus was the Messiah, Gabe said, "You sure know a lot of Jewish history for a Gentile."

This jarred me. I grew up knowing that the Jews were the chosen people. I was as familiar with the notion as I was with my own name. But when he said this, it pressed me up against a window of a party I wasn't invited to, even though I knew all the guests: Jonah, Elijah, Noah, Moses, David, Esther, Mary Magdalene . . . Jesus. How could they not invite me? And why was it okay to have a chosen people in the first place? Wasn't Jehovah supposed to love everyone?

Even so, I continued to press the point. It's not like I had a choice—salvation was mandatory.

But Gabe refused to be swayed. He said he believed in himself. His father had hit him when he was little and, after he died, he became, according to his mother, a misunderstood man. He wasn't, Gabe told me. He wasn't misunderstood; he was mean. I tried to convince him that nobody could be all mean, but Gabe disagreed. His dad was all mean and that was that. "I won't be," he said. And he wasn't. He believed a person chose to be the person they were.

Sometimes Gabe tried to derail my one-track mind with poetry or philosophy, but I remained firm. There was only one path to truth.

"You still like to argue?" he says now.

"No," I say quickly. "Not at all."

"I don't believe you."

"Oh, it's true."

"Why not?"

"There's no point. Everything is set, I think."

He laughs, and this irks me in a visceral way. "What does that mean?"

I sit straight. "It doesn't mean anything. That's my point. Forget it."

"Now you're mad."

"I'm not mad," I say. "Of course, that's a little like telling someone to relax. It just makes people mad when you say they're mad even if they're not."

"But you're not arguing here, right?"

I have to smile back, and then I become aware that we're sitting too close. I can feel the heat of him. I shift around on the log, ostensibly to look at him. "When you're a kid, you think what you do, say, feel, matters. It doesn't make any difference how little you are in the world, you know you matter. But that's not true. The truth is that we live for a very short time and then we die and we're gone." As far as ideologies went, this was a little short of the complete, revealed Truth of God, but it was something I could live with.

"Everything is set *and* meaningless? I can't decide if you're a determinist or a nihilist."

"I'm on the fence."

"Whatever happened to *Beauty is truth, truth beauty. That is all Ye know on earth and all Ye need to know.* I thought we'd at least agreed on that."

"You wanted me to agree," I say, quietly. I look up at the

small patch of blue sky above us, and I let my leg rest against his.

"Did you really think you didn't love me?" he asks, as quietly.

Before I can answer, Maxi leaps at her father from behind, like a bear cub. "Are we riding or sitting?"

Gabe stands, with Maxi clinging to him like sap on a tree. Julia watches them tussle. I know she's thinking about her own father.

"Shall we continue?" Gabe says to them.

We gallop through the woods; Maxi and Julia whoop like wild creatures. It's the sound of unfettered joy. Like the spiced air earlier, the sound fills me now and makes me braver. I need to talk to Des and I need to do it before I lose my nerve.

Gabe and the girls remain at the barn to rub down the horses. I say I'll go ahead to warn Des of loud, starving savages, but really, I can't wait a minute longer. I need to talk to her. I've waited for twenty years and an extra moment seems unbearable now. It suddenly seems this simple.

When I reach the bend of the path and the house comes into view, I notice a new car in the driveway. I don't recognize it but I do recognize the shock of impeccably highlighted hair. Kate is here.

fourteen

I watch Kate as I move down the path. She takes a compact out of her purse, applies lipstick, and fixes her hair. Des and I used to complain about how much time—months, we figured—her perfect page had cost us over the years. A bad hair day—or worse, a pimple—was good reason to skip school, and with her mother's blessing. Physical perfection was a minimum requirement in the Doerksen household.

The Doerksens were also raised to win. This was complicated by the *first shall be last* bit in the Sermon on the Mount, but they got around it by being the best darn servants in the church. Nobody contributed more to the church budget than Dr. Doerksen, and Evangeline's Christmas Charity teas were legendary. The Doerksen children sang and entertained the congregation with their musical talent, made the best grades (without cheating), participated in school government (not a whisper of malfeasance), and were top-notch athletes (without resorting to violence, although Lester's mental game was, according to Jake, without match). All of

133

GAYLE FRIESEN

this was accomplished with enough humility that one got the impression it wasn't that winning was important to the Doerksen clan so much as it was inevitable.

I walk up to Kate now and lean over her shoulder so that my reflection appears in the curve of her mirror. She looks awkward for a split second, like she's been caught, and then she smiles.

"Hey," I say, giving her a hug. "What the heck?"

She hugs me back, then twists to look at the house. "I called your mother. She said you were here. She still gives the worst directions, doesn't she?"

"Some things never change. But you're here so, again, what the heck?"

She shrugs. "Well, Mark was back, so my house chores were done."

"Thanks," I say. "I owe you."

She waves this away. "He thought you could use some support."

"Ah," I say.

"He worries about you," she says.

"I know, I know."

"Besides, once my mother saw you in church, well, wasn't she on the phone the next day, reminding me that it had been far too long since my last visit."

"Did she cry?"

"Is the Pope going to hell?" She pulls her hair back off her face. "So, how's it going with Des? Was that weird? When your mom told me you were here, I was ... surprised."

I smile at the understatement. If I was good at avoidance, Kate was a master at compartmentalizing. Marci would give her a gold star for letting go. "Pretty good. Mostly surface

134

stuff, but that's probably my fault. It's strange, being back. And you, your folks, how is that?"

"Dad's taken up sailing. He looks quite dashing in his nautical getup. I figure it gets him off dry land and, well, my mom's afraid of water . . ."

"Now that's a blessing," we say at the same time and laugh.

"Mom's taken up golfing."

"Looking terrific in checkered shorts?"

"Complete with matching visor."

"Shoes and belts and everything," we say, again, in unison.

"How's Lester?" I ask.

"Still living in the Valley, making money on his money and blissfully married."

"And Lydia?"

"No fairer maid in all the land. Her two kids are gorgeous and well adjusted and brilliant. Their dog actually sleeps beside their cat." Kate shakes her blond hair as though she's trying to get the image out of her head.

"*Quelle surprise!*" I laugh, but I squeeze her arm.

Kate's inability to have children was the death knell to ongoing membership in her family. That and her divorce. No one had ever left a Doerksen without being in a casket. When it was revealed that Preston had had an affair, the family shifted its position and Kate was promoted to victim. After that, it didn't matter what she accomplished in her life, Kate would always be *Poor Kate*.

I had thought they had a good marriage. She and Preston gave great parties and looked stunning together, but mostly Kate seemed happy. She had everything she wanted. But then, after two miscarriages and a year of fertility testing, the doctors decided that Kate would never be able to carry a baby to term. She was devastated and baffled. "Why me?" she said. "I would have been a great mother. It's all I've ever wanted."

This was true. Des and I did anything to escape baby-sitting, but Kate loved it. Children adored Kate, especially the little ones. She calmed the rowdies, drew out the shy, distracted the crazies, and bedazzled the rest. They were drawn to her beauty like everything is drawn to beauty, wanting more.

Occasionally, Kate could convince Des and me to help out during Children's Church. I agreed on the condition that we could do dramatic re-enactments of the Old Testament. We chose famous duos: David and Goliath, Cain and Abel, Mary and Martha, and, once, Elisha and The Cloud The Size Of A Hand, although this ended up being a little hard to pull off.

Kate's only condition was that the stories be upbeat. We tried to go along with this edict, but when she insisted that Goliath be knocked unconscious instead of dead, I refused to continue the production. "A farce," I think I said.

Kate was putty in the hands of children. When she received the final assessment from her doctor, she called me over to share a bottle of wine. She stared into the swirling crimson contents of her glass and said that having children would have made her better. What she didn't say, but I knew to be equally true, was that her inability to have children robbed her of the chance to show her mother how it could be done.

When Preston left her for a dowdy woman named Marg, who, according to a mutual gynecologist friend, could "deliver a Chevy," she almost seemed to expect it. She packed two large suitcases and left her beautiful house. To my knowledge, that was all she ever took.

I went with her to the hotel. In the bar, I phoned Mark to see if he minded if I spent the night. "Of course not," he said. "But Julia wants to say good night."

Julia took the receiver mid-complaint about how she was allowed to wear her Halloween costume all day at school—only a couple of days away—but what was it going to be? Had I remembered? "A beautiful princess," she insisted. "That's what I want."

"Are you sure you don't want to be a ghost again?" I asked, costume design not being my specialty. "A beautiful, royal ghost? You could wear a purple sheet."

"Mommy, nobody is a ghost in the second grade."

Kate signalled for the phone with a twitch of one hand, as the other simultaneously conjured the waiter and ordered another martini. "Sweetie, it's Auntie Kate." The dullness in her eyes disappeared and her voice softened. I could easily imagine her thirteen again, whispering to the children that their mothers would be there soon. She would have been a very good mom. "You'll be the most beautiful princess ever," she promised. "Of course I'll help you. I have just the outfit."

I knew this was true. If she dug deep enough, I was sure Kate would find a purple silk cloak lined with ermine. She might even be able to rustle up a foxtail stole to toss across a princess's shoulders.

"You don't mind, do you?" Kate whispered to me across the table.

I didn't. Even though I couldn't hear Julia, I knew her fears would be quelled. Auntie Kate to the rescue again. This was something to be repeated throughout the years. On days when I couldn't get out of bed, Kate would be there to make things right for Julia.

"So, is it too weird being here?" Kate asks now.

"Just weird enough."

"Come on, fess up. How are you doing? Is Gabe still gorgeous?"

"Just gorgeous enough."

"Aren't you being evasive?"

"I'm not—" I begin to say, but Kate has her head crooked in a manner not unlike one of Marci's patient poses. "I'm hanging in there," I say.

She reaches over and touches my arm. "Well, I'm here now. Strength in numbers."

I nod.

Kate returns to the subject of her mother; I appreciate the diversion. She ends her litany of complaints with, "The good news is that she's adjusting to my divorce, or *the* divorce, as she refers to it. She thinks it happened to teach her something."

"Ah, this is about her. What a surprise. And what has it taught her?"

"We live in a fallen world."

"She didn't know that?"

"I guess she needed reminding. I swear she watches the evening news, hoping for the apocalypse. She can't wait."

"She'll look good on that cloud."

"Waving like the Queen."

We laugh, somewhat meanly, and order is restored. As different as our mothers are, it is here that they sit firmly on opposite ends of the continuum. Both believe in judgment: Evangeline, comfortable to judge, my mother to be judged.

"She's a horrible woman," Kate continues. "She'll never be satisfied with anything I do."

"That's right. You know that. So stop glowering."

"Hey there," Des yells from the porch. "Kate, is it you?"

It seems to me that Kate looks nervous as Des approaches, but then I think I must be making it up. Kate is never nervous.

"Kate," Des says, giving her a hug. "You're here."

"Surprised?"

"Not at all."

Kate pouts prettily. This look used to get us out of all manner of trouble, including a number of speeding tickets in Des's red station wagon. (Who'd give a ticket to Grace Kelly, we used to say.) "Why aren't you?" she asks, the playful look freezing on her face just slightly.

"Oh," Des smiles and raises an eyebrow. "It just makes sense . . . you being here." There's something behind her smile, and I wonder if Des's newly found bluntness will appear. "It wouldn't be the same without you." This is old Des, conciliatory Des. "You look beautiful."

Kate smiles her first completely relaxed smile.

"Personal trainer," I say.

"Bitch," Kate says.

Des shakes her head and laughs.

As we move toward the house, Maxi and Julia race down the path. We wait for them to join us.

"Auntie Kate." Julia throws herself into Kate's open arms. "What are you doing here?"

Kate hugs her fiercely. The bond between them is solid, strengthened by the times I've been too tired and too sad. I feel the old mix of guilt and gratitude. "I was in the neighbourhood, Sweetie. You look gorgeous. Love the whole equestrian getup."

Julia spins for her like a ballerina in a music box.

"You've lost weight."

Julia stops spinning. "Doubt it. Gran's been plying me with carbs. They live on starch out here."

"I gained five pounds as soon as I drove into town." Kate runs her hands along her hips, and Des and I share a look at the familiar ludicrousness of the comment.

"Kate, this is Maxi, my daughter." Des puts her arm around Maxi's shoulders. "This is Kate, my old friend."

Kate shakes Maxi's hand and scrutinizes her. "It's nice to meet you. I believe your mom's still a couple of months older."

Des rolls her eyes at this and we laugh.

"I love your boots," Maxi says.

They are magnificent boots: tan, butter-soft, Italian. Kate lifts a pant leg to reveal one in all its splendour. "Good shoes run in my family."

The girls groan dutifully at the pun, having no idea of the truth in it. Then, like two colts, they sprint up to the house.

Kate puts a hand to her cheek. "When did I turn corny? She's beautiful, Des."

"Spitting image of Gabe. Speaking of whom, there he is. Why don't you say hello and I'll see what the girls want to eat. Probably mac and cheese," she sighs. "We can eat out on the porch."

"Don't go to any trouble," Kate calls after her. As soon as Des is out of earshot, she whispers to me, "She's sure let herself go, hasn't she?"

"I guess."

It's true that Des has put on some weight, and her hair is now as grey as it is blond, but I think Kate's statement runs deeper. Des has let herself go on, and we haven't. But it's only a fleeting thought, obliterated immediately by Gabe's approach. He pulls his hat a little lower on his face as he approaches. "Well, if it isn't the final member of the Unholy Triumvirate. Let me warn the townsfolk now, before it's too late."

"Gabe, you handsome bastard." She hugs him. He looks at me over her shoulder and mouths, *Help!*

"When did you get in?" he asks.

"This morning. I just dropped my bags off at the new hotel and headed over. It's not a bad place, actually."

"Well, the town heard you were coming and built it just for you."

"And I appreciate it." She pouts again. "Why is no one surprised to see me?"

Gabe just smiles.

"I think lunch is ready," I say.

We make our way to the porch, where Des has set a table with a blue checked tablecloth, white linen napkins, heavy glass goblets, and brightly coloured ceramic plates. Again, there are bowls of olives and hummus and a basket of flat-bread. A tureen of steaming lentil soup sits in the centre of the table.

"You cook?" Kate says.

"She really does. I was here the other day," I say, taking a seat opposite Kate.

"You thought I was faking?" Des says.

"Anybody can get lucky once."

Kate looks at me, a little baffled, and I'm pretty sure I know what she's thinking. After all these years, why so chummy? But she says nothing to me. "Heavily influenced, I see, by your travels," she says. "How long were you in Israel again?"

Des ladles the soup into bowls. "Ten years or so, give or take."

"Tell me about it," Kate says.

I recognize the active listener post; it serves her well as principal. Kate can greet a pair of incensed parents who have arrived with the sole purpose of convincing her that Jimmy didn't do it and have them leave, fifteen minutes later, with their anger replaced by the sober knowledge that Jimmy did indeed do it and, likely, enjoyed himself. Kate is a good administrator.

Gabe pours wine as Des launches into the story I'd heard only days earlier. But, as I listen, I realize that the story involves only her time with Gabe and beyond. There's no mention of the time directly after high school, the years she would have been in Israel alone.

When the soup is finished, along with most of the wine, Kate voices what I've been thinking. "What about the early years? The pre-Gabe years?"

Des blinks, and a dusting of pink rushes to her cheeks. "I've talked enough," she says, glancing at Gabe.

"Besides, nothing of importance happened pre-me, right?" He brushes his lips with a napkin.

The colour on Des's face deepens. "We need more bread— I'll be right back."

Kate watches her leave and leans forward. "So, how did you guys hook up anyway?"

"I was travelling and I heard that Des was in Israel. I looked her up," says Gabe.

Kate makes a *tsk tsk* sound with her tongue. "I know you're a man of few words, but we're going to need a few more."

Gabe looks at me. I look away.

"I heard she was working on a kibbutz, so I tracked her down and worked my magic. Swept her off her feet. How could she resist? Is that better?" he asks.

"Shameless," Kate says.

Gabe smiles. "I know. A Jewish mother *and* a Catholic father, and I can't compete with Mennonite shame."

"You've got that right."

Des calls from the house that there's a phone call for Gabe. He excuses himself but, at the door, he glances at me again. This time I don't look away and I feel a flutter in my stomach.

When he's gone, Kate says, "So, what was that look about?"

"There was no look."

"Oh, I know looks and that was a look if ever I've seen a look."

"Stop saying 'look.'"

"Is there still something there?"

"Kate," I say, lowering my voice, "not everyone is enjoying this stroll down memory lane, haven't you noticed?"

"The past is the past. Gone."

"So why bring it up?"

"They're married. It would have been strange not to ask."

I shake my head at this, but I have no response. Kate has an uncanny ability to reconfigure the past and, despite her earlier comment, is unburdened with guilt. Her mother, she says, had done one good thing for her and that was to saturate Kate with so much shame that she would never have use for it again. I envy this about her.

Gabe and Des return to the table together. "Sorry, girls. I forgot there's an auction I need to be at. Try to manage without me."

"You're not still afraid of us, are you?" Kate asks.

"Always have been, always will be," he says, kissing Des on the cheek.

"You got yourself one of the good ones," Kate says, once he's gone.

"I really did. I was so sorry to hear about you and Preston."

"Thanks."

"Great name, though," Des adds.

There's a pause before Kate smiles back. "Yep. Hey, do you ever see Jarnelle anymore? She was always so bossy."

"*She* was?" Des laughs.

I laugh as well.

"I was never bossy," Kate says. "I was organized."

The conversation turns to "Do you remember so and so and such and such?" until we're laughing so loudly that Maxi and Julia emerge from the house.

"Where's the cocaine?" Maxi asks.

"Oh, my cynical daughter." Des takes her daughter's hand and kisses it. "Haven't you heard the song, *Make new friends, but keep the old*?" Des begins to sing.

> *Make new friends,*
> *But keep the old.*
> *One is silver—*
> *And the other gold.*

Des's soprano rings out clearly alongside Kate's husky voice. I join in at the middle, as it's a round song, meant to flow continuously, with no beginning or end. The girls' faces shift from curiosity to horror, and then they flee. Kate and Des laugh as they leave and continue singing even louder. My throat closes around the words *keep the old*.

It's possible to lie, of course. And it's equally possible to live a lie. But it's nearly impossible to sing a lie.

fifteen

"It's great that Aunt Kate's here, isn't it?" Julia says as we make our way down the curving mountain road.

"Yeah."

"What was she like as a kid? She seems like she should be from somewhere else. Like Los Angeles, or something."

I smile at this. "Well, she did come from the city, but not L.A. And she never let us forget it."

I remember how horrified Kate was when she realized that Halloween was a forbidden holiday in the Valley. She insisted that we do something about this, since her only restriction was to brush her teeth more vigorously afterwards. Des was happy to oblige, but I had my doubts. Halloween was Satan's holiday.

We began the campaign in August. Begging, whining, logic, and persuasion were our weapons of choice. We ditched whining early on because we discovered that nobody likes a whiner. Begging and persuasion weren't any more successful. Logic was a lost cause due to several damaging Scripture passages that warned about the principalities of darkness, and any attempt to counter was a no-win situation because my mother could not be outshone in Name that Scripture.

But one year there was a weakening. My father granted provisional acceptance and my mother showed signs of fatigue. Des and I couldn't believe it. We could practically see the finish line, taste the caramel apples, feel the candy kisses brushing against our lips. But then another Sunday school teacher, Mrs. Andres, got wind of the situation and the next Sunday—only two weeks before Halloween—our lesson was not on the Good Samaritan, as indicated on the schedule. It was about salt and light.

But we would be light, we said—beacons in the darkness. And so salty—the saltiest trick or treaters the world had ever seen. Des whispered that we would also be the sweetest, but I just glared at her. I couldn't believe she'd risk a giggling fit at this delicate point in the negotiations. Eventually, our protests and promises wore Mrs. Andres down and she said she would check with the Elders. Des remained hopeful, but I knew all hope was lost when I heard this. We didn't have a chance inside the circle of Elders—it was the place where ideas went to die.

A week later we were informed that, upon prayerful consideration, trick or treating was un-Christ-like. So, instead of sending the children out on the evil streets, the Sunday School Department would host a Victory of Light over Dark social. Refreshments would be served and children would be permitted to wear a costume, provided it was based on a Biblical character.

When we heard the news, we decided to boycott the entire event, but our parents wouldn't hear of it. Given the turmoil we had put the entire church through, we would attend.

And so we did, cloaked in random bits of cloth. We told our parents we were beggars at the wall of Jerusalem, but when we arrived at the party we removed our outer layer and revealed our true costumes. Des went as Rahab, the Old Testament harlot; Kate was Judas Iscariot, friend and betrayer of Jesus; I, dressed in a flowing white garment, went as Sophia, Wisdom of God.

Des's choice was a little confusing, because she was still a bit of a tomboy, but she insisted that it went with her name: Desiree. She almost changed her mind at the last minute, but Kate talked her out of it, promising a tube of her mother's rose lipstick and, besides, she was going as Judas, wasn't she?

I found Sophia while reading Proverbs. I was flabbergasted to discover that God's wisdom was feminine. In our church, with the feminist movement raging all around us, women had progressed just slightly beyond head coverings. They were not allowed to preach or teach the men or even lead the singing. And the weird thing was, this didn't seem strange to me. It was just the way things were—kind of like having Mr. Johnson, the usher, pat your bum. Sophia was a real find.

When we asked Kate about her decision, she said she wanted to be Judas because he was misunderstood. He was a man who stood for law and order and, above that, action. She said she admired him for doing what he thought was right. Des disagreed, which was unusual for her. She thought Judas had been disloyal to his friend.

As usual, I floated somewhere in between. I agreed with Kate that Judas had been set up, but I also agreed with Des that he was ashamed. I wondered if Judas had killed himself to avoid dying to himself, the way Jesus was always talking about.

So we went to the party and doffed our rags, much to the dismay of Mrs. Andres, who really had worked pretty hard to get this party to happen in the first place. When they asked us who we were supposed to be, I proudly said, Sophia, Wisdom of God. Eyes narrowed, but I had my Proverbs reference at the ready. Des, shaking, said she was Rahab. This didn't go over as well. She was asked to remove the lipstick, put the rags back on, and change her name to Naomi. When they asked Kate who she was, she took one look at Des, who was trembling, and said, quick as a wink: Peter the Rock.

Des fled to the bathroom to remove the lipstick from her mouth, and I followed her. She was scrubbing it off when I entered the room, but there was still a stain of colour on her lips. When she saw me, her eyes filled with tears. "No one will see me," she said, looking down at her dress.

She'd put a lot of thought into her costume. It was made with satiny polyester and wisps of white chiffon (her old angel costume). It was beautiful but really so modest that no whore of Babylon would be caught dead in it.

I made an instant decision. "We're leaving."

"We can't."

"Oh, yes, we can."

"Really?"

"You bet your boots, Red Rider," I said, using an expression of my father's that made her laugh.

I found Kate and told her we were leaving. She said she couldn't. Her mother would kill her, otherwise she would. I believed her, didn't I? I said, of course I did.

"So you guys were all best friends?" Julia asks now.

"We were," I say.

"What happened, then? Why did you stop?"

Betrayal, I almost say. "Life," I say instead. I rub my forehead with my hand to stop the dull pain that's been growing.

"Another headache?" Julia asks. Her tone is without inflection but manages to sound sarcastic anyway.

"It's been a long day."

"Yeah, almost three o'clock. Time for your nap."

"That wasn't called for."

The hum of the tires becomes the only sound between us, but that's okay. The serpentine road is all I can handle. It would be so easy to lose control of the car. One wrong move—that's all it took to slip off a mountain.

"What's wrong with you?"

"Do you think I conjure up these migraines to inconvenience you?"

"Maybe."

"It's out of my control." The words sound empty and untrue.

"Is it happening again?" Her voice is so small that I can barely make out the words. "Are you going to get all weird again?"

I pull into the driveway at the farm just as my vision changes. Chunks of scenery disappear, creating a geometric puzzle, making Picasso out of everything. Cubist, my ass, the man probably had migraines. Big genius. "It's not my fault," I say.

Julia looks at me. Her eyes are cold, detached, as though she's a stranger. "Yes, it is."

I reach my hand out to touch hers, but she pulls away. Her lips tremble; she's trying to get herself back under control. She yanks the car door open and runs into the house.

I tell my mother I won't be down for dinner. She looks concerned and asks if she can bring up a tray. I say no. Upstairs, I get into the bed fully clothed and pull the covers around me.

The evening passes. When I hear a soft knock at the door and open my eyes, I'm surprised, as always, that my vision has been restored. Everything is in the right place, no missing chunks. And the pain has dulled. "Julia?"

My mother pushes the door open with her elbow. She's carrying a tray and, by the slope of her shoulders, it appears to be heavy. I'm so used to thinking of her as strong and capable, but her face looks tired; her arms no longer show the muscle definition she had long before it was fashionable. "I've brought you some soup. Chicken noodle."

"With your homemade noodles?"

"Phht," she says.

I try to pull myself up to a sitting position, but my head feels like it will fly off and roll under the bed if I keep going. "I'll have it later."

"Are you sure that's wise?" She places the tray on the dresser. "Sometimes it helps to eat."

"Sometimes it helps me to throw up if I eat."

"That never happens to me."

"You get migraines?" It hurts to talk, but this is news.

"Once in a while. They run in our family. My mother used to get terrible cluster migraines. Here, try a cold cloth." She removes a chilled facecloth from the tray and places it on my forehead.

The heat of my skin quickly absorbs the cold. I groan my gratitude. "What was she like?" I ask, eyes closed.

"She was busy. She had twelve children; she was a hard worker."

"But what was she like?" The picture of me in bed, asking questions, strikes me as surreal. It's a decoupage and directly behind one picture sits another and another and another. "What made her happy?"

"Phht."

"Who was she?" I press.

"She was who she was, Gloria. Now you need to rest. That's the only thing that will help. Good night." Her lips barely brush my cheek. Her skin smells like chicken stock and onions and aniseed.

She was who she was? Really? Not who she should be? Lucky woman, though, if it's true.

When I open my eyes, my mother is still in the doorway.

"I couldn't talk to her," she says. "We didn't speak the same language."

I sit up at this, about to say, *Hear, hear, I get that. Very common with mothers and daughters.* But she continues.

"She spoke German and I only knew a few phrases."

"So, literally, you didn't speak the same language? Why?"

"Well, she didn't want to learn English and I did."

"Why?"

"Oh, Gloria," she sighs. "You and your whys." She leaves the room, shaking her head.

sixteen

Marci says that it is the nature of depression to leave. It always leaves.

"Marci, Marci, Marci," I said, in my best Cary Grant impression. "It always comes back."

She didn't smile at this because she thought humour diluted truth. She also thought that I hid behind my humour. (Maybe Julia and Marci watched Dr. Phil together.)

"Depression always leaves," she repeated, somewhat sternly.

Once, during a particularly bleak period, we went over the checklist of depression's minions: insomnia, loss of appetite, agitation, fuzziness, and suicidal thoughts. When she stated the last one, there were two deep creases in her forehead. Had I ever had suicidal thoughts? I told her that my suicidal thought was that killing yourself was extremely optimistic. She asked if I was joking and I said I wasn't. I did think it was optimistic to believe that suffering ended with death. (I would have brought up hell again, except that I knew she was committed to hell as metaphor.) She grew concerned and began to talk about meds in earnest, something we had avoided until then.

She presented my pharmaceutical options with the zeal of a used car salesman, each model sounding more brilliant and fuel-efficient than the next. She was convincing, and convinced, that I could be saved. I tried to tell her that I'd been saved before, many times. This would be different, she said. My problem was quite likely chemical.

She had no idea what she was telling me. She didn't hear herself say—as I did—that my depression was contained within my very self, that it had crawled inside my DNA, tucked itself into my bones, was submerged within the molecules of my watery being. She didn't hear herself consign me to my original state: my lacking, sinful self.

The concept of original sin was one that was as familiar to me as any of the Old Testament stories. I knew about it before I learned how to ride a bike. It was part of our home, our church, even though St. Augustine came up with it and he wasn't even a Mennonite. We were born pre-stained and pre-ruined—predestined for salvation. Simply: Eve plucked, Adam swallowed, and Humanity was cursed. I was a sinner before I even poked my tiny head outside the birth channel.

But I didn't bother getting into this with Marci. She considered my religious upbringing to be little more than an interesting aside, a rich source for her metaphors. It wasn't the problem.

And so I have been Prozac-ed, Ativan-ed, Xanax-ed and clonazepam-ed to within an inch of my life. The dark cloud lifted and I became less filled with dread, less prone to binges of complete self-loathing. I became a nicer—if stoned—version of myself. But eventually each form of salvation wore thin because, although I was happier, more and more of my growing energy was earmarked to manage the side effects of the drugs: tremors, anxiety, excessive sweating, sexual dysfunction, increased headaches, loss of appetite, increased appetite, agitation, and joint pain. It seemed to me, I told Marci, that the drugs were returning me to a place I'd already been. It also seemed I was taking new drugs to combat symptoms that were a direct result of the old drugs. So, essentially, the drugs were cloning themselves into the very same symptoms I'd started with and eventually would create a whole new me outside of myself, much like Dolly the sheep.

It felt like a conspiracy, but I was smart enough to keep this to myself. The last thing you want to mention to your therapist is anything remotely paranoid, because that's when they bring out the big guns: the anti-psychotics. And I wanted to steer clear of those. So I kept my concerns to myself, even though I was pretty sure that keeping my concerns to myself was what had driven me to Marci's office in the first place.

She finally agreed that the meds weren't really working for me. What I likely had was a milder, chronic form of depression. So, now, apart from a handy bottle of anti-anxiety pills, I am drug-free. The depression itself, however, has remained virtually the same: unmoved and pitiless.

In the meantime, I've developed a few theories of my own. My theory of Depression as Place goes like this: Depression is a destination, a place where you go when you hate everyone, yourself most of all. It's a relief to go to this place where hatred is allowed, but it's a horrible destination all the same. It is a place without expectations; no false hopes, no brave faces, no heartfelt appeals. Hatred oozes, meanness thrives, bitterness rules. It is a dank, solid, grave of a place, but it is real.

Then there's my theory of Depression as Guest: she arrives with no warning, no plans, no set time of departure. You, the hostess, are too polite to turn her away and so you fix up the guest room and prepare for an interminable visit. The days run together as you cook, clean, and do laundry for someone who shows no sign of leaving. She's uninformed and ignorant; all she wants to do is to sit in the overstuffed chair, drink your coffee, and gaze out the window, making disparaging comments. She enjoys soap operas but not game shows. She tells your family that you prefer her to them. She isn't a teacher, she isn't a friend, and she certainly isn't a lover. She's just a nasty house guest to whom you are distantly related, and therefore obligated to with irrational allegiance, to the end of time.

One day, equally out of the blue, she leaves. No form of payment, of course, not even a thank-you note; only a messy house, a sink full of dishes, and a dull sense of dread that informs you that you've done such a wonderful job as hostess that one day—and make no mistake—she will return.

Finally there's my theory of Depression as Truth. It's a short theory, and the most depressing one of all.

Marci doesn't enjoy my theories. When I go on a rant about them she straightens in her chair and cocks her head so that all her thoughts will rush to the same place; she grows stern and tells me that depression is a fight-or-flight response—our most basic defence mechanism. It's a state of alarm and, as such, not our natural state, although she allows that we have been fighting or fleeing since the Garden of Eden.

It was my turn to straighten when she said this. She had my attention. If a state of alarm was not our natural state—and what was original sin if not an alarming state—then what was?

Happiness, she said. Essential happiness was our original state and our true birthright.

I felt a surge of unsettling hope when she said this. My posture must have shifted, because Marci rushed forth to say that essential happiness was unconditional, dependent on nothing else in order to exist. I tried to remember that state.

Marci knew about Jake, of course. What would he want? she asked. Wouldn't he want me to be happy? she answered.

"Jake wanted to live," I said.

"But what would Jake want you to do?"

"He wouldn't want me to do anything."

"That's not right," she said.

It infuriated me when she said this. Fury slithered through my skin, infused my blood, and crawled through me, feeding every cell. In a way, I was relieved because I was finally feeling something other than fear. But I couldn't remain in that state. It was too powerful, too hungry. It changed the blood to something acidic. Water to wine. No, that was Jesus's party trick. Maybe if he had been a little more careful—thrown his tricks and miracles around a little more discreetly—he would have saved himself a trip to the cross. That's what it always came back to: Jesus suffering for me. Maybe this was when my essential happiness was permanently doomed. He paid the price for my sins, I was told. He saved me. I knew I was indebted forever when I finally understood this. And, what's more, I was meant to be grateful for this sacrifice every day of my life.

The blood of the lamb was spilled to save me. He suffered and bled and died for me while his father sat idly by, watching.

~

Jake and I were only four or five when our mother came into the bedroom and asked if we were ready to be saved. Jake shrugged and said, "Sure." He knelt beside his bed and prayed the prayer of salvation with our mother. *Dear Lord Jesus, come into my heart. There is room in my heart for Thee.*

My mother stood and watched, her hands pressed to her face. She smiled as broadly as I'd ever seen her smile. This made her happy, not just glad. Then she said to me, "Do you want Jesus to come into your heart?"

I couldn't move except to shake my head. She seemed disappointed but said it was all right, I'd come to Jesus when I was ready. She turned the nightlight on and closed the door behind her. By the glow of the tiny light, I found my way to my brother's bed. He was already asleep. I tried to shake him awake, but he was a solid sleeper.

I was horrified that someone—this Jesus, this Thee—had crawled inside my twin. Where would Jake go? How could there be room for him and this whole other Thee inside his heart? Even so young, I knew the heart was that thing that beat inside me, booming when I had a nightmare or now, as I climbed into bed beside my brother. Jake didn't stir, even when I put my head on his chest and listened, desperate to know if he was changed. I found what I was looking for, the steady thump-thump of his heart, and I knew he was still Jake.

I've wondered if this was how we were in the womb. Was my head pressed against his heart? Did it soothe me even then like the ticking of an eternal clock?

In the middle of the night I woke up terrified. I rushed to my parents' room, jumped into the middle of their bed, and cried, "I want to be saved."

I prayed the prayer alongside my mother, who was in curlers, and my father in red plaid pajamas. After saving myself, I added: *Dear Lord Jesus, save everyone.*

seventeen

The next morning, Kate comes by in her rented convertible. It's a beautiful day, not a cloud in the sky. I go outside to meet her. She's wearing a pair of cream pants, a T-shirt that will have cost a hundred dollars, maybe more, and a butter yellow sweater tied around her neck. Designer sunglasses. As always, she looks stunning. I tell her she looks like Malibu Barbie.

"Watch out," she says. "That makes you Midge."

Barbie's plain friend. "That hurts."

"I'm going to Abbotsford to visit Lester and his brood. Want to come? They have a pool." This last bit of information is directed at Julia, who has joined us on the porch.

"I'm not really up to it. But Julia can go, if she wants."

"Can Maxi come?"

"The more the merrier," Kate says, with a magnanimous stretch of a well-defined arm.

Julia runs off to make a phone call. I notice that she doesn't try to persuade me to join them.

Kate sits beside me on the porch steps. "Another migraine?"

"Yesterday. Now I just have the dishrag hangover."

She makes a sympathetic clucking noise. "Sure you don't want to come?"

I shake my head as my mother comes out of the house to say hello. Kate chats comfortably with her until Julia emerges from the house with her backpack. She announces that everything is set. Maxi can go. Gabe will meet Kate at the bottom of the hill so that she won't have to drive so far out of her way. "Let's go, let's go, let's go!" she shouts.

"Dinner tonight, right?" Kate says, following Julia to the car.

"I told Des we'd meet her at the restaurant."

"Sounds good. Take it easy, okay?"

"You guys have a good time." I wave as the car leaves the driveway. Julia's hand flies up in the air, catching the wind, but she doesn't turn. She's already in full conversation with Kate. Her words, though indecipherable, drift back to where I'm standing.

I tell my mother that I'm going for a walk. She offers to come with me, but I remind her of her rising dough. As I pass the barn, I hear my father's tenor voice. He always sings when he's feeding the cows. He says it aids their digestion. "Trust and obey," he's singing, "For there's no other way to be happy." It's a good voice, not strong, but it holds a tune and it holds me now. I almost follow it inside but resist. I need the walk. And a clear head.

The entrance to the hollow within the woods is almost overgrown with blackberry bushes. The bright fuchsia rhododendron is still there, standing sentinel but giving away the secret passageway. It was a better secret when the rhodo wasn't in bloom. We used to slip past the branches and walk lightly when we entered; we even closed our eyes for the first few steps because we wanted the first sight of the hollow to come as a surprise.

I keep my eyes open now because I'm not in the mood for a scratch from the blackberry thorns. The path is still easy to find and leads me to the rock where Des and I used to sit.

Jake would follow us, hoping to catch us telling secrets or sneaking a smoke. But we were careful with our secrets and only tried smoking once, after making the mistake of choosing unfiltered cigarettes. We were too scared to bring the package back into our houses and too Mennonite to waste perfectly good cigarettes, so we smoked them all in one sitting. Des threw up, while I sat ashen-faced. By the time we had drenched ourselves with Green Apple perfume and chewed a pack of Juicy Fruit gum to mask the tobacco scent, we had decided it wasn't worth it. Besides, Albert Loewen had been excommunicated only a few years before for smoking.

I liked having a place—this grove—that was mine the way Jake had his mountain. Sometimes I imagined that the pre-birth world we shared was like another planet, except fixed, with one side facing the sun: Jake's side. He was never moody or unreasonable. Sometimes he got angry, but he was never ugly. His sins were mild: dirty knees, torn clothes from tree-climbing, excessive teasing. When he was older he might disappear into the forest for hours at a time without telling anyone where he'd gone or when he'd return. Our mother scolded him, but half-heartedly, and when he grew stronger and bigger he would lift her up mid-scold. He got out of a lot of trouble that way.

Jake was so happy, in fact, that when we were much younger, people wondered if he was retarded. "He's not," I said. "He's just Jake."

Our property abuts a paved road and beyond it is Jake's

mountain, the place where he used to disappear for more afternoons than we could count. Sometimes I went with him. We'd take a bag of our mother's fresh buns and bottles of Coke. He knew the mountain like he knew himself.

One of our favourite places was at the end of an old logging road. It was partially logged; as many stumps as old-growth trees dotted the face of the mountain like a receding hairline. Machines had been left behind to rust in the rain; weeds grew around them like flowers planted lovingly in memory of. It was as though progress surrendered and nature smiled, maybe a little smugly. Jake liked this place because he thought time had passed it by. But who cared about time anyway, because it was just a device, he said. "It keeps everything from happening at once."

This made no sense to me.

"You want everything to make sense," he said. "You have to know everything."

What about the Bible, I'd counter. Didn't it know everything? Wasn't that the whole point of it in the first place? And wasn't it our job, to know? And then to pass the knowing along so that everyone else would know? It wasn't my plan, I pointed out. We were just following orders.

As we sat at the top of the mountain, letting the rays deepen our tan, we talked about eternity. *When we've been there ten thousand years, bright shining as the sun, we've no less days to sing God's praise than when we first begun.* This was Jake's favourite hymn. He used it as evidence for the non-existence of time in heaven.

Ten thousand years of church. A forever of singing, praising, and the relentless strumming of harps. "Forever sounds exhausting," I moaned.

"That's because you're stuck in time."

163

"We're all stuck in time, Jake."

"We are," he allowed. "But that doesn't mean that time is stuck in time. It's just how we understand things. Time and space, they're not absolutes."

He tried to persuade me that the slowing of time actually did happen. The faster you went, the more compressed time became. He talked about the unknowable nature of light. Light didn't obey the same laws as everything else; it wasn't bound.

"What?" I asked. "Huh?"

"Light has no mass, right? Everything else has mass, so it can't travel at the speed of light. The faster something moves, the greater its mass becomes, and if an object were ever to reach the speed of light, its mass would become infinite. But light has no mass; it is the only thing that can travel at the speed of light. Einstein said that, from light's point of view"—and this was when I wished I'd paid attention in science class instead of arguing the Creation story—"light travels no distance and takes zero time to do so. Therefore," Jake concluded with a flourish, "whatever light is, it exists in a realm where there is no before and no after. No time. Only now."

"But why?" I asked, after all that.

"Why what?"

"Why any of it? Just why?"

"That's the point. Light might be the very edge of what we can know."

But I knew he was wrong. Einstein was wrong. Quantum physics was wrong. Everything was knowable. It had to be! It was why we were banished from Eden.

Jake stood at the edge of the cliff then. He waved his arms

around him like a deranged Old Testament prophet and launched into his Wonders of the World speech. All of life was a miracle, he said. Just look around. Listen. Pay attention. It was a mystery, didn't I see? A miracle. It all fit together and that was amazing. If you stood completely still you could feel the vibrating of the atom, the movement of the planets. "It actually shimmers, Glo. The world shimmers. You don't have to understand it to feel it. You just have to fall into it. It's like love. Whoever questions falling in love?"

"Yeah, yeah, yeah," I said. "Get away from the edge." I refused to continue the conversation until he was sitting beside me again. "*Why* is the only question worth asking."

"Because it's the only question that can't be answered?"

"Exactly."

"So what?"

"So why do we care about *Why* if there's no answer? I care. I know you care. Why are we made to care so much about something that can't be known? It's a cheat. It's—"

"Not fair?"

"It isn't."

"Can you see your nose?"

"Jake."

"Seriously. Can you see your nose? It's big enough."

My nose was actually quite pert, but I humoured him. "Yes, I can see my nose."

"Right now. Are you looking at your nose?"

"Yes."

"Who's looking at it? Your eyes? Your brain?"

"I don't know, my brain."

"And who is your brain telling this to, this news that you have a big nose?"

"To me."

"So, who is *me*?"

"Me is me, you idiot."

"Explain that, Miss-Too-Smart-for-Relativity. Are you invisible, then? Is the visible, physical 'you' telling the invisible 'you' that you have a big nose? Hmm. Could it be the soul? Could it be the light? Could it be the unknowable? Did you know that Einstein said that the imagination is more important than knowledge? Knowledge is limited, he said. Imagination encircles the world."

"Well," I said, needing to think fast to combat this surge of energy from Jake. His theories scared me. They were veering into dangerous territory. And anytime he went searching into these uncharted places, I wanted to return to the place I knew. "Einstein is dead," I said. "I just want to know the truth."

"No, you don't."

"Don't tell me what I don't want. The Bible is the truth, right? It's just a question of understanding it. You're making everything complicated."

"No, it's not. The truth isn't complicated. The Bible, those are stories, Glo. They hold the truth but they're not the truth. Nothing can hold the truth completely, because truth is liquid, it's light, it's—"

"I just want to know why, that's all. Why are we here? What does it mean?"

"Why isn't it enough that we're here?"

"I never asked to be born," I shouted, surprising even myself.

He looked at me with one eye squeezed shut, as though he was thinking hard. "You don't approve," he said, finally. "That's it, you know. You're pissed off that God didn't ask your permission."

Well, I could practically hear the gates of heaven slam shut at this. Being angry with God was going too far. Pastor Reimer preached that it was the unforgivable sin to turn your back on God, and when Jake said what he said, my blood turned cold. "Jake, don't say that." I tried to sound casual, but I was close to hysteria. "Take it back."

He sat in the grass with his hand shielding his face from the sunlight. When he took it away, the full force of the sun illuminated him. He lay in the grass, closing his eyes. "Glo," he said. "You and your big, stupid nose and your big, stupid *Why?* Wouldn't it be funny if the answer was *Why not?*" He laughed at his own joke and then promised that if he died first he would go right up to the throne of God and ask why. "Listen," he'd say. "I couldn't care less, but my sister? She really needs to know."

This was another huge difference between my twin and I. If I were to approach the throne of God to ask why, I'd back down immediately. If I managed to squeak anything out, I would ask: Do you know who I am?

I lay on the grass beside my brother, but he was done talking.

~

A horn blasts. I'm standing in the middle of the road and there's a tractor to my right. The driver looks friendly but still, he'd like to move past. I back up, embarrassed.

He stops the vehicle and turns down the radio. "You lost?"

"Oh, no," I say, with a wave. *Move along.* I smile at him reassuringly. I know where I am.

He revs the engine and I disappear into the woods, where

I find the path that leads to the farm. Light, here, is freckled on the ground; it moves across the forest floor in a slow dance. I prefer this light to the bright sunshine.

I move quickly through the woods until I see the rhodo sentinel. The entrance is now my exit; I push through. On the other side, I feel relief. The farmhouse is still there, solid and unchanged.

eighteen

I find my mother in the kitchen, surrounded by industry. Cookie sheets on the counter are covered with raspberries; water in the sink is bobbing with crimson. She must have gathered the fruit sometime between the leavening and kneading of her cinnamon buns, which are browning in the oven and, from the smell of it, almost done. A chicken carcass simmers in a pot on the stove. Eventually, she'll eat the neck and the feet. If the chicken had a soul she would find a use for it as well. Use everything. Even the air is busy with commingling aromas.

"Look at you," I say.

My mother glances over her shoulder, but her hands keep moving.

"You get so much accomplished in one day. The buns, the jam, the soup—you work so hard."

She pulls a tray of buns—golden brown, rife with cinnamon and sugar—from the oven and places it on a square of unused counter space. "Idle hands are the devil's workshop," she says.

"Yep." I glance around the room to see if this is sewn on a plaque somewhere. Nope. But there is one I hadn't noticed before.

I will set before myself no sordid aim
I will reject all crooked thoughts.
I will have no dealing with evil.

No one could ever accuse these walls of housing low expectations. "Seriously, Mom. This is amazing." I join her at the sink and sort berries.

She stands beside me and wipes her hand on the apron around her waist. "It has to be done."

I separate the defective, mushy berries from the chosen ones. "But how do you know what has to be done?"

"What kind of question is that?" She lifts the lid off of the simmering pot of soup and adds a fistful of freshly cut dill. It looks like a random amount. A sharp aroma spikes the air. "The berries are ready. They have to be picked. They have to be used. It's simple."

I look out into the yard. My dad is on the tractor, heading toward the back field. There is work to be done out there as well. "That makes sense, I guess."

"Phht."

I fill a colander with pristine berries and bring them over to a cookie tray, where I line them up in the same military manner as the others. I hand a bowl of lesser fruit to my mother, who tips them into a pot and stirs. She adds sugar directly from the plastic bin; measuring cups are an unnecessary convenience. "You don't even have to think about it, do you?"

"I've been doing this for years, Gloria. Practise makes perfect."

I think about this. What have I been practising for the last twenty years? Being sad. But that can't be it, can it? That can't be the only thing I'm good at. "Are there more to be picked?"

"Another row or so, but they can wait for another day."

"Could you use them now? If I picked them now?" I sound so eager it's almost embarrassing. My mother looks surprised. Then she laughs. My mother's laughter is as rare as an idle pair of hands on this farm; the sound fills me with accomplishment.

"Go on, then," she says. "The flats are still by the barn. Wear something to protect your arms and pick clean."

The last instruction sounds like the voice of the Straw Boss from the old days. She calls after me. "It doesn't have to be finished today."

The path to the berry patch is hard-packed with the ruts from tractor tires. I go to the branches that are heavy with the season's last ripe, unplucked berries. It's a small patch now, only a few rows. My parents used to farm acres and acres. In the month of July, kids from the neighbouring farms and town made pocket money by picking berries. Des was the best picker, I was mediocre, and Kate was abysmal, grumbling the whole time about how the thorns ruined her perfectly tanned arms. The days seemed to last forever as we tangled with bugs, mould, mud puddles, the sizzle of the midday sun, and aching backs. As much as we grumbled, though, there was a sense of achievement as we compared hole punches at the end of the day. (This is a story that never fails to irritate Julia when I try to pass on a semblance of the work ethic I grew up with.)

On the hottest days we headed to the lake for a picnic afterwards and let the cold of that first plunge strip the day's dust from our skinny legs and arms.

The sun beats down now. It's been a long time since I've been in the sun without a hat. We never wore them then and our noses peeled a hundred times over. We told stories and sang songs to pass the time. Eventually, Jake or Gabe would start a berry fight and at the end of the day it was normal to find a flattened, mouldy berry stuck between the waist of your cut-offs and the elastic of your underwear. But Jake never threw berries at Des. His crush was in full bloom by then. And if he didn't have a full flat at the end of the day, he gave all his extra berries to her.

When I'm convinced that the only remaining fruit is green and rock hard, I take my gleanings back to the kitchen. For the rest of the afternoon we work side by side. We freeze the best fruit and make jam with the rest. We finish baking the buns, regular as well as cinnamon, and the soup smells ambrosial by the time we're done. For the most part, we work in silence.

"Oh," she says. "Mark called while you were in the berry patch. He sounded tired."

"He's a busy man."

"Are you taking good care of him?"

I cringe, but say nothing.

She takes a tub of bleach from beneath the sink and swipes the countertops. The perfume of our afternoon's enterprise is sacrificed to the rising fumes of bleach. "Now, I know it's not popular to say that, so don't scowl at me." She's felt my scowl without even turning to look. "You need to take care of each other."

My eyes prickle at the compassion in her voice, and I want to talk. I want to tell her that my husband has turned into a stranger. When he touches me, it's the hand of a stranger because nothing touches me anymore.

"*A good wife is the crown of her husband.*" She recites the Scripture and it's no longer just the two of us. King Solomon has arrived.

I'm tempted to remind her that Solomon would have needed a separate palace to house all the crowns of his many wives, not to mention concubines, but instead I hear myself ask, "Did you always love Dad?"

She actually stops working and turns. "What kind of question is that?"

An accidental one. It's this place, its smells and memories; they've made me careless. "Never mind," I say, quickly.

"Of course I've always loved him. What a question."

I take a deep breath into my tight belly. Damn Marci and her tight belly of sorrow. I hate it when she's right. "It's just a question. You don't have to get all defensive."

"Phht. Defensive," she mutters, now cleaning the stovetop. "You and your psychology."

"Well, Freud started it. So, strictly speaking . . ."

"I don't know about Freud." She turns to me with the cloth in her hand, like maybe one good scrub and this conversation would disappear. "But I know that a wife should love her husband. Is that so unpopular these days?"

"No, Mom, it's not. I'm sorry. I just wondered, that's all, if you always love him or do you ever take a break?" Now I'm rambling.

"Take a break from loving your husband?"

"Have you ever wondered if he was the one?"

"Well, of course he is. I promised to love, honour, and obey. I took a vow."

I try to see the logic of this, the connection, but before I can respond she says, "Do you know what your trouble is, Gloria?"

"No, Mom." I sigh, but there is a part of me that really hopes she can answer this correctly. I have spent thousands of dollars on this particular question. "What?"

"All your wondering."

"Ah," I say.

We clean in silence, and then the phone rings.

It's Kate. She's wondering if she can take the girls to an afternoon movie. She might be late for dinner. "Julia will love that," I say. "Take your time. How's Lester?"

"Complete and unabridged. I am now up to date on the real estate situation from Abbotsford to Langley. Cherry served a wonderful luncheon à la Stepford wife." The words come out in a flurry.

"So you've had a good time?"

"Oh, the best."

"But they didn't show you their pictures of Europe."

"Now that's a blessing," she says.

"Well, have fun with the girls. And, thanks, you know?"

"I know," she says, and hangs up.

I knew Kate was dreading the visit with her brother Lester. He has the life she thought was meant for her. She was the one who was going to end up in the grand house, raising gorgeous offspring. Des and I used to say we would use her future palace as a meeting place, a hostel for the transients we were meant to become. Kate said she would keep a candle in the window.

That wasn't the way it worked out, but Kate had kept her promise of the burning candle. I could always count on her.

I go to the living room and sit down at the piano bench. I hear the click of the screen door and my mother's footsteps outside on the gravel. She said she wanted to take some jam next door to Mrs. G. I wonder if she's told my mother about seeing me come out of the pub the other day, and then I wonder if I'll ever grow up here. Maybe my mother is right; I need to stop wondering.

I run my fingers across the polished wood, through and around the intricate carving of the music stand. The metronome is still there; I pull the metal band and listen as it measures the time. And then it stops. I wind it until the key is tight. It would continue only as long as it was wound.

Time is an illusion, a device. Jake's words. *You're stuck in time.* I position my fingers over the yellowing keys. The ivory of middle C is cracked where I dropped the metronome; the crack has turned grey. My mother handed out the standard punishment: sitting in the corner, reading the Bible. Jake offered to take the heat for me, but I didn't let him. I actually believed in the punishment.

"But you're so grumpy when you're reading the Bible," he complained.

"This is serious. Listen to this one." I turned the flimsy pages of the book to a passage I'd pretty much memorized. "*So after all this Jehovah smote him in his bowels with an incurable sickness.* Do you even know what smote means?"

Jake sighed, his hopes for a day of possible fun dashed. He clambered up onto the piano bench, clutched his stomach dramatically, and fell onto the ground beside me. "I've been smoted," he gasped. He lifted his head and dropped it once more for effect. "I've been smoted again."

"Don't joke," I reprimanded, still reading.

He pulled himself up and sat beside me on the bench. He grew serious. "Don't be so scared all the time, Glo. Relax already. You should be shining."

My hands find their way to an old sonata now; the music echoes through the empty room. Sunlight finds Jake's picture. The photographer captured his wavy hair, his carefree grin, and the single dimple on the left side of his face, but not his spirit.

The music dwindles—I've forgotten the rest of the piece—and then my mother is in the doorway. I jump as though I've done something wrong.

"I thought you were playing," she says, glancing around the room as though she expects to see the music. "Maggie's come by."

"Mrs. G?" I say.

"How many Maggies do you know?" she says, brisk again.

"Thousands," I say, for no reason. My mother looks perplexed at this. "I'll be right there."

I liked Mrs. G: her loud bray of a laugh and her girth—a woman of excess who wore it proudly, plunging into my mother's baking with unabashed glee. She was a church lady who never acted like one. Every Christmas, Mrs. G appeared at the door with a bottle of sweet sparkling wine—Christmas cheer—and my mother would accept a glass in the spirit of Christmas charity. On those evenings my mother was actually silly—and it amazed me.

"She's drunk, stupid," Jake whispered on the stairs one Christmas.

I was outraged even more than usual. "She's not," I hissed back. "She's had one glass. She's being polite."

"Polite? Glo," he said, "you're so stupid." He patted my head the way you would a large, bumbling dog.

I return to the kitchen. A grin lights Mrs. G's face when she sees me. "Gloria," she says. "It's so good to see you." She whispers, "Again," as I lean over to give her a hug. "These chairs keep getting smaller," she says, settling back in.

"It's true," I say.

"Oh, you're thin as a rail, Gloria. Here—" She pushes the plate of cinnamon buns across the table. I take a small piece, which doesn't escape her notice. She clucks disapproval.

"Will Julia be home soon?" Mom asks.

"Kate's taken the girls to a movie."

She looks disappointed.

"They'll be home soon."

Mrs. G politely asks me about my life in Winnipeg. I give her a few tidbits and then the conversation switches to local gossip. I lean back with my cup of tea, knowing that my part is over. Mrs. G was always the best gossip of all my mother's friends, which is not to say that the others had no flair for it, far from it, but their news was always prefaced by: *I really shouldn't say this*, or *I don't mean to be judgmental but—*. Then there was the prayer-chain disclaimer: *We should pray for Sarah Johnson, whose sixteen-year-old daughter, Libby, was seen going into Dr. Brandy's office for a pregnancy test*. Mrs. G's gossip had no qualifiers. She loved to talk about people and that was that.

I replenish the teapot as Mrs. G leans closer to the table, or as close as her belly will allow, and begins: Sandra Meiers went to the dentist for a root canal and came out with a pulled tooth. She's considering a lawsuit. Henry Ferguson (Hank and Evelyn's boy) is being treated for cocaine addiction, and Joe McAllister's son, Sean, is living as a woman in the city—Chantal now.

As I listen to this, drifting in and out of attention, I have to admit that the local gossip is keeping up with the times. Then Mrs. G mentions the old Sunday school superintendent, Tina Wiebe. "The doctor said she had two months to live and do you know what she did?"

"Mrs. Wiebe?" I ask. "She's sick?"

"Didn't I tell you that she died?" my mother asks.

"No."

"I'm sure I did. Liver cancer, spread to her bones."

"Well, anyway," Mrs. G says. "When she came home from the doctor, what do you think she did? After finding out that she had two months to live?"

I take the bait. "What did she do?"

"Started cooking dinners for that good-for-nothing, holier-than-thou husband of hers, Helmut." My mother tut-tuts a little, for my benefit, I'm sure, and Mrs. G furrows her brow. "You know it's true, Liz." My mother says nothing. "Cooking and freezing and labelling—like she was going on a trip! And do you know what he said when he found her working hard like that?" She spreads a look equally between my mother and me, with another pause.

"What did he say?"

She extends the moment by eating the remaining morsel of bun, chewing it thoroughly, and then swallowing. Her timing was always impeccable. "He said, 'What about desserts?'"

Appropriately, my mother looks horrified and they both take a sip of tea at exactly the same time. Inappropriately, I want to laugh.

My mother clears away the dishes; her lips are a thin, straight line. "He always was a mean-spirited—" She stops herself.

"Son of a bitch," Mrs. G finishes.

I expect my mother to tut-tut the curse, but she just nods. I guess a curse is acceptable under some circumstances; it seems I should know this about my mother.

The conversation turns lighter and Mrs. G soon has us laughing. The lines on my mother's face soften and her hands, always busy, cross comfortably in front of her, except when she uses one to cover her mouth, which is opened too wide in laughter.

When Mrs. G has to leave to make dinner for her husband, whom my father calls Silent Bill, I offer to walk home with her.

"I'll give you some fresh eggs," she says.

"You've got a deal."

The sky is mowed into swaths of pink and mauve. "It'll be a nice day again tomorrow."

"I hope so." I rub my head. I wonder if I'll pay for today's sunshine in the berry patch with a headache tomorrow.

"Your mother said you're going through some rough times with Mark."

"She did, did she?" I slow my pace as the larger woman's breathing shifts from huffing to outright puffing.

"Well, we talk about most things, you know. No need for high-priced, fancy therapists for us."

I give her a sidelong glance.

"Not that your mother's mentioned that . . . ." she backtracks, ". . . too much."

We both laugh and she takes my arm as we cut through the pasture. The smell of sweet grass follows us as we follow the path to her home, a path worn by two friends travelling back and forth. *A path of communion*, I think, like the one Des and I wore to the creek. There's a lot to be said for a friend who will travel the same way so many times. "You've been a good friend for my mom."

"Well, it's gone both ways, dearie. If our kitchen walls could talk, well, it's probably just as well they can't."

I can't imagine that anything too shocking would be revealed by either set of walls, but I nod all the same.

"When I had my miscarriages your mother was always there with a pot of soup, an apple pie, and a shoulder to cry on."

"Miscarriages?"

"Five or six," she says. "Six. I just kept trying. Even when the doctor told me to stop. But your mother let me cry. Your mother waited so long for you—she understood that kind of wanting."

"What do you mean?" A spasm of guilt passes through me.

"Well, she was in her late thirties when she finally got pregnant. She waited a long time."

"I never really thought about that."

Mrs. G just smiles. "Children sometimes think their parents just appear the day they're born, don't they?"

I nod at this.

"She was so good to me, Gloria," Mrs. G is saying. "Even nursed me through some hangovers, though I knew she didn't approve. But she never judged me, just brewed up a strong pot of coffee. Thank the good Lord for coffee. Coffee and good friends. And brandy," she winks.

When we arrive at her front porch, I wait on the stoop

while she goes inside to get the eggs. I think of the other women, my mother's other friends, who visited our house. Mrs. G's name came up frequently, their concern bordering on the obscene as they rooted about for details. I can see now how discreet my mother had been, not saying much, occasionally agreeing that prayer was in order. I remember thinking how pious that sounded, how antiseptic. Now, I wonder. Maybe she was just trying to tune out the noise.

And I wonder, was it my mother's own need that recognized the need in her friend? And what did she need that we were unable to give?

When Mrs. G comes back with a double carton of fresh brown eggs, I thank her. She gives me a crushing hug. "It's good that you've come back. You take care of yourself."

I retrace my steps. The sun has dipped behind the mountain, subduing the light. Shadows have grown longer in the time that's passed.

nineteen

When I reach the house, Kate's car is pulling out of the driveway. I wave but she doesn't see me. I'm supposed to be at the restaurant in less than an hour, so I rush up the stairs to change. My mother calls up that Julia is home just as I open the door and see her sitting cross-legged on the bed with a book on her lap. "Hey you," I say, suddenly so happy for a present life rather than the constant sifting through the remains of another. I wonder if she's forgiven me. "How was your day?"

She hesitates for only a second. "Fun. Kate's brother is rich. Rich looks like fun."

"Rich does look like fun."

"Cherry, that's Lester's wife, made us hamburgers with ketchup eyes and mustard smiles. It was kind of creepy." She scowls into her lap. "But tasty."

"I'm glad." I go to the closet and swing open the door. "What are you reading?"

"Some old storybook of yours. You dotted your name with a heart!"

I immediately recognize the frayed jacket, yellowed and

stained with time. I can see the title from here, in big bold letters: *Bible Stories for Children*. It should have been called *Tales to Terrify Tots*.

"Look," she says, pointing to my signature. Sure enough, Gloria with a heart.

I sit at the foot of the bed. "We spent a lot of time together," I say, taking the book from her. "I didn't know it was still around."

"I was reading that Jonah story. Dad would call it a 'whale of a story.'" She groans.

"Yes, he would." The thought makes me smile.

"It's a good story."

"Is that . . . that isn't the first time you've heard the story, is it?" How bad has her religious training been?

"I guess not." She shrugs. "I mean, I knew the Jonah in the belly of the whale bit, but I never knew what a miserable guy he was."

"Really? I always felt sorry for Jonah, being ordered around and then digested by a fish until he said uncle."

"I don't know, wouldn't you think he'd be kind of honoured to have God talk to him? You'd think he would feel special. He seems so stubborn, kind of a whiner. And mean! Jeez, it's like he was eating popcorn while he waited for God to take out the city."

"Well, maybe he didn't think God was being fair."

"But God, Mom! I mean, it wasn't like Joe Schmo sending him on an errand!"

"Maybe that's how he felt, like an errand boy?"

"But it was a good thing. A quest, you know? One of those Holy Grail deals, find a good man, save a bunch of people, be a hero."

"Save them from whom, exactly? Joe Schmo?"

Julia doesn't answer at first. Her mouth moves back and forth the way it does when she's thinking. "But in the end, God didn't kill anyone and Jonah was still pissed off!" Her eyes narrow and she looks hard at me. "Maybe God was trying to save Jonah."

"Hmm," I say. "He didn't give him much choice though, did he? Three days inside a fish? Not exactly subtle."

"Um, it's a story, Mom? You're so literal."

I look into those deep blue eyes, almost navy, with lines of gold strewn randomly through. "That's exactly what your uncle always said."

Jake would have added stubborn. When he grew to his full height, he'd get me in a stranglehold: *Say mercy and I'll let you go.* I was unable to break free and he was unwilling to cause pain, which would have been the only thing that would get me to cry mercy. Finally, he would almost plead with me. "Just say it and I'll let you go." But I was stubborn. Finally, in disgust, he'd open his arms. I always wondered if he knew that if he'd pressed a little harder, I'd have given in.

"I wish I'd known him," Julia says, picking up another, slimmer book. "Look what else I found."

"You've been busy, haven't you?"

"Your high school album!" She holds it overhead with a wicked grin.

I lunge for it, but she pulls it close to her chest and folds her arms around it. She looks amused; her eyes are dancing. She's so beautiful. I almost say it, except that I know she'll accuse me of being sentimental and of trying to reassure her.

"I've already looked through it, so if you're worried that I'm going to mock the flippy hair, well . . ."

"Yeah, yeah. You have no choice, I know." I sit down and she moves over. I whip through the pages to my graduation photo. "It was just post-Farrah. You have no idea how long I had to argue with your grandmother to get her to let me go to the hairdresser; she didn't approve of the layers."

"Go, Gran," she says. "Seriously, Mom. Take a gander."

I smile at the word, but, when I lean in, I have to agree. "Well, it looked good at the time."

"Okay," she says doubtfully. "Look at Aunt Kate." Julia turns quickly to Kate's picture. Her pageboy hairstyle is lacquered with hairspray, but she is still beautiful. The teenaged promises she made are beneath the picture: *Career, handsome husband, fabulous house, kids.*

"That's not right that she can't have kids," Julia says, running her fingers over the picture. "She'd make an awesome mother."

I feel the gnawing pressure of jealousy when she says this, and instantly I'm ashamed. Kate deserves my gratitude, not jealousy. "You're right about that."

I fan the pages until I find Des's photo. Her dimples are framed with badly straightened hair parted down the middle. The caption beneath her photo is: *To be.*

Julia grabs the book again. "Look what somebody wrote in the margin." She scans her finger across a page that's covered in autographs: neat, rounded, girlish greetings of overwrought sentiment and promises, and the angled, messy signatures of boys who were too cool to put any effort into sentiment or penmanship. "Here it is." She clears her throat and reads. "'*All a person needs to be happy in this life is to be who they are.*' And look how it's signed. *God*! Who wrote that? Who signed themselves God?"

"Gabe."

"Maxi's dad?" Julia flips furiously again and finds the photo of Gabe. I look at the picture and my first thought is of how many times I kissed that face and ran my hands through that unruly hair. The pulsing vein on the side of his face.

"We were kind of an item."

Julia sighs. "This place is turning into a soap opera."

I smile. "Little bit."

I turn back to the annual, to my picture and to the words I chose for my own promise. Des and I had discussed our answers before submitting them to the yearbook committee. Kate was mad that we hadn't included her. I look down at what I wrote: *To see.*

Jake looked at the inscription and laughed. "That's a joke." He took out a pencil and crossed them out, and then added his own version. I erased it immediately, but when I look closely I can still see the indentation of his scrawl: *To know.*

~

I'm the first to arrive at the Country Inn, a restaurant that specializes in schnitzel and other heavily fried foods. The maître d' seats me and promises that he will return either with the rest of my party or a magic trick. "Can I bring you a drink before the others arrive?"

I order a glass of wine. With a grin, he hands me my watch. I look down at my wrist. Sure enough, watch-free.

"Very nice," I say.

He returns with my wine, and Des, within minutes.

Des points to my glass. "I think we're going to need more of that," she says. "Quite a bit more."

He offers to bring a bottle and then leaves.

"He took my watch," I say.

"He does that," Des says.

I take a gulp of my wine and reduce the contents of the glass by half.

"Thirsty?"

"A little."

Des leans back in her seat. "Me too."

I take another swig and then the waiter arrives with a bottle. He opens the wine in silence, pours two full glasses and leaves.

"It was nice of Kate to take the girls to Lester's place." She sips her wine gratefully. "I haven't seen him in years."

"He's a real estate baron now."

"Oh, I know. His face is on most of the bus stops in town. I've sat on him, I just haven't seen him." She smiles, taking a longer sip. "This is a little weird, no?"

"I don't know how you can't hate me." This is nothing short of a blurt, but Des doesn't even blink.

"Hate you? Never."

"How is that possible?" I feel something shifting inside me, and it jars me; a not-so-quiet voice tells me to back up before the crack widens.

"No." She shakes her head. "I shouldn't have told you about Jake and me, not that way, not at the funeral."

And there it is—the pain. Pain is punctual, you have to give it that. Like it never left, it nestles up against my breastbone and presses heavily against my lungs. I sit taller in my seat so that I can breathe deeply.

Kate arrives two steps behind the ebullient maître d'. "Martini. Gin, straight up, with a twist. Bombay, if you have it," she says, as soon as she is seated. "How's the headache?" she asks me.

"Gone," I say, looking at Des, who has adjusted her expression.

"You're not feeling well?" Des asks.

"I had a migraine yesterday. I'm fine now. Really." I take the bottle and top up our glasses.

"Horrible things," Kate says. "She gets them far too often." She goes on to describe a new drug she's read about that I must try. As she speaks, her voice gets smaller. Or maybe I'm getting smaller. Barely here. And then I see that they've raised their glasses. I lift mine as well. For a second, all I see is my arm; it's as though it hovers. Somehow it has managed to detach itself. Kate is offering a toast. "To friendship," she says. We clink our glasses together. The sound is unnaturally sharp and the words hollow. We don't make eye contact.

"What a day," Kate sighs. She goes on to describe the Stepford brunch: the three-car garage; the stainless steel appliances; the original—albeit ugly—artwork; the statue by the pool.

"Statue?" Des repeats.

Kate nods, shrugs, and knocks back the martini. She pours herself a glass of wine.

"Julia said the hamburgers had ketchup eyes and mustard smiles," I offer.

"Oh." Kate sits up straight. "And french fry pigtails! At first I thought they were sidelocks. I asked her if they were orthodox burgers."

"Did you unsettle her?" I've heard enough Cherry stories over the years; it's a fair question. Kate enjoys unsettling Cherry.

"Maybe when I asked for a splash of vodka in the orange juice."

"What did she say?"

"She said that they don't partake of alcohol."

"She said 'partake'?"

"She could use a stiff drink."

I offer a toast to stiff drinks and the wine starts to take hold. My arm reattaches itself and the fissure begins to close.

Kate looks at Des. "You never were very bitchy, were you?"

"I'm working on it. Having Maxi around helps. Gabe calls it the Five Stages of Bitchy."

We drink to the Five Stages of Bitchy.

There is silence as we put our glasses back on the table.

"So," says Des, filling the void. "What's life like on the tundra? We haven't even talked about your life there."

Right. Winnipeg. My life. I draw a blank. My life there feels as frozen, suddenly, as one of the endless winters.

"Glo and I went to the opera the other day," Kate answers.

"Oh," I laugh. "What a disaster."

"Which one?"

"*Tosca*," says Kate.

"I liked it," Des says.

"The opera was fine. Kate and I. We are disastrous opera-goers."

Kate looks a little hurt. "Oh, come on. Grab a brain, Tosca. The guy who's trying to get into your pants tells you that he's going to use fake bullets in the 'mock execution' and 'pretend' to kill your lover, who also happens to be his arch-enemy? Please."

"But the music, oh, Kate. The music," Des laughs. "What about you, Glo?"

"Sadly, the same reaction. I wanted to tell everyone to stop the music and just take a moment, just a breath, and think. Be reasonable."

"Mennonites at the opera. Not a pretty sight. Heaven forbid that passion should rule the day."

"Heaven forbid," I repeat.

"Oh, brother," Kate sighs. "Passion, my ass. *Days of our Lives* would take one look at the script and say: *Too much*."

Des shakes her head.

"You have to remember that this is the woman who knows why the *Mona Lisa* was smiling," I say.

"You do?"

Kate holds out both palms. "Sex. Either before or after. No mystery."

We all laugh at this.

"You were always so sure of yourself," Des says. "Do you guys remember devotions?"

"Every morning," I say, looking at the wine in my glass and how it catches the light.

"Who prays for wisdom when they're fifteen years old?" she asks.

"Who knows that 'glorifying God' is the only answer?" I respond.

Kate finishes her wine and reaches for the bottle with one elegant gesture. "You guys were so earnest," she says, pouring another glass for herself.

"Is that such a bad thing?" Des asks. "I mean, look at Maxi. She's earnest. Mostly about body piercings and tattoos, but still, she knows what she wants."

"Which is?" Kate asks.

"To be herself. To stand out."

"Like everyone else."

"True enough. But it's a start. You have to start somewhere."

"Maybe we started too high," I say. "Like you said, who prays for wisdom when they're fifteen?"

"I never prayed for that," Kate says firmly.

"Well, you never had to," Des says. We all laugh at this. "What *did* you pray for, Kate? I've always wondered."

Kate groans. "I don't know. Peace on earth, good will toward man."

"C'mon," Des pushes. I wonder what she's getting at.

"I don't remember."

"Really?"

"Really." Kate leans forward, her elbows on the table. "I do remember being totally ripped off about losing the Angel of the Lord to you. I had it nailed."

We laugh so loudly at this that the maître d' comes rushing over to see if we're all right. We say that we are fine and order another bottle.

"I'm sorry about that," Des says. "I never wanted the job, you know. You have no idea how nervous I was. I practised that line in the mirror so many times: *Fear not. I bring you glad tidings of great joy.* I really wanted to be convincing."

"You were," I say, remembering the look on every person's face in the congregation. Not to mention Jake's. I shudder.

Kate puts her hand on mine. "You okay? Is it another migraine?"

"I'm fine."

Des watches us, an expression I can't read on her face.

During dinner we talk about Kate's career, my funny job as school secretary—you can only grow up to be the school secretary if you agree to have a sense of humour about it—and Des's fledgling herb-growing business. She says that it was tough to get started because people were suspicious of the herbs at first.

This makes me laugh. "Why?"

"Well, you know, first it's cilantro in the salad and echinacea for a cold, but then it's ginseng in the bedroom and the next thing you know it's devil worship."

"A natural next step," I add.

Des and I laugh, but Kate doesn't join in. "So, you're still part of that world."

Des's dimples disappear even as her smile remains. I always wondered how she did that. "Uh-huh," she says.

"How could you go back after everything that happened?"

I can't believe Kate's said this. I stab at the remaining bean on my plate.

"I guess I had to go back because of everything that happened."

"But you were excommunicated," Kate says, and now I have to look up. Kate is a lot of things but she isn't careless. Her cheeks have gone shiny red and this is unusual as well. It so mesmerizes me to see her this way that I forget my own discomfort. In fact, stranger than that, I draw strength from it and watch as though I'm across the room. Des doesn't take her eyes off Kate. "Why would you want to go back to something that didn't want you?"

"I needed to figure some things out. I was married by then and we'd moved back with Maxi. I went alone."

I meet her gaze, wondering if she's looking for strength, but it's like she's looking through me.

"It wasn't really a big deal. In fact, nobody even said anything to me about it. At first I was disappointed. I wanted the big showdown." She smiles. "I was sitting in the back of the church, stewing about it, and then the music started and the announcements and the sermon. It was all so familiar." She toys with the stem of her empty wineglass. "Do you remember the old carpet?"

"The ugly gold one?" I say.

"The very one. Remember when they replaced it?"

"Everyone was horrified because it was purple. It was too purple," I say. Kate still hasn't said a word. "But we really liked it."

"That's right. But it would have cost too much to replace it so eventually we decided to keep it and call it burgundy."

"That's right," I say. "Don't you remember?" I graze Kate's hand but she moves it away to brush hair from her eyes.

"No, I don't."

"Well," Des continues. "I sat there and I thought, *It's purple. I really don't care if anyone else sees it.* I kept expecting to feel the old hurt again, but I never did. I just looked at that stupid rug and thought, *It's purple, it really is. And it's beautiful. It doesn't matter what other people call it.*" She shrugs. "After that, I just kept going. It reminds me of good things, true things. Dance with the one that brung you, I guess."

"I don't think so," Kate says. "Sometimes you have to cut your losses. Move on."

Des looks evenly at Kate. "What about forgiveness?"

"It's not about forgiveness. If people don't want you, you don't want them. Besides, people change." Kate's colouring has mysteriously returned to her smooth, even, Estée Lauder porcelain-beige, and she matches Des's gaze.

"I don't think we do—not really," Des says.

"Of course we do," Kate insists. "I'm not the girl I was. None of us are. I can barely remember the old days, if you want to know the truth."

"Really?" Again, there is a slender, fine edge of steel to Des's voice.

"The past is who we were, not who we are."

"But who we are comes from that."

Kate shakes her head. "Let the dead bury the dead, right? Leave the old life behind. Help me out here, Glo. Memory verses were your specialty."

"Actually, I always thought that verse was particularly heartless. The poor sap just wanted to give his father a funeral."

"Well," says Des, "I guess you just need to make good and sure the dead are really dead."

For a split second the restaurant seems to grow quiet and Des, for the first time this evening, seems to have surprised herself.

"On that macabre note, I'm going to the bathroom," Kate says suddenly. Before she leaves, she flips her credit card onto the table. "Dinner is on me. Listen, we could go back to my hotel room, if you guys want. We could stop at the drugstore and pick up some hair colour, Des. We'll have you looking ten years younger in no time."

Des looks into her empty wineglass as Kate leaves the table.

"She didn't mean anything by it," I say.

"It's okay."

"Really, she's still upset about the divorce. I don't think she ever thought anyone could leave her. It changed her."

"It's okay, Glo. You don't have to explain Kate. I know her."

"It's just that Kate's been so good to me and Julia and Mark. There have been days—weeks, even—I haven't been able to take care of Julia. Kate's been there."

"She always did that, didn't she?"

"Did what?"

"Took care of you. Whenever you were sick—it was important to her to be the one who took care of you."

"I don't remember that."

"I remember everything."

Des's eyes are so clear. Both Kate and I have lost that bluish white translucence, but while the rest of Des has taken on signs of time, her eyes are still brilliant. She never did miss a thing. It's ironic that I was the one who chose *To see* as the promise in our yearbook.

⌣

Outside, we try to persuade Kate to let us pay our share of the bill, but I recognize the set of her jaw and give in, saying thanks. Des thanks her as well. I offer to give Des a ride home, even though her place is on the way to Kate's hotel. Kate hasn't offered, in any event.

"So, when are you heading back home?" Des asks Kate.

"In a couple of days." Kate turns to me. "Oh, Glo, your mom asked me to come to the farm day after tomorrow."

"She did? When?"

"Today, after I dropped Julia off."

"She invited us as well," Des says, quietly.

"She mentioned that," I say.

"Is that okay?" Kate asks.

God, I think, *I am so tired of the delicate looks. So tired of being fragile.*

"Sounds good," I say. "Sounds like a party."

"Social," Des corrects.

"Get-together," Kate says.

"A shindig," I add.

We laugh and I remember that night at McGann's pond. We'd stood in a circle and held hands. We chewed our bubble gum furiously and blew three bubbles, moving closer until each bubble touched. And then we stood perfectly still, connected by our sticky spheres. Kate's was the first to burst, then mine. Des's bubble lasted the longest—even with our bits of gum clinging to it—but finally hers exploded as well, sticking to her upper lip, her nose, and even her eyelashes. We laughed until we cried and promised to stick together forever. And believed it.

twenty

A crescent moon hangs above the mountain and offers a wan light. A handful of stars have been tossed across the narrow sky; some hover above the peaks, others slip behind. On the prairie every star is in full view. On the prairie you can picture yourself standing on the surface of the world, held by gravity. You know where you stand.

The silence is a relief from the clattering din of the restaurant. Neither Des nor I says a word as we get into my car and drive, but I know we're both thinking about Jake.

We're almost at her place when she says, "Do you remember that time Jake slept outside under the stars?"

"Which time?"

Starlight illuminates her half-smile. "He wanted to know what the other Jacob felt like. Stone pillow and all."

"Wrestling with an angel. 'I am not leaving here without a blessing,' he said. I was shocked by that."

"Jake wasn't. Both of you were so into those stories, weren't you?"

"I guess."

"You guess?" Des laughs. "You can't have forgotten that. How many times did we play Adam and Eve in the Garden of Eden? I just wanted to climb the tree."

"I was obsessed with the stories, I guess. I didn't think Jake was, though, not as much."

"Oh, he was the same. You guys were so alike. Well, the twin thing." She smiles. "And what about Abraham and Isaac? That was the story he loved the most."

"I was horrified that God would ask Abraham to kill his son."

"And Jake couldn't get over Abraham's faith. 'Doubt will destroy you,' he used to say. Remember?"

That word is starting to bug me. It's all I can do these days after years of successful forgetting. "Jake's faith was unshakable. We used to get into huge fights about it." It comes back to me. As usual, I complained about God's unfairness and how he toyed with Abraham, taunted him, and made such an unreasonable request. Jake said that, as usual, I was missing the point. Abraham knew, he insisted. He knew that God would keep his promise: Isaac's children would fill the earth. Grandchildren, Abraham was promised grandchildren. Abraham never doubted God, even when his hand was raised in the air. I insisted that Abraham couldn't know how it would turn out.

"He didn't have to know how. He had faith," Jake argued. "Besides, it's a story, Glo. A story."

We've reached the gravel entrance of Des's driveway. The star-strewn sky blinks at us between the surrounding hills. I see Gabe's outline as he sits on the porch. When he sees us, he waves.

"Come in for a bit," Des says.

"No," I say, too sharply. "It's late."

"I shouldn't have said what I did about making sure the dead are really dead. It was crass."

"No, please, Des. Don't apologize." I know that's my job and the words are waiting to be spoken. Still, they wait.

"Okay," Des says quickly, as though filling the gap. "You know, Glo, about Kate? Just because you really see someone doesn't mean you can't love them."

"Um?"

"Kate loves you, I understand that."

"I'm not following you, Des."

"Yeah, well, I'm talking in circles. It's just—I'm just going to say this, okay?"

Oh, so not okay, I think. But I nod.

"How do you think everyone found out about Jake and me? I only told you."

"Oh, Des." And then my throat closes. How is it that I've never wondered about this, not once. It didn't occur to me that the church, like God, doesn't see everything. "I told Kate. I was the one . . ."

She waves her hand. "You had to tell someone; I get that. But she told her mother, which was like broadcasting it on the evening news."

I let these words settle. They make sense. "Des, I'm so sorry."

"Honey, don't be. It's just that tonight, watching you, I remembered how you always believed the best in everybody except yourself. But Kate? Kate takes care of herself."

"I don't know what to say."

"Just come in for a while. There are so many things we need to talk about. Things I need to tell you."

"It's late, Des."

She looks like she wants to persuade me, looks exactly the same as she did that evening, standing beside the pew. Alone. "Okay."

And I drive away, leaving her again.

On the winding road, I get lost, but at least I know I'm heading down. When I reach the foot of the mountain, I still don't recognize the road. I pull onto the shoulder and step out of the car for some fresh air. The land has recently been sprayed with manure. The air is familiar, at least, if not fresh.

I lean against the car and watch a thin cloud drift past the curve of the crescent moon. The rest of it is in shadow.

I think about Des's parting words. Kate has become such a part of my present life that I hardly ever see her as part of my past anymore. I thought I left all that behind me with the mountains and the rain. She is my boss at work; my confidante at home; the caretaker of my child. I need her in my present. There was no room for the past. But right now, the line between the two feels like an arbitrary distinction.

I remember when I was thirteen or fourteen and came down with the flu. Kate brought me her mother's chicken noodle soup. She put a cool cloth on my forehead and fed the soup to me. She stood in the doorway before she left. "You know," she said. "I like it when you're sick. You're so . . . gentle."

It was meant to be comforting, but the words come back now: *I like it when you're sick*. I walk over to a knoll at the side of the road and sit in the grass. One time, just as I was crawling out of a particularly dreary hole, Kate was over, cooking dinner. As per normal—my normal—I watched her in my kitchen with a mixture of gratitude and self-loathing. As she marinated the prawns, cooked the pasta, and tossed the salad, all seemingly at the same time, she reminded me of my mother. Unflappable, competent, focused.

"You know," I said. "You're perfect."

She smiled as she tossed the salad, adding indiscriminate amounts of extra-virgin olive oil and balsamic vinegar.

"But here's the thing. Perfect doesn't exist," I said. "Not really." Clearly, the guest of depression had not quite left, a vestige of her meanness remained.

"What's that supposed to mean?" she asked, using her placating tone reserved for unrepentant fifth-graders and me, in this state.

"Well, how can it? It doesn't need anything. Perfect—even if it is possible—just is."

"Have another glass of wine," she said.

Well, I didn't mind if I did. When I was in the centre of the pit I never drank (adding a depressant to depression is a little pointless), but climbing out was a different story. The real world was always a little too bright, and alcohol was a good re-entry drug.

"I mean, it doesn't need to eat or drink or sleep or feel. Why would it? It already is everything it needs to be. Honestly, where do you go after perfect?"

She smiled at me again—the perfect, condescending, poor-you smile. And I'm not saying what I said next was right or good (or lovely or pure), but it was true. "You remind me of your mother."

Now, in my defence, I did mean to say "my" mother, and maybe it was the third glass of Merlot, but as soon as I said "your" mother I knew it to be equally true. But, oh my, did I regret it as soon as the words fell out of my mouth.

Kate poured herself a glass of wine, removed the prawns from the element, slipped the penne into the colander, and sat down opposite me. "I know this is a tough time for you," she said. "This is the disease talking. You can't help it, Glo. It's not you."

I thought about that. "So, then, what would *I* say?" It was a good question. Despite the Merlot, I felt remarkably clear-headed.

Kate looked at me and nodded her head the way she did when she was thinking a problem through. And I realized that she didn't see me anymore, just the disease. The thing she was saving me from. She couldn't see me. "Darlin'," she said, and this jarred me. She knew it was what Gabe used to call me. "Maybe you need to reconsider the meds."

"Ah," I said. I apologized, then, for saying she was like her mother, and I hated myself for it because—especially in that moment—it was true. So, maybe I did need the meds. An anti-truth serum.

It's getting late, my thoughts growing incoherent, yet when I look at the landmarks around me, I can see my way home now. But I don't get into the car. I'm too wide awake; sleep won't come for hours.

Sometimes I wondered if it was fear that kept me Kate's friend. Fear of what I would do without her. I'd lost Jake and Des and Gabe. My parents were lost in their own grief. Where did that leave me? Adrift. I wasn't raised to be adrift. I wasn't even conceived to be adrift. I was part of a unit even then, brought here sharing an umbilical cord, joined with another from the beginning.

I went to Kate's house the day after Jake's funeral, and I told her everything that Des had said about her and Jake. I cried and said I didn't know what to do. Kate held me. And then she said, "You need to get out of here." It never occurred to me that Kate might need my weakness for her to be strong enough to leave.

Des might not be wrong about Kate, but the truth was that we had both betrayed her.

twenty-one

It's past midnight when I pull my car into the driveway. My parents will have gone to bed hours before, but the porch light is still burning. I close the car door gingerly, steal across the yard, and creep up the stairs. The screen door creaks and I freeze at the sound—the old muscle memory still works.

"I'll put some oil on that in the morning."

My hand flies to my chest as the door snaps shut with a crisp bang. My father is sitting on the porch swing in the dark. I smell the faint odour of tobacco. He's smoking a pipe. "Does Mom know you're doing that?" I ask, taking a seat on the swing beside him. "What about your blood pressure?"

"What your mother doesn't know won't hurt my blood pressure."

"That's what I always thought when I was climbing down the trellis."

"Or the ladder," he chuckles. "How was dinner?"

"You knew about the ladder?"

He smiles.

"Dinner was good," I say.

"Des has grown into a fine woman."

"She has."

"And that daughter of hers, Maxine?"

"Maxi. Yes."

"Does she still have that piece of metal in her eye?" He points to his eyebrow.

"Yep."

He shrugs. "Found Julia on top of the barn today."

"I beg your pardon?"

"She said she wanted to feel the wind. Wanted to know if it felt different up there."

I struggle to find my equilibrium. What's stranger: the fact that my daughter was climbing barns today or that my father is chatting? "She said that?"

"She said she wondered what it would feel like to fly. I told her to get down."

I don't know what to say to this, but maybe it doesn't matter. My father is feeling chatty. The skin, folded at the base of his neck, is soft and vulnerable. His jaw was once strong and chiselled, but his profile is soft now.

"Reminded me of you and your brother," he says, taking a draw from his pipe. I remember this smell now, lingering behind the barn. I thought it was just another farm smell. "I didn't tell your mother. She'd have had the Bible open to the Tower of Babel quick as a wink. Your mother can talk about pride till the cows come home."

"Yep."

"Mark called again."

"I'll call him in the morning."

"He's a good man."

"Yes, he is."

"We just do our best, don't we?"

"We try. I saw Mrs. G today."

"That woman can talk."

"That she can. She told me, well, reminded me, I guess, how long you and Mom had to wait to get . . . for kids." Funny, I have trouble using the word *pregnant* with my father.

"Yep," he smiles. "That was a good day. You came out, kicking and screaming. The doctor said you were a stubborn little bugger. Jake came quick, like he was happy to be here."

"Yeah." It's not the first time I've heard this story.

He takes another draw from his pipe. Night fills the space: an owl, cricket song, the breeze in the wind chimes, and other soft sounds. "You know that my mother died when I was very young and then I had to leave?"

I know this story as well. I take his hand the way I used to. The skin is still rough and calloused but thinner. "Your father couldn't take care of you and all your brothers and sisters, so you had to live with another family. And then your stepmother died and you thought you'd have to leave again." I feel his nod. "So you packed your suitcase and waited in your bedroom for them to take you away. But your father came—your new father—and said you belonged with him, that you were home. Your home would always be with him." I hadn't thought about my father's past for years. I had tucked it away with everything else. "That's such a sad story."

"Oh, Gloria. It's a good story," he sighs. "You were always such a fighter. Life was so serious for you." His hand tightens around mine.

Our hands remain wrapped together, and I lean my head

against his shoulder. The night sounds deepen; the breeze is cool on my face. "Jake was easygoing," I say.

My father chuckles. "Now where do you suppose he got that from?"

An unnerving thought hits me. "Does that make me like Mom?"

He chuckles again.

"You're kidding, right? Mom is so hard-working, so unswerving in her faith, so . . ."

"Stubborn?"

"Oh."

"Do you remember that ark you made me build?"

I nod. I haven't thought about it for years. "You worked so hard on it."

"So did you."

I don't tell him that this is where my faith first began to swerve, and doubt crept in.

"Don't stay up too late," he says, patting my hand as he rises from the swing. He stands at the door. "I watched a movie with Julia tonight."

"*Sound of Music?*"

"*Moulin Rouge.*"

"You watched the whole thing?"

"The whole shebang."

I laugh and he presses a finger to his lips. "Some catchy tunes in it," he says. "Don't forget to lock up."

"Since when do you lock up?"

"Things change, Gloria." He enters the house humming, "Come What May." At first I think this is a hymn but then I recognize the tune from *Moulin Rouge*.

The screen door clatters shut and I listen to the fading

melody, amazed that Julia has managed to draw my father into her world.

The thin moon is brighter, offering a more generous light with the deepening night. I remember the ark now, and how determined I was to recreate it.

I pitied my school friends for their Santa Claus and their Easter Rabbit. I had my Garden and it didn't have fairies or talking frogs or sleeping, waiting princesses. It was a world where "once upon a time" really meant something, because it was all true.

Once upon a time, there was a man in the land of Uz, a good man who feared God and stayed away from evil. Once upon a time, in the town of Bethlehem, there was a man named Jesse who had a son, David, who would be king, who brought down a great giant with a single stone. There was Daniel, who stood in a fiery furnace without so much as a singe on the hairs of his arm, who dined while lions watched, and who understood the dreams of kings. And that was just the beginning. There were so many more, each one more fantastic than the one that came before. The stories started with time and continued through eternity.

Other children had their dollhouses filled with miniature furniture and cribs populated by plastic people. I begged my father for an ark, and I wanted it built to size. I read Genesis 6 and took copious notes. I stood in the middle of the kitchen while my dad finished his coffee. "Okay, Dad," I said, anxious to begin. "The length shall be three hundred cubits, the breadth of it fifty cubits, and the height of it thirty cubits."

"It shall?" he smiled.

"Yes, it shall. That's what it says." I didn't know why he

was smiling; there was so much work to do.

"That might be a little bigger than we need," he said, as he got up from the table. I followed him to the mudroom.

"We could use the backyard."

Jake said no way. He wasn't about to lose his rope swing or the rabbit hutch that took up a huge chunk of the yard. I was prepared to fight him for it, but then my mother observed that it wasn't necessary to have a full-size ark since God promised he would never send such a flood again. I couldn't argue with her logic, because it was in chapter nine of Genesis.

I gave up the backyard grudgingly but remained determined to stay as close as possible to the original plan in every other way. "It has to be resinous wood," I reminded my dad. "And sealed with tar." It was all so precise, so careful, so beautiful. Only a caring God, I thought, would pay such attention to detail.

We worked on Project Noah, as Jake called it, for weeks and weeks. My dad collected different wood that was left over from carpentry jobs he took on when farming was slow: mahogany, teak, cherry wood, oak. When my mother grimaced at the extravagance, he reminded her that it was discarded wood left behind to rot.

There were three levels, as decreed. A bottom level for the bigger beasts: elephants, rhinos, tigers, and such. (I was careful to arrange partitions in a way that made sure that natural enemies were as far away from each other as possible. No sense causing a stampede on the high seas.) The middle level was for the smaller animals: dogs, rabbits, squirrels, etc. I was concerned about the skunks and porcupines until my dad suggested we find a quiet spot for them at the stern of the boat. The top level was for family members; we decided to use the nicest wood for these quarters since the family would be so closely confined and, likely, get on each other's nerves.

We sanded and polished and cut the wood so that it fit together perfectly. Near the end of construction, I borrowed one of Jake's bunnies, for trial purposes. I carted him over in my old lunch kit and was preparing to put him in one of the pens when Jake flew out of the house and ordered me to release him. "You don't put animals in cages," he said.

"What about your stupid hutch?"

"They can run around in there. That's different." And then he looked worried. "Isn't it?"

I shrugged.

That night he let all the animals go.

After the ark was completed, my father started whittling all the different species. My job was to paint them when he was done. This was where my faith began to falter. There were too many animals. I asked my dad about it, but he said it wasn't a problem. The Lord knew every hair on a person's head, every grain of sand, didn't he? I didn't see the connection.

He whittled, and I painted, out on the porch for hours. He would sing and sometimes I sang along when I knew the words. I tried to ignore the little voice that told me this was a fool's task.

One day, Jake came running out of the house. "Come watch! It's the Beatles."

My eyes flew open and I looked at my dad. He just smiled. "Go ahead."

"No," I said. "What about bugs? I forgot all about the bugs."

He stared at me for a second and then laughed so hard I wondered if he would ever stop.

The next day he showed me a couple of ladybugs that he had carved after I went to bed. They were very cute, intricately carved, and I admired them. I didn't let him see my disappointment. I could tell he just didn't get it: there was no possible way that this Noah story was true.

After locking the back door behind me, I make my way quietly up the stairs. The sixth stair creaks, as it always did—only noticeable in the dead of night. Upstairs, I walk past Jake's room. I place my hand on the doorknob and a wave of the past crashes over me.

Jake knew his mountain, sure-footed as a goat, and then he slipped. Des and Gabe thought he was fooling around, because it was hardly more than a tumble down a mossy slope. But I felt him leave and it wasn't mysterious. Jake was here and then he wasn't. It was a purely physical sensation, like someone walked up and pulled my arm from its socket. I denied the knowledge immediately. Shock, I guess.

Gabe climbed down to where Jake lay. He pulled a rock from beneath Jake's head and I saw the blood. The look on Gabe's face confirmed what I was trying desperately to ignore. Des screamed and then Gabe was between us again.

"Darlin'," he whispered.

"Go get help," I said.

For the next twenty or thirty minutes—however long it took, forever—Des rattled on about how mad Jake was going to be if he had to miss grad. How mad she was going to be, because she had such a beautiful dress, which he would love. But maybe he'd get out of the hospital in time and have a big, white bandage on his head that would match the awful James

Bond tux he'd picked out. She talked about their first date, first kiss, first fight. I'd heard most of it before, but never like this, never with such tender ferocity. I knew she was trying to keep him with us. All I could think about was Lazarus and how his sister pleaded with Jesus to raise him from the dead. And so I prayed for this.

Des started to sing in her pure, imperfect soprano. When I didn't join, she grew stern. "What's wrong with you? You know how to sing." Shaking, I added my equally imperfect alto. I don't know how long we waited, singing every song we'd ever learned. We were on the last verse of "Amazing Grace" when the paramedics arrived.

They scrambled down the hill while the three of us remained huddled together looking down on Jake as though we were having his out-of-body experience. Then one of them said that Jake had a heartbeat, and I knew everything I had ever been taught was true. Jehovah did care. He was with us and he did grant miracles. I had lost faith but never again. I apologized silently all the way down the mountain, ignoring the fact that my limb had not been restored.

In the waiting room we met my parents, who were sitting in the corner with their heads bowed. We gave them the good news: Jake's heart was beating. I expected my mother to say, *Phht*. But she only said that we needed to pray.

When the doctor entered the room, we knew that Jake was gone. It was written not in his face, but in the unprofessional, defeated slump of his shoulders. "We lost him," he said. It occurred to me that, in this moment, *I* became *we*. I wondered if that was how he talked when a life was saved, or if death had the power to make every last one of us band together, trembling in fear, a *we* by necessity.

Des collapsed and my parents rushed over to her. Gabe hugged me, but I couldn't feel him. All I felt was my missing limb and an emptiness I'd never imagined could exist. *That was mean*, I prayed, *taking him twice.*

twenty-two

I wake the next morning to the smell of nutmeg. When I enter the kitchen, my mother is making muffins for breakfast.

"You're up early," she says.

"I guess I am."

"Could you pick a few apples for the muffins?"

"Who picked your fruit before I came home?" I tease.

"Your father, mostly."

I leave the kitchen, wondering if she's made a joke. I pull a pair of boots on and wander over to the apple tree. The spice of early morning dusts the air; a chickadee lends his two-note song. As I walk across the dewy lawn, I whistle my father's hymn, "Trust and Obey." It's official then; the place is getting to me.

The tree is heavy with fruit. I touch the apple closest to my hand, but I don't pluck it from the branch; it's not ready. I look for one that's ripe. It doesn't take much of a yank and it's in my hand. When I take a bite, I remember that this is the tree Des and I labelled The Tree. She was right; we re-enacted that story over and over again.

I always argued that Eve's choice was the only one she would have made, with or without the serpent's cajoling. The Tree of Knowledge? How could she not? It was irresistible. How could God not have known this? How? He knew everything. It was the ultimate set-up, I said, like a pie cooling on a windowsill. Des didn't care about that. She liked to wonder what life was like before the first bite.

We took turns being Adam or Eve. We'd go to our secret creek, sit on the bank, and name the creatures with the same freedom we imagined our namesakes possessed before they threw it all away for knowledge. We thought up new names for birds, flowers, trees, rodents, and fungi; anything alive was up for grabs. Strictly speaking, we knew that Eve hadn't had much to say during this part of the story, so we changed the rules. We didn't think God would mind. He was our companion as well—just as he had been for Adam and Eve in the cool of the evening. Flowers were named for their colour and scent; berries for their taste; animals for personality quirks. At first we faithfully wrote these names in our own little book of life, but it all kept changing and we couldn't keep up. It was a bigger job than we realized.

At the end of the day, we would review our work with pride, but sometimes I felt unsettled. Had we made the right choices? What if something was other than what we decided it was? I'd want to go back and change the names and that's when Des would get bored and want to climb the tree.

We only reprised the actual climax—the plucking and eating of the apple—occasionally. Now that I think back, we may have done it only once. Des was Eve that day. It was warm and muggy; we wore bathing suit bottoms. (Unlike Adam and Eve, we had begun to be aware of our nakedness.)

We approached the tree cautiously. I was nervous; Des was excited. I can still see the look on her face as she wrapped her small hand around the reddest apple. "Should I?" she asked. Her voice was quivering with emotion.

"I'm Adam," I reminded her. "I'm not here, remember?"

The apple didn't come easily. Des had to tug, and then it was in her hand, red and juicy. We both stared at it for a second, and then we ran, giggling nervously, back into the heart of Eden. We waited until we caught our breath, but Des couldn't bring herself to take a bite. She held it between us. That's when we remembered that our game lacked an essential character: the serpent.

"You be the snake," she said.

"But I'm Adam."

That's where the memory flickers. I search my mind for the lost, essential detail. Did Des take a bite or did she resist temptation? We had toyed with new endings; what did we decide?

She did. She took the bite. I don't remember seeing her do it, but when she handed the apple to me some of it was missing. I can see this. I dropped it to the ground, refusing to take a bite. I said I didn't want to know, after all.

After Jake's funeral, the house filled with people who came to share our grief. They came to offer their condolences and to whisper, *Why?* But it was only a whisper and it was always followed by an answer: God's will. Thy will be done.

I left the house to find fresh air in our garden. Des found me sitting under the apple tree. She said she had something to tell me.

Fifty people could have wandered out of the house and joined us at that moment, or I could have listened to the sudden lurch in my gut that told me the time was wrong. I could have just said, "Des, let's sit here. Let's not talk."

"Jake and I slept together," she said.

At first I thought I'd heard wrong. But she looked at me with her aching blue eyes and I knew I hadn't. I didn't know what to say.

The imagination is boundless. It conjures up stories for relief; any story will serve when an explanation is absent, and there was no explanation for Jake's death. As soon as Des told me that she had slept with Jake, a link formed in my mind: cause and effect. Sin and consequence. Jake and Des had sinned, and I knew there had to be a consequence. There had to be a sacrifice.

"Maybe I shouldn't have said anything," Des said, almost immediately. "I just wanted you to know."

I felt my heart harden. Jake and Des had broken a divine law and they were being punished. We were all being punished.

She tried to take my hand, but I pushed it away.

"Don't," I said. I stood up. I wiped the grass off my dress and walked into the house without a backward glance.

Nobody expected Jake's family to go to the church that day, only weeks after the funeral. The Elders had found out about Des and Jake and called a meeting. Normally, these things were handled in a small room with ten dour, middle-aged men, but nobody expected it would be more than Des repenting of her sin. The church could then forgive her and let the healing begin.

The sanctuary was full. I sat at the back with my parents. I looked down at my lap, at the narrow lines on the corduroy of my brown skirt. I couldn't bear how everything was changing. The church had always been a sanctuary. Maybe that's why I went. Maybe I thought something miraculous could happen there.

Des was at the front with her parents. Pastor Reimer and Helmut Wiebe questioned her in a way that was meant to be loving and instructive. They asked her if it was true, had she had premarital relations with Jake? My skin crawled when I heard the words—how chilled and sterile they sounded, like they were prepping Des for surgery. Someone recalled the Halloween party where Des had dressed as a prostitute; another mentioned her jokes about the Second Coming. There was a silence after this and I pleaded, inwardly, for it to be over. Finally, Evangeline said, with only a slight hesitation, that she'd always wondered about Des, ever since the star had fallen on her head and she had laughed.

Des didn't respond at first, and then I heard her clear, small voice. "I'm not sorry. I loved Jake." I listened as she walked down the stairs, down the purple carpet to the back of the church. She stood briefly beside our pew, but I couldn't look up. She paused. "Glo," she whispered. "I'm leaving."

I knew I should get up and go outside with her. My heart was so sure. My mind as well, for that matter. I knew I should jump to my feet and say, "You bet your boots, Red Rider."

But something stopped me. Something made me believe that Des deserved this, had somehow caused this. Or at least, the sin had caused this. And I couldn't believe that there shouldn't be a sacrifice.

I return to the farmhouse with a bowl full of apples I don't remember picking. The landscape around me is still in one piece, but it's shivering at the edges. Something will probably drop away soon—a tree or a clump of grass—and then the pain will arrive.

My mother is sitting at the kitchen table reading. At first, I assume it must be the Bible, but then I realize that it's one of Julia's magazines. I would actually doubt my own vision at this point, except that my mother looks up, guiltily, and closes the magazine. Jumping up, she takes the bowl from me. "I wondered what was keeping you."

I sit at the table and pick up the magazine. I can't help smirking at my mother, who frowns.

"It isn't right," she says.

My smile fades. I really am not in the mood to hear my mother say that Julia shouldn't be reading such trash. "What, Mom?"

"A woman shouldn't have to look like a girl," she says, pointing to the cover, which boasts both Madonna and Jessica Simpson.

"You're absolutely right," I say, unable to disagree.

"We deserve our wrinkles."

"Every single one of them. So . . . this party tomorrow."

"It's just lunch, Gloria."

"Right."

"Des talked to you?"

"Kate, actually."

"So Des hasn't spoken to you."

"She mentioned that you had invited them as well. My question is, why wasn't I invited?"

"Phht."

"You can't really 'phht' your way out of this, Mom."

"Well, you're here, aren't you?" she says.

It's hard to argue with this sensible comment. "I guess I am."

The absurd exchange reminds me of every conversation I've never had with my mother. Jake was always the go-between, my father the buffer. Both of them, I see now, kept us from each other. I wonder, now, if I'd ever really talked to her. Where would I begin? How did you feel, Mom? When he died. How did you feel, Mom, when they sent Des away? How did you feel when I went away and didn't come back? What did you feel?

"You need to talk to Des today." She stops, I think, because she sees the tears in my eyes. "Are you . . . what's wrong?"

"Nothing. Why should I talk to Des?"

She looks at me. And there is a moment here; I feel it. But she turns and peels the apples. "She called earlier. Maxi wants Julia to come riding before you leave."

And then Julia flies down the stairs and informs me that Mark is on the line.

"Oh," I say.

"Mom." She's looking at me as though I've already said the wrong thing. "Be nice."

I go upstairs without a word and take the phone. Julia hangs up immediately.

"El? Hi." Mark's voice sounds different, softer.

"Hi."

"How are you?" We say this at the same time. He chuckles, and it's such a warm sound that it makes me question everything. I should be there, at home. At home working on my marriage, on my real life.

"I'm good," I say. "How are you doing?"

"I miss you, El. When are you coming home?"

I begin to tell him about the party tomorrow, but he tells me that Julia's already filled him in.

"I miss you," he repeats. "And Julia," he adds.

"Are you okay?"

"Sure. I just miss you guys."

"We do too."

I hear him breathing at the other end. "I know it's been rough, El. I'm sorry."

"I haven't been around," I say, with a lowered voice. I move deeper into the chair. "It hasn't been your fault."

Marci, who has been uncharacteristically quiet, urges me to remain silent and let him speak, and so I let the uncomfortable space widen. I try to picture what Mark is doing, thinking, feeling. What he looks like. A panic clutches at me; I'm forgetting him. And then I realize I can't see his face anymore. I look at the family photo that's hanging on the wall. It was a rushed day when it was taken; the strain of getting there on time is written in our body language. Still, there he is. Smiling at me. My pulse slows as I look at his handsome, steady features. It should be the other way around though, shouldn't it? Shouldn't my heartbeat skitter the way it did at the sight of Gabe? "Mark, are you there?" I say, quickly.

"Come home after the party, okay?"

"It's tomorrow, Mark. You could still come. Jump on a plane! It's not too late to catch an afternoon flight." It's a brilliant idea. Sometimes I surprise myself. "Really, I could pick you up at the airport. Julia will be thrilled. We could drive back home together." My voice grows stronger as the idea builds.

Having Mark here would solve everything: conversations I didn't want to have with Des, feelings I shouldn't be having about Gabe. Memories. Most of all, memories. And my parents loved Mark; Julia would be over the moon with excitement. This was exactly why people got married in the first place: it was the ultimate Plan B.

"I can't get away, El. I'm getting ready for the fall session."

"Then fly home afterward. It would be fun." My tone is still buoyant, but the manic momentum is fading. Suddenly, the reasons for this separate trip are back. We are stuck, he and I. Far beyond the breezy fix.

"It won't work. I'm sorry." His tone is conciliatory. "We'll get away for a weekend when you get home. How does that sound?"

"You just let me know when it's convenient for you, Mark. You set it up."

"You're angry."

"I'm not."

Mark reminds me that this was the plan. I say I remember it was the plan, but sometimes people make new plans. New plan then trumps old plan. He repeats that he thinks that I'm angry and I repeat that I'm not and the whole thing gets stupid. Sometimes marriage is stupid.

"I'm just disappointed," I finally say. Marci whispers for me to go further and *excavate those feelings*.

I hear him sigh. "Have a good time tomorrow," he says. "Are you looking forward to it?"

"I guess so. Listen, my mother's calling," I lie. "Breakfast."

"Right. I forgot. It's two hours earlier there, isn't it?"

"Yeah. I'll see you soon." I hang up before he says goodbye. Before he can say, "Right" again.

I feel foolish as soon as the line goes dead, but, for that moment, I believed he could jump on a plane and save me.

twenty-three

Julia comes to my room to convince me to let her go riding. She has her arguments neatly organized and concludes with the fact that Maxi is an experienced horsewoman.

"Horsewoman?" I say.

"She's been riding for years."

"And you haven't."

"We'll be fine."

"You have to promise me you'll wear the helmet. And you won't gallop."

"Mom." She draws out the word for a very long time.

"I'm not bending, Julia."

"Yeah, yeah. Do you know how many times a day you say that?"

"Six or seven?" I guess.

She almost smiles. "Fine. Joke. Anyway, it's perfectly normal."

"What's perfectly normal?"

"Women, you know, menopausal women tend to get easily unnerved by life. It's like everything is suddenly careening out of control and you just want to grab some of it back. You're not a freak, Mom."

Julia frequently comes up with explanations and/or cures for me. Everything from raw foods to homeopathic remedies (dilution of snake venom and sea sponge, administered by Dr. Nell) to, one Christmas, yoga classes, where I discovered that not only am I truly not flexible, I have less than a five-minute capacity for meditation.

"You're wicked," I say.

"Really. I've read about it. You could be going through a midlife crisis."

I cover my ears with my hands. "We're not actually having this conversation, are we?"

"It can last, like, ten years."

"How do I look?" I turn around to show Julia the third outfit I've tried on this morning. She doesn't know this, of course. I can only imagine the mocking.

"Good."

"Really?" I twist in the mirror. "When did I start looking like the mother of the bride?"

"Hogwash."

"Hogwash?"

"It's the new bullshit. Here, try this." She throws a black T-shirt at me that is probably the better choice for the skirt. "Who are you trying to impress anyway?"

"Nobody. So, tell me I look fabulous and freakishly young and we can go."

"I'm supposed to lie to you?"

"Yes, you're supposed to lie to me. And when you're ten months pregnant, retaining water, and bloated, I will tell you that you glow. That's the deal."

"Right," she says, sounding exactly like her father. "You look practically prenatal."

"Thank you."

"Oh! I want to show you something." She jumps up and runs out of the room.

I check out the mirror one last time. "Menopausal, my ass." I look great, I decide. I need to look great today. It feels like one of those days when it might be necessary to look better than I feel. *Fake It Till You Make It!!* A book I didn't quite get through.

Gabe knew how I was and never pressed, but on the day I bought my graduation dress I felt a rare stirring of maybe. I was wearing the prettiest dress I'd ever owned—shimmery pink—and while I'd never seen myself as a pale pink kind of person, it was obvious from my reflection that I was. Gabe would love it because it showed my shoulders and collar-bone—the hollow just above. And I thought: maybe. Maybe there was room for something other than shalts and shalt nots. Maybe it was okay to dream, or better, to not know. And maybe there was such a thing as luck. Standing there, dizzy with all the possibilities, I liked this maybe the most. I thought to myself, *I love him*. It was as though the world itself lifted a veil and I couldn't believe how simple it was. Why didn't anyone ever tell me how lucky love was?

I had spent my life trying to figure out how I could be worthy but, standing there in that boutique in my gradua-tion dress, I wondered if maybe I didn't have to do anything. Maybe love was freedom.

Less than a week later Jake was gone and Des told me about their night together. It was as if I'd never learned what I did; felt what I had. In a second I forgot all of it, because

Jake was gone. There was no freedom in love. Jehovah was not that kind of love. He was to be feared and I knew that. I had just forgotten for a dizzy moment in a pink dress.

Gabe came to see me the night of the funeral in the rain. He wore jeans and a plaid shirt. His hair was curly from the damp. He'd been to the house during the day along with everyone, but we had barely spoken. After I had left Des under the apple tree, I went to my room. My mother told him that I needed to be alone. He came back later and waited. I watched him through my window. I hid behind the curtains and the roses that continued to climb without the trellis. The perfume was stronger in the rain. He waved for me to come down to the porch, but I couldn't move. I knew I would walk straight into his arms and never leave, and I didn't deserve that kind of love because I didn't believe in it anymore.

But he remained. Finally, I went down and told him I didn't think I loved him anymore, that I needed to be out in the big, wide world. As with Des only hours before, I didn't look back.

～

When Julia flies back into the room, she sees my face and stops in her tracks. "Mom, are you okay?"

"Just a little headache," I say, smiling quickly. "I'm fine."

"Oh. Okay. Look at this. It was with some pictures . . . I was going to show you the other day and I forgot. Look at you. Now that's young, okay? And look how happy you were." She holds a photo out to me. "Almost weird happy, like someone else happy."

"Okay, okay, I get it," I say. "Show me this uncharacteristically happy picture of myself."

She's right. It's a picture of Des, Gabe and me. Gabe is standing in the middle and has his arms around us. His head is turned, poised to kiss me. My eyes are closed and I'm grinning. Des's eyes are fixed on Jake, who's taking the photograph, and she's giggling. I can hear it.

We were on the mountain only weeks before the accident. We had had a picnic. Des and Gabe slept afterwards while Jake and I debated. Time, perhaps. Or the nature of light. Any one of a thousand stories. Water to wine, that was it. Jake argued the metaphor; I argued the miracle.

Des finally just shook her tangled mane of curls at us. "Who cares, you guys? Who cares? It's a miracle right now."

Jake grabbed my camera and walked to the edge of the mountain. I was worried about how close he was—too close. I said I'd take the picture, but he ignored me.

"Am I beautiful, lover?" Des asked, tossing her hair.

Jake took his eye away from the viewfinder and looked at her. Gabe and I had disappeared. "*I am overcome by one glance of your eyes, by a single bead of your necklace. Your lips, my dear, are made of honey . . .*" he said. And he looked exactly the way he had the night the falling cardboard star brought Des to her knees. And my brother to his.

"Take the picture already, man," said Gabe. I smiled, eyes closed. Gabe kissed the air. Des laughed. The shutter clicked, a sliver of eternity captured in time.

As we walk along the lavender-lined path to the barn, Julia reassures me that this ride is a good idea. She keeps talking, I know, to distract me and to forestall the possibility that I could change my mind. She's a smart girl.

"They are so big," I say, when I see the horses saddled up and tied to the fence.

"They haven't grown in the last few days, I'm pretty sure of it. Hey, Maxi, have the horses grown?"

Gabe gives the girls some final instructions and I, against every bit of good judgment I possess, remain quiet because Julia looks so happy.

Once they've left, Des turns to me. "Don't be nervous, 'kay?"

I smile at the old word. "'Kay." But then I notice that Des looks nervous as well, fidgety and unsure, the way she used to be before an exam she hadn't studied for. "Are you all right?"

"I'm good. I'm fine. Listen, Gabe needs to go to town for some groceries."

"Has been ordered to go to town . . ." says Gabe, joining us.

"Yes," she sighs. "I'm such a dictator."

I realize that, besides nervousness, there is tension in the air. "What's up?" I ask.

Des shakes her head. "I told your mom I'd bring a lasagna for tomorrow. And maybe bake something."

"I'll help you."

"No, honey, I'll get started. You go with Gabe. And when you come back, we'll talk, okay?"

Ah. "Yes," I say.

Gabe and I are quiet as we head down the mountain. Sitting beside him in a truck is a visceral memory. The air feels different—charged. I open a window and fresh air pours in. Better.

"The girls will be fine," he says.

"I just get nervous."

"You always were."

"Really?"

"Well, maybe not always."

I want to ask when, but it's a dangerous question. In his arms I was never nervous.

I turn my thoughts away from this particular memory now, before I tell him that there are days, still, when I think about those kisses and how they meant far more to me than his poetry.

In the parking lot, Gabe grabs a cart with gusto and it makes me smile that he still manages to look like a cowboy. "What are you laughing at?" he asks.

"Nothing."

I take the list from his hand and, when we enter the store, we immediately argue about where to begin. I feel strongly about ending with produce, due to squishing potential, but Gabe points out that we have a large cart and a short grocery list. Why not just start where we are?

"Whatever." I sigh.

"Now you're bitter."

"Do it your way. You always did." I sigh again, a little longer.

"Me?" He laughs. "That's funny."

I stick out my tongue.

In the middle of the tomato sauce aisle, he chuckles again.

"What now?" I look up from a label I'm pretending to read.

"I was just remembering your views on *Romeo and Juliet.*"

"It's a stupid story."

"You're the only person I've ever met who could argue with Shakespeare."

"I have nothing against Shakespeare. *Tomorrow, and tomorrow, and tomorrow creeps in this petty pace to the last syllable of recorded time and all our yesterdays have lighted fools the path to dusty death.*"

He nods his head. "*Macbeth.* But nicely done."

"He had some good stuff to say."

"*Way.*"

"I beg your pardon?"

"*Lighted fools* the way *to dusty death.*"

"Fine. Path. Same difference."

"I don't think so. There are a lot of paths, I think. Only one way."

"Aha! You're finally admitting there's only one way."

"You can take the girl out of the church, but you can't take the church out of the girl," Gabe smiles. "Anyway, we were talking about dusty death."

We move to the dairy section in a growing silence that even the store PA system can't quite pierce.

"I just thought it could have had a different ending," I say, picking out parmesan.

"Something a little more upbeat?" Gabe smiles, standing too close.

"More sensible. Honestly. Check the pulse—really be sure—before you plunge the dagger in the chest."

"Exactly."

"Don't look at me like that," I say, feeling his eyes.

"You're not even looking at me," he says. It's the same thing he said that night in the rain.

In the checkout lane, I insist on paying for the groceries. Gabe gives in. When I leave the store, the truck is waiting out front. He reaches across and opens the door for me. I place the bags between us on the seat and he smiles.

When the town is behind us and we're on a back road, surrounded by the ridiculous confluence of green, yellow, and purple, Gabe pulls the truck to the side. Then, despite the grocery bags between us, his curly hair is wrapped in my fingers, and his lips, a scarlet thread, are on my mouth. *This is wrong,* I think. *And right. This feels like happy,* I think. *What it used to feel like.*

I pull away first.

Gabe runs a hand through his hair and pulls the truck back onto the road. "It was a bad ending," he says, and he's not talking about *Romeo and Juliet.*

"I know," I say, looking out the window.

As we climb the road to his house, I am torn between which commandment has just been violated. *Thou shalt not commit adultery* or *Thou shalt not covet.* It was almost a draw. Really, it would have been so much simpler to just have one commandment: *Thou shalt not want.*

We're almost at the driveway when his phone rings. "Yeah?" he answers gruffly, pushing his hand through his hair again. His face shifts to concern. "There's been an accident."

twenty-four

"Julia fell."

Gabe turns the truck around and then we're speeding back to town. Julia has broken her arm in a fall. Des has taken her to the hospital. This is all I hear. Gabe is still talking, but the words are as blurry as the green rushing past the car.

"But she's okay," I say. "She'll be fine."

"Maxi wasn't sure if she hurt her head."

"But she'll be fine."

"I'm sure she's fine." His voice is unsure and this undoes me.

The world speeds by. Houses and strip malls rush past, and I wonder why we're not moving. Why is the truck standing still? I reach for the door handle, but Gabe puts his arm across me. "Glo, we're almost there. Can you hear me?"

I push his arm away. I rub my legs until I can feel something akin to pain. I try to pray. For the first time in years, I try to pray. What are the words again? Why can't I remember the words? *Our Father who art in heaven* . . . then nothing. "Was she wearing her helmet?" I ask.

"She wasn't."

I'm grateful for the galvanizing rush of anger because it will keep me where I need to be. I cling to it as we approach the emergency entrance of the hospital.

My parents are there. They look ancient. A wave of guilt passes through me. How could I have left Julia alone? All those years of watchful diligence are worthless now. How could I have let my guard down? I feel my fingernails dig into the palms of my hands. A ragged nail grabs hold of a scab; a berry-picking scratch from the other day. When I reach for my mother's arm, I see the blood. Why is there blood? This is so unlike her. She is usually so fastidious.

My mother takes my hand in hers and then there is blood on her hands as well. Where is it all coming from? She tries to hug me but I pull away. And then I see the gash in my hand where my nails have torn a hole. "I'm sorry," I say. "I'm so sorry."

She looks frightened. This unnerves me. She shouldn't be going through this again. Julia must be gone. Gabe was lying.

I sink into a chair because my legs won't hold me. Gabe kneels in front of me. "She's fine, Darlin'. Just fine."

My father takes a handkerchief from his pocket, wraps it around my hand, and presses hard. "I'll take you to her," he says. His chin is trembling.

Doorways, gurneys, trays of hospital food pass by in a rush. There's far too much white: white walls, white uniforms, white sheets. No faces on the people, only expressions. I suddenly see that everyone is the same except for different expressions, but it means nothing to me because they're not real. Just masks.

On the way to Julia's room we pass Maxi and Des sitting

in the hallway. Maxi's face is ashen. She springs up from her seat when she sees me. "It's my fault," she says. "We were going too fast. I'm so sorry, Glo. It's my fault."

I move past her. "She should have been wearing her helmet," I say.

Des tries to hug me, but I push past her as well.

My father stops and takes Maxi by the hand. "It's not your fault," I hear him say. "It's nobody's fault."

Then I'm in her room and relief overwhelms me. She is perfect. She is fine—only a cast on her arm. Her beauty stuns me, her perfection. Her small nose, that rosebud mouth, the sooty lashes smudged beneath her eyes. I go to her side, take her hand, and then I see that she's not perfect. Her eyes are wrong. She grabs my hand and pleads, "Can somebody just tell me what happened?"

My mother leans across the bed and strokes her arm. "You were riding with Maxi and you fell. You hit your head. You just need some rest."

"Okay," she says, rubbing her hands together as if she's cold. "Who's Maxi?"

I look at my mother, who says, "She's having some trouble remembering. The doctor says she has a concussion."

At this point a dishevelled-looking woman enters the room and introduces herself as Dr. Something but I can call her June. "What's going on?" I demand.

My heart races as she explains the bruising, the hematoma at the base of Julia's skull caused by the fall. There's no cause for alarm yet. She's probably just disoriented. These things usually correct themselves within a few hours.

"Yet?" I say. "Usually? Why isn't she remembering?"

"There's no point in getting overly nervous at this point."

"So, you'll tell me when I should become overly nervous? You'll let me know? That'd be great," I hear myself say.

"Um, Mom?" Julia's troubled eyes look up at me. "Do you mind telling me what happened?"

My mother repeats, calmly, the same thing she's said only moments before and the doctor asks if she can talk to me privately. Outside, she explains the situation with exactly the same words as before, and I explain that I'm not the one with the memory loss. My father tries to put his arm around my shoulder, but I move away. This is too familiar. It's all happening again. Of course it is.

"We just need to wait," he says.

Between his passivity and my mother's calm and the inscrutable expression on the doctor's face, I will scream if I remain here one second longer. "What are you doing about this?" I face the doctor.

"If things don't change in an hour or so, we'll run some tests. I've seen this a thousand times, okay, Mom?"

"I'm not your mother," I say.

She ignores me. "I believe the memory loss is temporary."

"Well, if that's what you believe, that's hugely reassuring."

"You need to be calm for your daughter," she says.

I feel like slapping her and then I think she might be right. I say I'm going for a short walk and will be back in a minute. My father says he'll tell Julia.

As I move through the hallways, avoiding the waiting room, I think about how thoughts are falling out of Julia's head and of how often I've wished my own memories would disappear. A thought that I've somehow caused this competes with the awareness that it's all—everything—out of our control. I find myself praying that Julia's whole life will return to her and this angers me more than anything, because I know this, too, is pointless.

I look around at the institutional white. I have no idea where I am or how long I've been wandering. But then I hear Des calling my name and I can't face her. I open the first door I see and slip inside. The room is filled with empty pews and an empty altar. A picture hangs on the wall: someone with long hair and a dreamy look in his eyes. Gentle Jesus, of course. I've found a chapel. "Well, fuck me," I say. The words ring out in the quiet room.

A sudden turn of a white head in the front pew informs me that the room is not empty. An elderly gentleman rises abruptly and scowls. I turn to say I'm sorry and I see that Des is standing behind me.

"I think you might have scared him," she says. She touches my arm. "She's remembering, Glo. She's going to be fine."

"She's remembering?"

"She is."

I crumple onto the hard bench. I lean my head on my arms and close my eyes. Now, in a rush, I remember kissing Gabe. And leaving Des. Jake on the mountain. Driving away. It comes rushing back like there's been nothing in between. "I'm so tired," is all I can say.

"Honey, my brothers have had a hundred concussions between the three of them and they're all normal. Well . . . for the most part." I hear the smile in her voice. "Come. Let's go see her."

My mother is waiting outside Julia's door and she's smiling broadly. "She remembers."

I rush into the room. I sit beside Julia's bed, but I can't find my voice.

"It's okay, Mom. I'm fine. Don't freak out, okay?"

"You're remembering now?"

"Yes. And you're bleeding all over my arm."

I look down. The handkerchief has come unravelled. I wind it tightly. "Why weren't you wearing your helmet?" I hear myself say.

"Mom," she says, urgently. "Not now."

"We'll wait outside," my mother says.

"No, don't go. Stay here," Julia pleads. "I want you here."

"It's a simple question." I have no idea why I'm saying this. Why I haven't wrapped her in my arms. What is wrong with me?

"Yeah, yeah, I get it. I screwed up, okay? Relax already. Go take a pill or something. I'm fine. Can't you see that? I'm not like you."

The room falls silent. Then the doctor steps forward. "She can go home soon. Just make sure you wake her up a few times in the night to see if she remembers where she is. The arm was a clean break. I'll write a prescription before you leave."

"I don't need a prescription," I say.

"For Julia. For the pain," she explains calmly.

"Yeah, Mom. For me. My pain."

Her pain. But I know that the pain in her arm is nothing against the pain I've put her through. She needs a pill for me. I back toward the door, where Gabe is standing. "I'll go home with Grandpa and Grandma," Julia says.

Gabe puts his hands on my shoulders, but I pull away. "I'll take you home if you want," he says.

"Fine," I nod. "A clean break," I say to the doctor. "So that's good." I follow Gabe.

Kate is coming through the revolving doors when we get to the hospital entrance.

"I called Mark," Kate says, immediately. Mark. I hadn't even thought of him. "He's okay," she continues. "I told him you'd call him later. Can I go see her?"

"Of course," I say, accepting her hug. "She'll want to see you."

She takes my bandaged hand in hers and presses. I wince at the pressure. "Are you okay? Are you going to be okay?" Her voice is meant to be soothing, I guess. The tone makes me wince, though, more than the squeeze of her hand. "Do you need something?"

"Go to her," I say. "Julia needs you." My head is throbbing now, although my vision is still clear. I'm grateful for that. I just need to get home. Pack up our stuff and leave this place forever. I'll be fine once we're on the highway. It's only one road home. I just want to go home.

~

Gabe says nothing as we drive back to the farm, nothing until we pull up in the driveway. Then he turns to me. The vein on the side of his head is pulsing. "It's just a broken arm, for Chrissake. She's going to be fine."

"Stop saying that. She's not fine. I'm not fine. We're not fine."

He doesn't respond. Just looks at me the way he always did.

"I just want everyone to leave me alone," I say, reaching for the door handle.

He guns the motor as I get out of the truck. I hear him say, "You always did."

twenty-five

The house is still. I stand in the kitchen and listen. It's the same sound that echoed in every room the days after Jake's death. We didn't talk about it, how absurd it was that he was gone. I'd enter a room and find my mother or father wiping away tears, but I don't remember seeing them cry.

We ate other people's food, left at our doorstep. That was strange to me—that the smells filling our kitchen weren't our own. The soup was bland, the crusts tougher, the bread tasteless. My dad didn't sing; my mother just sat in Jake's room. When I told them I thought I should go away to school with Kate, they nodded.

Nothing—only the stillness.

Be still and know that I am God. This was Des's emergency memory verse, pulled out when she was unprepared. "That's kind of funny," she would say. "Forgetting to memorize?" None of the Sunday school teachers thought so.

I remain in the kitchen and am still—knowing nothing.

"Glo, are you there?"

The words come from far away. I'm sitting at the piano

bench with a cup of untouched tea in front of me. I wonder who made it. I tried to go upstairs to Jake's room when I came home, I remember that, but the stairs looked as perilous as a ladder. Kate sits opposite me. "Where's Julia?" I ask.

"Your parents had to do some paperwork. She wanted to wait for them. They'll be here soon. Are you okay?"

"I will be once everyone stops asking me that."

"Sorry," she says, defensively.

"No, I am. Do you want some tea?" I push the cup over to her. "Have some tea."

"I made it for you. What were you thinking about? You've just been sitting there. It's kind of creepy."

I take a sip of the tea. It's cold. "Sometimes time just slips away. Does that ever happen to you?"

"Not so much."

"No, you're always in control, aren't you?"

She looks hurt.

"I meant it as a compliment. Honestly, Kate, you're a rock. Really, I can't thank you enough for that."

She smiles. "You don't have to thank me."

"Why, though? Why have you always been there for me?"

"You're my friend. I love you."

"I love you, too. But still, why?"

"You needed me."

"Ah."

"I'm going to get you some hot tea. I have no idea why it's supposed to help, but it does."

"Kate," I say, suddenly. "Why did you tell your mom?"

"I beg your pardon?"

"About Des and Jake sleeping together. I told you not to tell anyone." Kate had been annoyed that I would even ask.

"It was so long ago, Glo."

"It was yesterday. A day is like a thousand years . . ."

"You're overwrought."

"Yeah, I am, Kate. I need an answer."

She runs her hand through her hair; it falls neatly back into place. "I don't know. I always told my mother everything."

"Really?"

"I was worried about you. And Des. Listen, I don't know, okay? It was upsetting for everyone. I'm going to call Mark now."

"What's with you and taking care of everything?" My harsh tone surprises both of us. I'm about to apologize when I see the fear in her eyes. It's unmistakable, even though I realize I've seen it and missed it a thousand times. I've seen fear enough in my own eyes to recognize it.

And then it's gone. She takes a deep breath, gathers herself. Calmly, she explains, painstakingly, that the depression has taken its toll on Mark as well as Julia. She outlines every single transgression I've committed. I've been a neglectful wife and mother. I have left them for my own misery. Have I forgotten how much extra stress leave she arranged so that I could remain in bed? Is this what I wanted for Julia?

As she speaks, her voice speeds up but remains calm and I see that Kate has needed me to remain weak. And all those times she saved me, I let her save me.

"Take me to Des's," I say.

"Excuse me?"

"I left my car there earlier."

She blinks. "I think you should rest. Julia will be home soon. You need to be here for her."

"It's okay, Kate. I'll take a cab." I get up from the bench, uncharacteristically sturdy and clear-headed. There is no doubt in my mind.

"I'll take you," she says.

We don't speak as we drive the now familiar way to Des's house. With every turn I expect Kate to say something, a reasonable explanation for why we left our friend when she needed us the most. But Kate's jaw is set. She's hurt and it's up to me to make it better.

"I'm not blaming you," I finally say. "I didn't have to leave."

Her hands are firm on the steering wheel as she turns into the driveway. "I don't see the point of this, Glo. We were eighteen years old, for God's sake. We both needed to leave this place. I just don't see the point of looking back." She says this with the same certainty she uses at school to keep grumbling teachers and students alike in tow.

"Oh, Kate," I say. "I don't think it's looking back. I think it's all around us."

She only sighs. "Do you need me to come with you?" She stops the car.

"No, Kate. Do you want to come?"

She shakes her head but makes no move to leave. She looks as if she wants to say something.

"What?"

"I really did always tell my mother everything."

"Okay."

As I watch her drive away, Roy bounds up to greet me. I pat his soft snout. "Good boy," I say. The dog seems pleased, as though he's done his job. He's a welcoming dog; not a very good guard dog.

The night air is crisp: a hint of fall and pine, fading

flowers. I take a deep, cleansing breath before I ring the bell.

Des doesn't seem surprised to see me and opens the door wide for me to enter.

Maxi is at the kitchen table. This is the first time I've seen her without dramatic makeup. She looks like she's twelve years old. "How is Julia?" she asks.

"She's fine. You can come visit her tomorrow. She'll want that."

Her eyes brim with tears. "So, she's fine?"

"She's perfect. You're perfect. I'm sorry about . . . at the hospital. I wasn't . . . I was wrong."

She crosses the room and buries her head in my chest. I rub her back. Des watches us.

"And you, Des. I'm so sorry."

"No need. If it were Maxi I'd have been deranged."

"Pretty much business as usual?" Maxi says, still sniffing.

"Let's go outside," Des says.

I sit in the willow chair and wait in the twilight. Des brings tea and a pitcher of steamed milk. She hands me a cup; I take a sip. The warmth infuses me.

"Can you ever forgive me?" I say.

"Glo, mothers are nuts where their kids are concerned."

"Not about that."

"Then what?"

"So much. I should have listened to you when you tried to tell me about Jake."

"You were in shock."

"And I should have left with you that night at church. You stood there and waited for me. I wanted to go with you, but I just . . . I should have stood up for you."

"Glo." She pulls her already messy hair. "I knew you couldn't come with me."

"And tonight, I kissed Gabe." This just tumbles out of me before I even know if it's mine to tell.

"I know."

"Gabe told you."

She nods. "It's okay."

"It's okay?"

"Well, it's not great . . ."

"It was wrong. I don't know what I was thinking . . ."

"Maybe that Gabe was yours first? That you weren't done?"

"No, Des. Honestly. You have to believe me."

"I do believe you. I've always believed you." She smiles. "I've wondered if I took him from you. He was such a mess after you left."

"That doesn't make it right."

"Oh, honey," she says, tired. "Enough with the wrong and the right already. There is something in between, you know. Entire lives happen between those two points."

"But I didn't stand up for you, I didn't listen to you, I . . ."

"Fine, fine! I forgive you. Jeez, except for the listening part, because you're still not listening! You never did listen to anything or anybody except that stupid little voice inside your head that told you that you were crap. Honestly, Glo, you were grieving. Everything we thought we were going to be . . . it all fell away when Jake died."

"You're mad at me."

"I am. I am mad at you. Why didn't you answer my letters?"

"I'm sorry."

"Do not be sorry. Do not be that. I am so not interested in that. Why?"

"Honestly, I don't know. I'm . . . " The look on her face stops me short. "Something other than sorry, I guess. I don't know."

"Did you blame me?"

"Yes," I say, finally. "You broke the rules."

Des doesn't blink. "And that's why Jake died?"

"No, of course not."

"Of course not why?"

"I don't know why."

"Exactly. He just did. You don't have to know why or explain why. You don't always have to explain things, Glo. There isn't always an explanation."

"I don't believe that."

"I know you don't. And that's what I love about you. It's what Jake loved about you. But it's not your job to explain. Sometimes we just have to accept. Jake died. It was his time."

"I hate that! That makes no sense to me. He slipped off a mountain he knew like a mountain goat."

"Glo, he died because it was his time. Honestly, how can you argue with that? How the hell do you win that argument? He was an eighteen-year-old boy and that was his life. Eighteen years. You know what I hate? I hate it when people say that someone died before their time. Like they know. Hate it. Why not let it be his time? His brief, glorious time. Why take that away from him?"

"I never thought about it that way."

"Of course not! You never read my letters!"

I have to smile at her fury. Even enraged, her dimples flash. Suddenly I see her face when she took the bite of the apple, I see it between us on the ground. "Okay, what else didn't I want to know?"

She sighs. "Love, I think. We were taught what God expects of us, how we need to measure up. But we just have to measure up to love. That's it."

"You're kind of magnificent when you're angry."

"Yeah, well, it's a stretch. Listen—"

I hold my hands up in surrender. "I'm listening."

"I have something to tell you."

"Then tell me."

"Are you sure?"

"I am."

Des cradles her cup and takes a deep breath. It was a warm night, she says. She and Jake walked up the logging road to his favourite place. They brought a blanket and a bottle of cheap sparkling wine. They called it champagne. "But we didn't drink much of it," she says. "We were already pretty stoned."

I'm surprised at this, of course.

"Oh, honey," Des smiles, patting my hand. "The wind was warm. Balmy—not usual. We didn't plan it, not really. Or maybe." She colours slightly. "He was so sweet and tender. He was afraid he would hurt me, but he didn't. He asked if I was okay. I told him it felt natural and he said he felt the same way. It was pretty corny. I think we believed we were the first ones to feel that way." She stops, remembering. "When I tried to tell you, that day? I just wanted you to know how he felt. I thought . . . I don't know. That it would comfort you, maybe."

"It does."

"And then everything turned so crazy."

"We sent you away."

"Glo . . . "

"I'm not apologizing. I'm just saying."

"Okay, fine. That was hard. But the weird thing is, it's not like I didn't understand. It's what they believed—"

"It's no excuse."

"Yeah, it is. If you truly believe you know better, best; if you truly believe you're saving someone, you do some pretty dumb-ass things. I understood the idea. I just never understood how they could all stop loving me at once."

Tears fall down my face.

"Tell me now if you can't take it." Her eyes are naked. I get that old feeling: skin being stripped off me layer by layer. But I say I can take it.

"I went to Israel after that. I'm not sure what I expected to find. Absolution, maybe."

"Des, you did nothing wrong."

But she doesn't seem to hear me. "I travelled around, hitchhiked mostly. Slept with as many boys as possible, which was easy to do back then. I didn't know some of their names." She looks at me. "We used to think we had to save everybody. I didn't think about that. They were saving me. It was awful and great at the same time. But it wasn't enough.

"I ended up at a kibbutz close to the Sea of Galilee. There was this pond, like McGann's pond, only I was alone. They said it was fed by the Jordan. I thought, *If I stay underneath long enough, that's all it will take. I'll just breathe the water.*"

"Baptism by suicide." The words are out of my mouth before I hear how crass they sound.

"Yeah, I guess. I never thought of that. Trust you," she says. "I just wanted to be done, you know? I thought it was what I wanted, but then it wasn't. Suddenly, I was gasping for air like none of the rest had ever happened. All I wanted to do was to get back to the surface again, to breathe again. No matter what had happened, or what I had done. Just to break through and breathe." She stops and gathers herself.

"Then what?"

"Well, I dried off," she says. "A little anticlimactic. I was a little surprised to see myself still here."

"I feel like that most of the time."

She stops smiling. "I know you do. Your mom's told me."

I'm surprised at this. "She told you I get depressed."

"'A little down', she says."

"Sounds like my mother." I shake my head. We laugh. Then we compare illness notes like two keen students reliving an exam they were not prepared for. Turns out we've had a very similar chemical history, slept with some of the same meds. I tell her about my lowest moment, a sleepless night, one of many.

"The three o'clock wake-up call?" she says.

"Worst hotel service ever," I nod. "Heart pounding, ears ringing . . ."

"Elephant on the chest?"

"King Kong."

"Can't think in a straight line. Sweating . . . "

"Like you're ready to face a firing squad." I stop because I haven't told anyone about this night, not even Marci.

"It's okay."

I take a breath. "It's the same old, same old—except worse. I go downstairs to read, watch TV, something to take my mind off . . . to turn my mind off. I grab the Bible and turn to a random page. Remember that?"

"Oh yes." She closes her eyes and jabs a finger through the night air. "The surefire way to truth. The verse of the pointing finger."

"Yeah, well, it sounds silly when you put it that way," I say. "But, Des, we really believed, didn't we? We really did."

"We couldn't have believed more."

"I felt like Jacob, honestly. *I am not leaving here without a blessing.* I actually said it."

"So what was the verse?"

"You know what's weird? I don't even remember. I just read it and thought, it's not enough. It's just not enough. We're done."

Des straightens. "You broke up with God?"

We laugh for so long that Maxi comes out of the house to check up on us. Des waves her away. "Oh, honey," she finally says. "And I thought I was brave."

I wipe my nose on my jacket sleeve. "So, what did you do?"

"I kept reading. Everything I could get my hands on. And then I discovered the Gospel of Thomas, the doubter, no less. *That which is within you that you bring forth will save you. That which is within you that you do not bring forth will destroy you.* I knew it was true. I had to figure this out for myself. I had to forgive myself."

"For what, Des? For loving Jake?"

She puts her hands on top of mine, and I feel the pressure and the warmth. "No," she says, taking a deep breath. "When I left here I was pregnant."

"Pregnant." The word feels heavy in my mouth.

"Turns out everything they said in Guidance class was true. It can happen the first time."

"Oh, Des."

"I'm sorry. I'm so sorry that I . . ."

"Do not . . . be that."

"Okay." There is trust, finally, in her eyes. "I should have told you, though. I wanted to."

"You would have."

"Yes," she nods. "But by the time I knew, really knew, you were gone."

She explains how her dad was already sick by then, and her mother couldn't help her raise a child. Who knows if they would have anyway, but this is what they told her. She was to remain with relatives and then give the baby away.

"But I wouldn't have," she says. "I couldn't give Jake's baby away."

"And my parents?"

She shakes her head. "They never knew. I was going to tell them when I came home with the baby. First things first, I thought."

"And . . . but?"

Des takes a deep breath, then another. "I went into labour at my aunt's house. I didn't tell anyone at first, about the pains. I didn't want to complain."

"Des."

"Trust me, I made up for it when Maxi was born. I asked for every drug they had then."

I take her hand in mine. "Go on."

Her eyes brim with tears, but her voice is calm. "She came right away. Grace—the girl. I knew it would be a girl and I knew she would be Grace. A bit of Jake. I was so happy when I saw her, Glo. And then there was another pain, ripping me apart."

"The placenta?"

"The boy." Her voice is small. "He was tiny, barely alive. They didn't know. He was so little and weak. I couldn't separate them, Glo. I couldn't. Not after you and Jake. And I couldn't care for them both. I mean, that's what I thought at the time, but maybe I could have . . . maybe I should have been . . ." Tears splash down her face.

"Maxi," I say, sternly.

"What?" Her eyes shimmer through the wetness. She twists around to see if Maxi has joined us.

"Think of Maxi a year from now. She's pregnant and you're not there. She's going to take care of twins?"

"Oh my God," she says, eyes wide. "Not a chance."

"Okay, go on."

She grips my hand tightly. "Oh, I wanted you there. You would have told me what to do. You were always so sure."

I fight back my own tears. Now is not the time. "What did you do?"

"I gave them away."

I don't even hesitate. "You did the right thing."

"I don't know. I've never been sure."

"Sometimes what we do is the only thing we can do."

And then there is an abundance of tears, a full-blown, unequivocal, waterfall of salty tears. We cry. Like Bridal Veil Falls, we cry.

Finally, she says, "I named him Jacob. It was my only condition—they had to keep the name."

"Of course," I say, shaking my head. "Because we haven't cried enough."

And then we laugh, stupidly, through our tears. The sound stretches to the valley below.

twenty-six

Des left the hospital alone. Two months later she was on a plane to Jerusalem. Before she left, she wrote their names on a birth certificate under my brother's name.

And there's more. Des has found the babies. Or, rather, Grace has found her. She contacted Des a couple of months ago. Des immediately flew out to Calgary to meet her. Her brother, Jack, was travelling in Turkey at the time; he had no interest in meeting his mother. He already had a mother, he said. Grace said this apologetically and explained that he just wasn't ready. But they were planning to move to the West Coast to study. They would be here tomorrow. Grace couldn't promise, but she said she would try to convince her brother to join her.

Tomorrow. I struggle to take it all in, but it's too much. Instead, I try to remain focused on Des. "How does Gabe feel about all this?"

"Well, you know Gabe. He takes care of things. He can't take care of this."

"I don't understand. He's had years to get used to the

idea of the babies . . ." Des's face stops me. "He hasn't had years."

"A year ago. When I put my name on the Adoption-Find website."

"Oh."

"Yeah. Big oh."

"Why?"

"Didn't I tell him? I tried, a hundred times. I couldn't. The words just got stuck."

"Hmm. You lost Jake, Kate, and me and the entire church in a month. Maybe you were afraid you'd lose him?"

She shakes her head. "It's been hard to talk about Jake. Gabe calls him the Holy Ghost. Gabe believes in moving on."

"Ah."

"Will you talk to him?"

"What do you want me to say?"

"You'll think of something," she says. "But maybe no kissing." And then she grins and she is the old Des and we're back in Sunday school, singing, "Verily We Roll Along."

～

Gabe is in one of the stalls with the grey mare, brushing her coat. Des said the barn was his church, that he built it himself; he needed to build a place that was his own. The high ceiling and the aisle between the stalls is spacious, lit by a couple of dangling light bulbs, a flickering of light. Dust is in the air, straw all around. It's more an inn than a cathedral.

I choose a brush from an adjacent wall. Animals breathe in the corners: wheeze, whinny, snuffle, a breath, a sigh—subtle

255

signs of life. Do animals sigh? Probably not. "Do you need some help?"

Gabe doesn't seem surprised to see me. "Grab one of the—"

I hold up the brush in my hand.

"Smooth, even strokes," he says. "She's old."

"Not what she used to be?"

Gabe looks up.

"The old grey mare?" I say. "*The old grey mare, she ain't what she used to be, ain't what she used to be, ain't what she used to be . . .*" My voice cracks.

"You never could sing."

"You're right."

"Whoa," he says. "I'm what?"

I stop brushing. The mare turns as if she's wondering what happened to her massage. "Sorry, old girl," I say. I continue brushing, pressing down on her hide so that each movement releases more of the musk. "You're right," I repeat. "I never was much of a singer. Or much good at saying sorry."

"Still aren't."

I look at him over the swayed back.

"That was pretty lame," he says.

"I'm sorry." I say this slowly.

"Heartfelt. So moving."

"Were you always such an asshole?"

Now he stops brushing, and the old grey looks at him like she is getting a little ticked off.

"I'm sorry I pushed you away. You and Des . . . tonight, at the hospital."

"Tonight." He leaves the stall, pushes the gate open with a booted foot. I follow him into the nave of the barn.

"Say something," I say.

He stands with his shoulders thrust forward. His shirt is just another shade of plaid. It could be the same shirt, the same body, except it's not raining. He doesn't dig his hands into his pockets this time. Instead, he reaches out and hurls the grooming brush at the wall. It hits an aluminum basin and clangs loudly. The sound echoes in the room.

Instantly, he looks embarrassed. "That was a little more dramatic than I intended. Sorry, Darlin'."

The word surprises me.

"The mare," he explains. "Old Darlin'."

"You named an old nag Darlin'?"

"There have been a few of them," he says. "Over the years. It helped. *The last weird mystery that held him with wild fascination and pounded his soul to flakes. With her his imagination ran riot, and that is why they rode to the highest hill and watched an evil moon ride high, for they knew then that they could see the devil in each other. But Eleanor—did Amory dream her?* I memorized that, in case you came back. Why I thought *that* would impress you, I don't know. I should have memorized the Psalms." He walks over to a bale of hay, sits down, and pulls out a bottle. He twists it open and takes a drink, then passes it to me. "We were both such fanatic romantics. It's probably a good thing we didn't end up together."

"*I* was a romantic? I don't think so. I mean, I tried, but it never quite took."

"Maybe you were just a fanatic."

"Maybe we were both trying to convert each other."

"And failed."

"No, I don't think so. You made me really happy, Gabe.

257

You always told me I was perfect. It was way too much, but still, you tried."

"To me, you were."

"Oh, boy. See, this is what you're good at. You made me believe there was more."

"Then why did you leave me for the wide world?"

"Stupid. Stupid thing to say. Maybe I thought it was the only thing you'd hear. I just didn't believe in happily ever after the way you wanted."

"Do you now?"

"I'm trying. Gabe, I am sorry that I left—that way."

"You were blindsided by Jake's death. I get that. Everything else gets sucked away. I know that."

"So then why are you so mad right now?"

"I'm not mad."

"The vein, Gabe. The vein never lies." I brush the pulsing blood at his temple with the neck of the bottle.

He takes the bottle from me, brushing my fingers with his. "I've spent my life trying to follow the footsteps of a ghost, sweeping up." He takes another, longer draw. "First my dad's and then Jake's."

"And now the babies."

"Jake's babies. Des went out there alone. That's the way she wanted it. She didn't need me." He cradles the bottle in his hands like he needs something to hold onto. "She's never met the boy, you know." I nod. "Just the girl. She needed to do it by herself." He takes another drink. "And the Holy Ghost."

"Yeah, that's what Des said you call him," I say. "You call the old nag Darlin', and my dead brother is the Holy Ghost." I take the bottle briefly, a short sip, and return it. "I speak from experience when I say you may need therapy, my friend."

He laughs shortly. "You may have a point."

"You always did the right thing, Gabe. Why change now?"

"I should have gone after you."

"No. I wanted to leave the pain. I didn't want anything or anyone from this life following me."

"How's that working for you?"

"Well, mostly I've tried to stay numb. And I'll tell you something, *that* really does not work."

He takes a long draw, says nothing.

"I never knew how much alike we were. We both wanted things to be fair and right. We had different ideas about how to get there, but we both wanted to fix life. Tonight, or last night—what time is it?—Julia's life kept falling out of her brain. One little bump on her head and suddenly part of her life was missing. All I could think was that she should have been more careful."

"If only she'd worn her helmet. If only Jake hadn't slipped?"

"Exactly. But it's a bad idea, trying to live retroactively."

"Not to mention impossible."

"Not to mention that."

"Did you really not love me anymore?" he asks, abruptly.

I take the bottle and a larger sip. "No."

"Thank you. Thank you for that."

"How could anyone not love you?" I say, with all my heart. "How would that even be possible? How could anyone be with you and not think it would all be okay? You do that, Gabe. You take care of people. You always have."

"I would have taken care of you."

"I know. And I would have let you. I would have let you save me—I would have expected it."

"And that's wrong?"

"Yep."

"Why?"

I smile, take another drink. "I don't know."

"That's your argument?"

"It's new. Des doesn't need you to save her, you know. She just needs you to be there."

"I don't like . . . doing nothing."

"Well, the best cowboys never do. You might have to be a bad cowboy tomorrow."

He leans over and pushes me with his broad shoulder. "She's a good sport though, eh? About the kissing?"

"She really is."

twenty-seven

I park my car in the driveway and walk to the house. But when I get to the porch, I can't make myself go inside. I sit on the porch swing, careful to not make a sound. I'm not ready to see Julia. The look on her face—she'd finally given up on me. *Take a pill,* she said. *I'm not like you.* All the times I've run away press together simultaneously in my mind like an accordion.

My parents are sitting at the kitchen table: I can see them through the window, sharing a sandwich: night lunch. The scene is familiar and distant at the same time. And then, for the briefest of moments, I can see Jake's head as well. His wavy chestnut hair, the deep brown eyes full of life and mischief. He would have them both laughing at something he'd done during the day, and my mother's eyes would be full of adoration. She would discard that word with a brisk shake of her head, but it was true. She adored him; we all did.

My mother gets to her feet when she sees me come in. "Can I make you something to eat? A fried egg sandwich?"

I consider asking her about the babies, but they both look

so tired I haven't the heart. "I'm not really hungry," I say. "Where's Julia?"

"She's resting. She's had a rough night. She was just upset, Gloria. She didn't mean anything."

"Yeah, she did, Mom." I sit down at the table, suddenly exhausted. "I deserved it."

"You've raised a wonderful daughter."

"She is. But I haven't given her enough."

"Have you given her all you could?"

"Yes."

"And it's never enough, is it?"

"You're right about that." I wait for a response. My alligator brain anticipates a verse of some kind, but it's late and I can't even guess what King Solomon would have to say about this.

"You really should have something to eat," she says.

"Maybe I'll fix myself something after I've seen Julia."

"Call your husband," I hear her say as I climb the stairs. "He's been phoning all night."

~

I open the door quietly in case Julia is sleeping. "Are you awake?"

"Hey, Mom." Her voice is gravelly. When she sees me she bursts into tears. "I'm sorry about what I said at the hospital. I was just really, you know, like, it hurt! And I couldn't remember anything. It was freaky. But I shouldn't have said—"

"Hey, stop it. You didn't do anything wrong."

"But I didn't wear my helmet and then we were going so

fast. It was so great, Mom. It was so . . . with the wind, like flying, you know?"

I look into her eyes. "Oh, Sweetie," I say. "I think you're flying right now. You're a little bit stoned."

"Nooo."

"Yeah, you are, just a little."

"No, I just took two. They're so little. And cute."

"They are cute. It's okay."

"But I'm sorry."

"You need to stop saying that. Listen to me, Jewel, I'm proud of you. Honestly."

"Huh?"

"I'll probably have to tell you again tomorrow, but I really am. You're so brave, you know that?"

"I am?"

"You are. And beautiful and so strong. And stubborn."

"Nooo."

I pull the covers up and tuck her in, something I didn't think she'd ever let me do again. "You need to rest now."

"Don't go," she says, but her eyes are droopy. "Tell me a story." Her eyes close. "But not the whale one. It pisses you off."

Instead, I tell her the story of my brother and of Des and how, once upon a time, they loved each other so much. I tell her about the babies—the lost twins—she only murmurs. "You'll meet them tomorrow," I say.

When I'm at the door, though, she opens her eyes again. "I shouldn't have said I'm not like you."

"Sweetie, most of the time, I don't even want to be like me."

"That's not right," she says sleepily.

No, probably not, I think, closing the door behind me.

I try to convince myself that it's too late to call Mark. He'll be sleeping. He knows Julia is fine—there's no need. And then I remember he's been phoning all night.

He answers on the first ring. "El?" he says.

"Glo," I say, automatically.

"What?"

"It's me," I say. "Just wanted to let you know that Julia is fine. She's sleeping."

"What is it? You sound funny. Is she really all right?"

"It's late and it's been a crazy day."

"How are you holding up, El?"

"Glo."

"Right. Listen, *Glo.*"

I smile at the impatience in his voice—so much better than the concerned voice of the last number of years. "I'm listening," I say, seriously.

"I should have come out there. I don't know why I didn't. It was wrong. You needed me and I wasn't there for you."

"Oh, brother."

"I beg your pardon."

This is his professorial voice and it makes me giddy, suddenly. The night is, officially, catching up with me. I just want to giggle and I don't know why. And then I do giggle.

"Are you okay?" And there it is—the concern.

"Argh," I say. This does it. I stop laughing. "I am so tired of that question. I'm not okay, but listen, Mark. You have been there for me since the day I met you. I haven't been there for me, but there has never been a day when you weren't. Maybe you're tired of it."

"I'm not."

"You should be. You should be tired of it. I am."

"For better or worse," he says.

"Well, Sweetie, a little better would be nice now and again, don't you think?"

He chuckles at this. "I could use a little better."

"Do you love me?" I say.

"I do," he says instantly.

"Why? Why on earth do you love me?"

There is a pause. "I have no idea. Let's face it, you're kind of crazy."

Good answer, I think. "I am."

"No, really."

"I know. I'm agreeing with you."

"But I like that. I mean, I don't like how sad it makes you. I don't like how you don't get who you are, but I respect the crazy."

"Why?"

"You're true to it, I guess."

"Well," I say. "I'm trying."

⌣

I sit in the chair next to Julia's bed and listen to her breathe. With every rise and fall of her chest, I wonder at the miracle, wonder at myself for not having seen it every day of her life. Every so often I wake her up, ask her if she remembers where she is. Finally she gets annoyed and asks if I have Alzheimer's. This makes me happy. I listen to the clatter and ping of the wind and rain on the window all night long.

Close to dawn, I hear the screen door clatter shut. Must be time to milk the cow.

In the dim morning light, I walk through the soggy garden, between the regimented rows of carrots and lettuce and squash—my mother's work—and past the splashes of colour from the flowers that my father insisted upon: aster, begonia, daisy. There's life here in every corner. I hear music, faintly. I can't make out the words, but the tune is familiar. I follow it like a path, one that resonates more surely as I near the barn.

"... and to my listening ears all nature sings and round me rings the music of the spheres. This is my Father's world: I rest me in the thought of rocks and trees, of skies and seas ..."

He stops singing when he sees me approach the corral where he's milking our one remaining cow. He looks embarrassed. "She gives more milk this way—"

"Well, who wouldn't?" I lean over the gate. "Keep singing," I say. "It sounds nice."

He coaxes milk from the cow, who is now stamping a hoof impatiently. Her tail flickers past, but he avoids it with a subtle shift of his head; he's used to her ways. "She's a little shy," he says. He resumes the song, but humming.

I walk through the place that used to be a hive of activity: chickens, a pig, sheep, everything our family once needed. Most of the animals are gone, but their scent remains. As I pass the empty stalls, I remember the names that Jake and I came up with: Goliath, the hog, for obvious reasons. We named the chickens after the twelve tribes of Israel, but my mother drew the line at calling the rooster Abraham. My favourite was a sheep named Bathsheeba. (How could we resist?) Her stall was at the far end of the barn. My favourite time of year was when the lambs were born. The worst was when they were sold. I think it even made my father a little sad, but he tried not to show it. My mother shook her head over our sentimentality. "They're just animals, for goodness sake," she must have said a thousand times. But she usually cooked something particularly nice on those evenings when the lambs would disappear and, if it contained meat, she disguised it.

The sweet smell of hay is no match for the ripeness of manure. My stomach flips as I walk to the end of the barn for fresh air. And that's when I see it, nestled in the stall where Bathsheeba used to be: Project Noah.

I glance over my shoulder. My father is still at work. *In the rustling grass I hear him pass; He speaks to me everywhere.*

It doesn't gleam as it once did, but it's the same. Well, I only suppose it's the same. The truth is, I don't remember it looking like this. The ark stands as high as my waist; it would have seemed even taller then. The deck is solid oak, golden, with flecks of orange. The planks—laid tongue-and-groove—have hardly separated with weather or time. The railings are mahogany; the family quarters are burnished cherrywood—stained glass in the small windows of the cabin. I don't remember these. The gangplank is exactly as I remember it, though. It was the final and most important feature on the vessel.

I vetoed all of my father's suggestions when it was time to make the gangplank. It had to be exactly right. Jake said that we should use plastic because it was just going to get covered with animal crap anyway. I called him an idiot, and we were both sent back to the house to sit in the corner. I didn't mind. It was satisfying to have Jake there, legitimately, for a change.

I passed my corner time by poring over Genesis for the perfect material. As soon as I read the part about the dove and the olive branch, I knew. When the timer went off, I tore outside to tell my father. "Olive wood!" I gasped. "It has to be olive wood." He said this might be a little tough to find, but I hugged him tightly around his middle. I was sure he'd do his part now that I'd finally solved the mystery.

Sure enough, the very next day there was a beautiful olive wood gangplank that could be lowered and raised with a pulley system that he constructed. He'd used the right thickness of rope, weathered just so. I remember falling to my knees with a zebra in each hand, because I'd already decided that these exotic beasts would be the first to be saved. Any doubt that was beginning to accumulate because of the prolificacy of insects vanished momentarily. This olive wood was a miracle.

I turn the small wheel now. It's a little rusty, but it still works. The gangplank lowers majestically. I run my fingers over and around it, and then I realize that the singing has stopped. When I glance up, my father is behind me, smiling.

"I caught heck for using your mother's nativity scene. She didn't speak to me for two whole days." His smile broadens and his eyes twinkle. "So that worked out a couple of ways."

"Did I know how beautiful this was?"

He doesn't answer right away. "Maybe not."

twenty-eight

I enter the kitchen full of good intentions. It's a good day—
I know this. Julia is fine, my father and I have had a nice
moment, Mark and I have had our first real conversation in
a long time, and Jake's babies, his children, will be here
soon. Jake's children. Jake has children and this hasn't
come up in conversation once. We are a strange family,
there's no other way to say it.

A pot of coffee belches softly in the corner, but there
are no other smells, no nutmeg or cinnamon in the kitchen.
Nothing is cooking or baking. My mother isn't here. People will be arriving in a few hours. She should be cooking
up a storm. An old thought that the Rapture has occurred
and all the believers have been whisked up to heaven
comes over me, but then I think that my father would
have been included, and I was just with him, besides
which, surely I'd have noticed something in the air. I
shake this thought, this old fear out of my head. I am so
very tired of old fears.

In the hallway upstairs, I see that the door to Jake's room

is open. Just a crack. My mother is in there. I can't see her, but I know it. When I peek inside, I see she is sitting in the corner doing needlepoint. She looks up, even though I've made no noise.

I sit, gingerly, on his bed. The springs creak. A picture of a wild-haired, wild-eyed Einstein peers back at me from the wall. Beside this is another, younger Einstein, considerably more relaxed, perched on a bicycle. Beneath, the poster reads: *Life is like riding a bicycle. To keep your balance you must keep moving.* How true, I think.

"What are you working on?" I ask.

She holds up her work, which is almost completed. "*I am come that they might have life, and that they might have it more abundantly.*" John 10:10.

"Ah," I say.

"Des told you about the babies," she says, calmly.

"Yes, last night. Why didn't you tell me? Especially since they'll be arriving in, oh," I look at my watch, "five or six hours."

"I wanted to tell you when we found out, but Des thought she should be the one."

I nod at this.

"Would you have come if you'd known?"

"Maybe."

She looks doubtful.

"I don't know," I say. "It's gotten easier to stay away."

"Life isn't easy," she says, her needle not breaking its stride.

"I know that, Mom," I say, my voice rising. "*That*, I actually know. I'm not completely sure you know it, though." I point to the needlepoint in her lap. "It's not always an abundant life. Sometimes it's really, really empty and meaningless. And sad."

She says nothing, but her hands are still.

"Why couldn't we just be sad when Jake died?" I say. "For just a while? Why did we have to celebrate?"

My mother looks up at this. "But we were sad, Gloria. Of course we were sad."

I shake my head. "When Mrs. Braun said that Jake was with the Lord, how Glory was having a good week because Jake was in heaven, you just stood there."

"Oh, Gloria."

I wait for the verse, something along the lines of the sweet by and by and where we shall meet on that beautiful shore.

"I wanted to smack her silly," she says.

"I beg your pardon?"

"Mrs. Braun is a nitwit," says my father, who is standing in the doorway. I don't know how long he's been there. "Married to a numbskull."

"Abe," my mother says, disapprovingly. She gets out of the rocking chair and sits beside me on the bed, still clutching the needlepoint in her hand. My father enters the room and sits on the other side of me.

"But we were never sad together," I say. As soon as I hear my dismal words, I feel an ache in my head. This is all too familiar, me sucking the air out of the room. I gather myself, what strength I have. "Anyway," I say briskly, "we have work to do, Mom." I begin to rise from the bed, but my mother puts her hand on my leg, stopping me.

"When Jake died I didn't have any answers for you."

"I wasn't looking for answers."

"You were always looking for answers."

I smile sadly at this and nod my head reluctantly. "Well, I guess that's true. Jake was so easy, wasn't he? I mean, sometimes I can barely remember him and other times it's like he's still with me, saying, 'Relax, already.'" I graze her strong, callused hand with mine. "And you got left with me."

"Gloria Elizabeth," she says, as sternly as she ever did when I left my muddy boots in the kitchen. "I don't ever want to hear you say that again."

"Oh, Mom, but it's true."

"It's not true."

I can't back down; as much as I want to believe her, I can't. "Jake was so full of light and happiness. Not just joy, Mom, happiness. He brought it into the house with him and it left when he did."

"Oh, for pity's sake. Jake wasn't perfect, Gloria. He was full of jokes and I loved him dearly, but you filled the house with talk."

"You never shut up," my father adds.

"You came home from school talking and you went to bed talking. Do you remember all your questions?"

"I thought they made you tired."

"Sometimes they worried me, and I didn't know where they would lead you, but you made life interesting."

This is a revelation. This is on par with Revelations. If a six-headed horse showed up at this very moment, I would be less surprised. And then, to my horror, I begin to cry.

It's suddenly all too much and I cry. It comes out of me in great, gushing, ugly sobs.

My mother puts her arm around me; it's unfamiliar, but not entirely. My father gets up off the bed and I think, *That's it.* This is too much for him. My mother will leave as well; I know it. It's too much crying. Too much sad.

But then I see that he's gone to Julia, who is looking scared in the doorway. He takes her by the hand and draws her into the room. They join us on the bed; four of us are sitting in a row. My father hands me a clean handkerchief. Oh, who would he be if he didn't have a clean handkerchief. Out of nowhere, a jolt of joy runs through me like a current. I blow my nose and start to laugh. "Look at us," I say. "Just look at us."

"Are you okay, Mom?" Julia finally speaks.

"Oh, I'm something, Sweetie," I say, blowing my nose. I look down at the plaque in my mother's lap. Abundant life. "Do you still believe that?" I ask.

"You have to believe in something," she says. "That's your—" She presses her lips together. I'm impressed that she hasn't finished the sentence.

"I've asked for two things in my life," she continues.

"Only two?"

She nods. "The first prayer was for a child. I was given twins."

"And then one was taken."

"Oh, Gloria. Death is inevitable. Life isn't. Life is a gift."

"Is that a verse?"

"Are you making fun of me?"

"No. Yes. Maybe."

"I believe I'll see Jake again one day."

"What if you don't?"

She looks at me, dry-eyed. "Well, won't I feel like a fool? I'll have wasted my life being content."

"*I have learned to be content in whatever state I am in.*" I can't believe I'm quoting St. Paul to my mother. I meant to be sarcastic, but it falls short of the mark because she's looking at me the way Henry Higgins must have looked at Eliza Doolittle: *By George, I think she's got it.*

"What was the second thing, Gran?" Julia asks.

"That your mother would come home."

The room falls silent and I feel the shadow of old guilt.

"So that's two for two," Julia says brightly. "Go, God." And we laugh. I reach over and grab her hand and squeeze. Then I pull her up from the bed.

"You know what we have to do now?" I hear myself say.

"What?"

"We're going to bake a pie," I say. "It's a travesty that your grandmother makes the best pies in the province and I can't even heat one up properly."

"Well, knock yourselves out," she yawns. "I'm going back to bed."

"Wilful child," I say, as she leaves.

My mother frowns. "I can't imagine where she gets that from."

～

Dawn stretches as we make our way to the front of the house to the old apple tree; a sliver of pink trickles across the mountains, dabbing the clouds with a rosy glow. It's just enough light for apple picking. We gather the fruit and bring it back to the house, where my mother turns brisk as she ties an apron around her waist.

I take the flour from the cupboard, full of good intentions, and then I'm baffled. My mother shakes her head at my ineptitude. "Shortening," she barks. "Salt, an egg, and water. Ice water. Make sure you run it ice cold."

I run the water cold with absolutely no understanding as to why. "So it's boiling water for birthing babies and ice water for pies?"

She shakes her head and says, "Phht." She puts me in charge of peeling the apples. When I display an unexpected talent for this, she smiles. "That's good," she says. "You're hardly wasting any of the apple."

"Use everything," I say.

While I cut the apples, I watch carefully as she cuts the shortening into the flour. She whisks the egg with vinegar and ice water and adds enough for the solid to adhere to the liquid. She sprinkles flour onto the surface of the countertop, then plunks the dough down. She hesitates.

"What?" I ask, still cutting.

She takes the knife from me. "You try it."

"Me? It'll be as tough as a house on fire."

She smiles at my mixed metaphor. "Don't knead. Just sprinkle a little more flour. There, that's it." She hands the rolling pin to me. "Spread some flour on the pin."

I do as I'm told. Trust and obey. I start humming the song.

My mother looks at me curiously, as though I might be mocking. But then she sings along. She knows the words. *Not a shadow can rise, not a cloud in the skies, but His smile quickly drives it away. Not a doubt nor a fear, not a sigh nor a tear, can abide while we trust and obey.*

I watch the dough spread beneath the rolling pin, tugging it first one way and then the other, careful not to cause a tear in the delicate pastry. It's so fragile—I had no idea. I take my time; there is no rushing this. Finally, it takes shape beneath my hands and it's lovely. I grin foolishly. "It's a pie," I say.

My mother snorts. "It's not a pie, Gloria. It's only dough."
She removes a metal spatula from the drawer and hands it
to me. "This is the tough part."

"Damn," I say. She scowls. "Sorry. Now what?"

She eases the edge of the spatula beneath the flattened
dough. "Carefully," she says, giving me the handle. I'm
even more cautious as I work the edge around the circle,
moving closer to the middle, freeing the dough from the
surface of the counter. I've almost finished when a corner of
the spatula rips through the centre. I'm disappointed. "It's
not perfect."

My mother pats the tear closed with an expert hand. "It
doesn't have to be perfect. It just has to taste good."

She shows me how to lift the dough onto the pie plate,
folding it first in half, and then in half again. She gives it to
me. I lower the quadrant of dough onto the plate. I unfold it
once, and then again, until the plate is draped with dough.
"Now it's a pie," I say, relieved and victorious.

"Now it's a crust," she sighs.

She adds brown sugar to the apples and then some white
sugar for good measure. Then she cuts a lemon in half and
tells me to squeeze it onto the mixture. Finally, she sprinkles
cinnamon and flour indiscriminately. "Until it feels right,"
she says, mysteriously. A quick stir and then I dump it into
the pie shell.

We repeat the rolling process and this time I don't tear a
thing. I dip my fingers in flour and scallop the edges of the pie
the way I've seen it done on TV. She tells me not to get fancy.

Finally, she tells me to cut a slit in the centre. "So that
some of the juice can be released," she explains.

"I think that's a good principle generally, don't you?"

She looks at me as if this is an unnecessary and unfathomable comment. She redirects my attention to the unbaked sphere. "Now it's a pie," she says.

twenty-nine

In the afternoon, Des arrives with a cooler full of food.

"I made pie," I say, holding it up triumphantly.

My mother snorts as she helps Des with the food.

"*We* made pie," I correct.

"Oh. You made pie?"

"Er, yeah, with my mom."

"Do you want a piece?" she asks.

My mom looks at me and says she's going to go outside and pick some carrots and peas.

"Don't you think we should wait until later?" I ask. Des has taken a knife from the drawer and is poised to cut.

"Oh."

"Looks like somebody could use a drink."

This seems to snap her back into the present. "Here? Yeah, I'll have a vodka martini with a twist."

"Brandy. For Christmas cake?" I open the top cupboard and root around behind the cereal. "It used to be . . . ah, here we are." I take a half-full bottle from the cupboard. I pour a small shot into two mugs and hand her one. "Breathe," I say.

"What was I thinking? Honestly, what the fuckety-fuck was I thinking?"

"Wow, never heard that before."

"I'm supposed to meet my son for the first time in front of all these people?"

"Well, now that you mention it . . ."

She looks stricken. "I knew it. I'll call them. Maybe they're still at the motel. Grace called last night to say they'd arrived. I invited them over then, but she said Jack wanted to wait because he's nervous. Nervous! Of course he's nervous. Why wouldn't he be nervous. He—"

"Slow down. Just a little." She looks at me like she is registering the fact that I'm speaking but has no idea what I'm saying. "This is good, Des. We're family. It's better this way."

She drains her cup in one gulp and clunks it noisily on the table.

"Okay." I put my cup down. I need to say something to distract her, because she's heading over to the bottle. "My parents are excited about this, Des."

She grabs the bottle and pours another shot. "Oh, I'm glad."

"You're saying 'oh' a lot." I take the mug gently from her hand. "It's probably best not to be too drunk when they arrive, right?"

"Glo, I don't know if I can do this."

"What do you mean?"

"I loved Jake so much. But I had to let him go, I had to. But now he's come back, I mean, you know what I mean. That first love, it's so powerful. What if I love them more . . . or not enough? Or what if there isn't enough love?"

I put my hand on hers. "Do you remember what you said to me last night?"

"When I got mad at you?"

"Yeah, that was fun. No, afterwards. You said that all we have to do is measure up to love."

"But what if I can't?" Her eyes fill with tears. "What if . . ."

"What if you can? You know what I think Jake would say?"

She shakes her head.

"I think that he would say you're on the edge of what you can know."

She takes a tissue and blows her nose. "He would say a dumb-ass thing like that."

Then she starts laughing and I start laughing and we laugh far more than it's funny, but we can't stop.

"I'm going to pee," says Des, just as Kate walks into the house.

She's carrying two enormous bouquets of flowers. I take them from her. "What's so funny? What have I missed?" she asks.

I notice immediately that something is different, off, with Kate. It takes a further moment to register that she's wearing no makeup and her hair is flat. From the look of Des's raised eyebrows, she has noticed it as well.

Kate begins to rummage through cupboards, but I can tell she's not really seeing anything.

"Kate, are you okay?" I have to admit that there is a part of me that's happy to be the one posing this question for a change.

She spins around. "I'm fine. Where are the vases in this house?"

I point to an open cupboard. "Right behind you."

She takes down a large crystal vase and begins filling it with water. It spills over the top, but Kate doesn't seem to notice.

Des takes over the job. "Sit down," she says.

Kate, to my surprise, obeys.

"What's up?" I ask.

Kate crosses her hands in front of her. She's going for the principal pose, but she's not pulling it off. Again, her hair is a distraction. First thing in the morning, last thing at night, sick with the flu, Kate always looked perfect. It was the first commandment of the Doerksen household: Thou shalt always look fabulous.

"Gabe just told me about the babies. Outside, just now," she says quietly.

"Oh, Kate, I'm sorry. I was going to tell you . . ." Des says.

Kate's chin trembles as she stares down at the table. "You were pregnant."

"Yes, that's the . . . way it works." Des looks at me for help.

"I didn't know." Kate's eyes brim with tears. She takes a deep breath. "I didn't know."

"Nobody did," I say, putting my hand on hers.

"Well, I did," Des says.

I smile at her.

"I should never have told my mother. I should never have told anyone," Kate says.

"Good grief, your mother would have found out eventually. The woman is, I'm sorry, a bloodhound."

Kate nods, sniffing. "But I know that. I knew that. I just . . ." she turns to me. "Honestly, I always told her everything."

I pat her hand. "You were scared of her, I think. We all were."

Kate shakes her head. "No, that's not it. It was her approval I wanted. Oh, I can't believe it." She runs her hand through her hair.

"Honey, it's okay. It really is," Des says.

"It's not. I'm so . . ." Kate twists her hands.

"Sorry?" Des says.

Kate nods. "I am. I was . . ."

"Wrong?" I say.

Des and I laugh.

Kate shakes her head. "I've spent my whole life trying to be better than her and all I've done is to turn into her."

"Oh, honey," Des says. "That's not true."

"It is. I'm judgmental, superficial, self-righteous . . ."

"Listen to me," Des places her hands on Kate's shoulders. "You aren't your mother."

Kate looks up at her.

"Your mother would never, ever, in a million years leave the house looking the way you do now."

Kate smiles wanly. "Des, you are a bitch after all."

We laugh. And I see the sticky bubble sphere holding the three of us together again.

Gabe comes into the room first and tells us that we don't get to sit together anymore. He says that they've arrived. And then Grace enters, followed by Julia and Maxi.

"My cousin," Julia announces with a flourish of one hand.

"My sister," Maxi adds, with her own outstretched arm.

"Hi," Grace says. She gives Des a big hug. "It's so good to see you again. I couldn't sleep last night, I was so excited. I tossed and turned and, oh, I was so excited." She turns to me. "You're my Aunt Gloria?"

I can barely breathe. All I can do is look for a trace of my brother. I begin at the feet, where I see the twinkle of a toe ring. She has strong legs and the peeking swell of her belly is pierced with something shiny. She is sturdy in her frame. Her shoulders are strong, like his. I am impatient and move to the top of her head, where a widow's peak arches above her forehead. Her eyes are green. She has Julia's nose—that's something.

I wrap my arms around her and hold her close. She feels warm, real. When she pulls away, I wonder if I've over-stepped. She scrutinizes me with a big smile on her face. "Ohmigod, I can't believe it. I can't believe I'm meeting you. I have so many questions; I don't know where to start. You're pretty. Who cares about that, though? I'm babbling. Sorry, I babble when I'm nervous." She gives herself a big hug, like she needs to do something with her arms.

I laugh and hug her again. "Don't be nervous, Sweetie."

"Hello," says Julia indignantly. "I thought I was Sweetie." We all laugh.

Grace laughs the loudest and says, "You are."

"We're going to show her the barn, okay, Mom?" Maxi says. "When's lunch?" The girls don't wait for a reply. They start to drag Grace away, but, at the doorway, she turns. "He's waiting outside, Des. He's being an asshole."

"Is he—okay?" Des asks.

"No, he's an asshole. He's under that tree. Go. It'll be okay."

They drag my mother and father and Kate with them, saying that Grace needs the full tour. Gabe and I stay with

Des, who can't seem to move. Finally, I take her arm and lead her out to the porch.

She stands there and watches the boy beneath the tree. "I gave him away," she says.

"And now he's come back," I say.

Gabe and I remain on the porch as Des makes her way to the solitary boy. I drink him in. He's tall and he slouches. He has dark, wavy hair. I can't see his face clearly, but, from a distance, he resembles my brother. I think he does.

"He looks like you," Gabe says.

And then I see it and I have to sit down. Gabe sits as well, but I can feel the tension in his muscles. He's spring-loaded, perched at the edge of the swing. He'll pounce if something goes wrong. "How are you doing?" I ask.

Gabe doesn't respond. The vein is working on the side of his head; his jaw is tense.

Des reaches Jack. She gives him a tentative hug, says something. He smiles.

"I guess I won't have to beat him up," Gabe says.

"Now that's a blessing."

"She's a nervous wreck."

"Go to her."

"She wants to do this alone."

"She needs you."

"I don't think so."

I brush the side of his face with my hand. "Beside her. She needs you beside her."

He takes my hand and kisses it. "Thank you, Darlin'." He crosses the lawn and, when he draws close, stretches his hand out to the boy. Then the entire gang joins them and soon the poor boy is swarmed. He seems guarded but polite, running his hand repeatedly through his hair until it's practically standing on end. Grace pats it in place with a sisterly gesture and Jack gives her a dirty look.

I can't move. I'm rooted to this swing. I hear Des say that lunch is ready and they make their way to the house. At the door, Julia pauses and gives me an exaggerated motion of her head. "Go," she whispers loudly.

Des says something to Jack and he looks my way. I wave, feebly, trying to keep tears from falling. Tears are inevitable, I know, but I also realize that I'm dealing with a teenage boy and sentiment is the enemy. I don't want to scare him away; it all seems so fragile. Like this could just disappear. I know it could disappear. I don't even want to blink with the fear of him vanishing.

Heavy feet, light feet, clamber inside the house—except for Jack's. He moves toward me and sits, tentatively, on the edge of the swing.

"Hi," I say.

"Hey."

"So you're Jack."

"So you're my aunt."

I search for the right words. "Your sister says you're an asshole." This is the best I can come up with.

But he smiles, and it's a great smile, and then I see the crease, the dimple, in the side of his face. It takes my breath away. "Yeah, well, she's insane."

"Sisters are like that."

"You were his sister."

"His twin."

"Yeah. Listen, I'm not really into this new extended family deal, okay? It's not my thing."

"My brother liked to be by himself, too."

"Yeah?"

"He liked to go hiking a lot. He may have been trying to avoid me, now that I think of it."

"I like hiking."

Des calls from inside the house that lunch is ready. Jack hesitates.

"It's okay, you know," I say. "You don't have to do anything or even talk. We're just glad you're here."

Grace bursts through the door. "Come in. The table is loaded. It's incredible. It's a feast! There's chicken and lasagna and pie! You can't even believe how much food there is." Then she looks at me. "Should I tell Des that I'm a vegetarian? I should have told her. Oh well, one wing isn't going to kill me. Come, Jack, now." She disappears back into the house.

Jack runs his hand through his hair and gets to his feet. He shakes his head and looks at me. "I won't have to talk."

"Um, Jack, would you mind if I gave you a hug?"

He shrugs.

I place my arms around him gingerly. He doesn't move and he doesn't disappear. He feels substantial—flesh and bone. His hand lightly grazes my back and I let him go.

"I'll be right in," I say.

The house expands with more noise as the girls greet Jack enthusiastically, each vying for attention. *He'll be fine*, I think. I listen to the noise and the laughter. I want to keep the moment a little longer. *Jake should be here*, I think.

thirty

It's almost dusk when the party breaks up. Jack seems relieved to go, but he's done well. He endures the farewell hugs. Grace goes on and on about how amazing the vegetables were and how impressed she is that everything is grown on the farm. Julia reiterates how environmentally conscious it is around here. I have to smile at how cool my mother has become. Both Jack and Grace promise to come back once they're settled in the city.

Kate and Gabe go back to the kitchen to help my parents clean up. Julia throws her good arm around me and thrusts the cast in my face. "See? They signed it."

I examine her autographed cast and Julia's beaming face.

"Can you believe it? We have a crazy family! Us. Oh my God, oh my God. Oh my gosh, it's spectacular, isn't it?"

"It really is."

"And Jack is so hot, not that it matters, I guess. He's my cousin, but still. Maxi's going to spend the night, okay? Des and Gabe said they'll pick her up tomorrow before we go, okay?"

"That sounds perfect. Have you seen Des?"

Julia points her cast toward the apple tree. "I think she's over there."

I walk over to the orchard. When I stand beneath the tree and look up, there she sits, tucked into the branches. When she sees me, she pretends to topple and I gasp. She giggles.

"Come up," she says.

"I don't climb trees."

"There's a first time for everything."

"We're practically middle-aged. This is unseemly."

"Shut up and climb."

"You are a bad influence," I growl. I take a branch in my hands and hoist myself up, a little proud of the upper-body strength that this requires. I climb farther and plunk myself down, legs swinging. "That's as far as I'm going."

"You can see it from here," she says, pointing.

Jake's mountain. Sure enough, peeking through the branches.

"I see it."

"You know what I think?"

"What?"

"I think Jake knows what's going on here."

"Maybe," I say. "Possibly. I don't know."

Des laughs at this. She grabs an apple and tosses it to me. "I dare you."

"Not funny," I say, catching it neatly. But I take a bite. "There," I say. "Satisfied?"

"Feeling smarter?"

"Maybe a little."

"Now that's a blessing," she says.

I drive along the dirt road to the side of the mountain, park the car. Wild roses peek out from the edge of the wood; I breathe the fragrant air as I climb. I wonder if the path will be hard to find, but it's clearly marked. I want to find the place where he left.

When I take what I think is the final turn in the path, I see a small white cross, nestled in rocks on the side of the hill. His grave has been well tended; I can see this from where I stand, unable to go further. My father's flowers grow in profusion around it. I force myself to move closer. All I can hear is the sound of the blood in my ears and the hum of insects. I breathe deeper. The message that's written on the narrow, weathered cross above the small headstone is simple: *Beloved son and brother. We miss you.*

"Well, that's an understatement," I say, sitting. I pluck out a few stray weeds. "You're also a father. You have a son and a daughter. I met them today. Her name is Grace; she's beautiful and strong. She talks a lot and she knows everything. She'd make you laugh. Jack is handsome. He's a little quiet . . ." My voice falters. It sounds false. I brush the outline of his name with my fingertips, but it doesn't help; this doesn't feel real. Jake isn't here. Jake is gone. He can't hear me.

I lay my head down on the small headstone as though it's a pillow. I look up at the sky, at the clouds. When we used to do this, the possibilities were endless: a dragon, a mountain peak, a chariot, a ladder. I was always looking for a face, of course. Proof. The eyes and mouth and nose of God. Just a glimpse. It didn't seem too much to ask. "I don't know how you did it. I don't know how you had such faith."

The setting of the sun infuses the clouds with tangerine and ruby and violet—a shifting canvas. As I watch, a cloud scuds by and the canvas changes again. The sun dips lower. Colours fold together. I could lie here forever and never see the same thing twice.

A breeze rustles the trees; it's growing chilly. *In the rustling grass, I hear Him pass. He speaks to me everywhere.* I push the words away, wrap my arms around me, but I can't get up. Maybe I'll turn into stone or a pillar of salt. That would be appropriate—she looked back as well. I hated that story. *Poor Lot's wife,* I said to Jake. *Didn't she even have her own name?* One little backwards glance and that was it for her—a permanent salt lick for passing deer. Jake, of course, thought the story was interesting. Endlessly interesting.

But that's the thing, Glo, it's a story: she looked back, get it? She should have kept going, kept moving. The stories aren't the truth; they hold the truth. And then he would close his eyes in the face of my interminable stupidity.

I look out at the valley below: amber tips of corn, flashes of purple fireweed and hardhack, a dash of red clover and yellow dandelion, and the green, the endless green in this place and how it all fuses together, in the ebbing light, into the impossibly beautiful.

"This is a crazy system you have here," I say. My voice echoes around me. "It's so beautiful—so heartbreakingly beautiful. Such care, such attention to the details." I pluck a buttercup from the ground and toss it into the breeze. The breath of God, I used to think. But the delicate weight of the slight flower and the pull of the earth draws it down to the place where Jake lay. "And the big picture—maybe you see that, too. But the middle part, the in-between part, that's the hard part."

My words travel back to me—*the in-between*. The hard part. Life. Life *is* hard. In which pew was I sitting, during which sermon was I giggling, when I missed this. I heard the part where it was all forgiven, but not so much where it was all lived. I didn't hear the part that said, Here we are and it's hard and it's amazing and meant to be felt deeply. Not just the grace but everything, everything leading up to it.

And then I feel a shiver, the footstep of a ghost. It's real and invisible and palpable and familiar—that raw feeling. My heart is racing, my feet are scalding, my hands are trembling. Skinless now, fear enters my bloodstream like a needle through water.

I let it happen, watch it happen. Or an aspect of me watches. If Jake were here, he'd say it was the *me* who looked at my nose who watches me now. Completely still, I watch my old enemy and companion, fear, slide through me like a serpent. I take shallow breaths, feel the heaviness and the staccato beat of my heart. And still I watch. I don't know when it will end, if it will end. As often as my brain tries to explain that it will be over soon, another whisper comes that this is endless.

But then my breath lengthens and my pulse slows; I feel the brushstroke of the wind. And I realize that I'm here—completely here. Completely alive. Not even a particle of myself is missing. And I'm not afraid. I feel the boulder slip away from my cramped heart. I look at the glistening ribbon of the valley below.

"Jake," I say. The evening light streams through a distant cloud the size of a hand. The valley stretches before me, no longer the valley of the shadow of death. It glows in the twilight, a thousand billion flickering atoms. "It shimmers," I say. "It really does."

As I climb down the mountain, I feel the song trickling through me like a river.

In God's green pastures feeding,
By the cool waters lie.
Soft in the evening
Walk my Lord and I.

It is as though it never left.

ACKNOWLEDGEMENTS

I'd like to thank Jane for seeing the possibility in the manuscript, Amy for committing to it, Janie for insisting on it (oh my, how she insisted) and Jane (full circle) for seeing it through to the end. It does, it seems, require a village to write a book.

I'd like to thank my mom and dad, who showed me that when belief and love are traveling together on a narrowing path, love leads the way.

GAYLE FRIESEN is the award-winning author of five novels for young adults, which have garnered critical acclaim in both Canada and the United States. *The Valley* is her first novel for adults. She lives in Vancouver, British Columbia.